jemma kennedy

skywalking

PENGUIN BOOKS

PENGUIN BOOKS

Published by the Penguin Group
Penguin Books Ltd, 80 Strand, London WC2R ORL, England
Penguin Putnam Inc., 375 Hudson Street, New York, New York 10014, USA
Penguin Books Australia Ltd, 250 Camberwell Road,
Camberwell, Victoria 3124, Australia
Penguin Books Canada Ltd, 10 Alcorn Avenue, Toronto, Ontario, Canada M4V 3B2
Penguin Books India (P) Ltd, 11 Community Centre,
Panchsheel Park, New Delhi – 110 017, India
Penguin Books (NZ) Ltd, Cnr Rosedale and Airborne Roads,
Albany, Auckland, New Zealand
Penguin Books (South Africa) (Pty) Ltd, 24 Sturdee Avenue,
Rosebank 2196, South Africa

Penguin Books Ltd, Registered Offices: 80 Strand, London WC2R ORL, England

www.penguin.com

First published by Viking 2002
Published in Penguin Books 2003
1

Excerpt from 'Dry the Rain', words and music by Stephen Mason, Steven Duffield, John Maclean, Robin Jones and Gordon Anderson © 1998, reproduced by permission of EMI Music Publishing Ltd, London WC2H OQY

Set in Monotype Sabon
Printed in England by Clays Ltd, St Ives plc

For Gerry, Polly, Zoey and
Morgan – the original line-up

'To be meaningful, life must move inevitably towards climaxes, possessing the quality of music'

Colin Wilson, *Adrift in Soho*

part one

1

There was a song in my head that held all the answers. A song as familiar as my own heartbeat, a perfect pattern of lyrics, chords and rhythm that encompassed every kind of reassurance and belonging I'd ever known, a melodic warmth tucked just out of reach in my mind. Only I'd forgotten how it went. And the more I tried to remember my redemption song, the more it eluded me. The notes kept fragmenting, shifting in and out of focus while I tried desperately to piece them together and make them whole, but the music was a silver-tailed fish which darted away into the shadows as soon as I touched a finger to its cool surface, leaving me floundering, bobbing, lost on the surface of the dream, while stray notes echoed back from the depths, teasing me. And then there was nothing but the wetness, the wet . . . wet cotton under my cheek where I had been dribbling into my pillow, and the dim knowledge that beyond my eyelids there was grimy daylight filtering through the curtains, and beyond the curtains, the dull monotone of the Camden Road and its slurry of early traffic.

Slowly, helplessly, I was dragged up through the well of sleep by my awakening physical demands. Uncomfortably full bladder. Tightness of head. Dry mouth, eyelids studded with slumber crumbs, imminent cramps in my right leg as I stretched and took the first shallow breath of the day. And underlying it all, a cement floor beneath the threadbare carpet of skin and nerve-endings through which consciousness crept moment by moment –

the familiar disappointment. I lay tangled in my sheets, paralysed by the horrible growing brightness of morning and the loss left behind by the fading, forgotten chords from my imaginary guitar.

Self-pity can be as strong an intoxicant as alcohol, and for a moment, lying there sucking in air with my mouth half open like a beached fish, it even eclipsed the painfully familiar sensations of hangover (a vicious cocktail of Guinness and tequila), and fag-over (surplus Benson & Hedges), which lay in my cranium and on my tongue, waiting to pounce. My whole body ached with a grey, eggshell fragility, the kind that makes you want to stay in bed for ever, watching daytime TV and waiting for your mum to bring you soup on a tray. But I was twenty-seven and hadn't lived with my mum for years. It was just the advent of yet another soupless day, an unfinished symphony of regret and self-loathing.

Flat on my back, trying to muster some saliva to dissolve the bitter sock that shod my tongue, I groped blindly through the cold vaults of my brain for inspiration – for music, quickly, more music, something real, something to replace the promises made by the dream song and distract me from its betrayal. Early-morning stereo selection was usually the first and most important ritual of the day, a way of easing out of the sluggish bowl of depression left behind by another disturbed night's sleep. But my head at this moment was too fragile to bear any sound, real or not, and so I was left with only the internal drip of my own unwelcome thoughts, a remembering of self, a sheet of negatives held to the light.

The same old daily litany of failure began, as I moved a hand to cup my balls and felt the beginnings of a hopelessly optimistic erection, with the fact that I hadn't had sex for over seven months. The only piece of journalism I had produced in two weeks was a badly written review of an Elvis Costello box-set. I was skint and desperate, while my best friend Lovell still owed me two hundred quid and as far as I knew had pissed off to Brazil, where he was probably working his way through the local population of under-age Amazonians. My bicycle, the only noble form of transport, had been stolen from Hyde Park a month ago and I couldn't afford to replace it, which had meant a succession of days spent mouldering alone indoors. And I couldn't even do this in peace, for there was an unlocatable and indeterminate smell of rot in my flat that grew stronger with every passing hour.

Hangover notwithstanding, I knew that this all-too-familiar morning melancholy, this deep-rooted cold-soulness, was something that effervescent vitamin C and a classic recording couldn't cure any more. Nor the fear which more and more frequently accompanied it, as in one of those nightmares when you're trying to run from something terrifying that's right behind you, breathing down your neck, but you find that your feet are rooted to the ground, and you wake yourself up because your psyche can't deal with the assault.

But what if you could never wake yourself up?

The underlying anxiety – that this was as good as it ever got.

In my mind's eye I sat bolt upright in bed, charged with fixing the meaning of all this dehydrated angst – the nightmare, the hangover, the feelings of despair all rushing into focus for a split second. In actual fact I lay still, twisted on my damp mattress, too nauseous to move. None of it was anything new, really – not the wrenching dreams, or the headache, or the unlovely awakening with its sour stabs of consciousness, which somehow always managed to remind me that there were a million people out there just like me, both eternally unsatisfied and paralysed by their own mediocrity.

Eventually I sighed deeply and gave in to the onslaught of morning, rolling on to my side and gently excavating my crusted eyelids. They opened upon a picturesque arrangement of a crumpled cigarette packet lying on the floor by yesterday's pants. Empty water glass, full ashtray. The *Sun* in disarray. There is nothing more brain-cluttering than the sight of an unfolded newspaper. I closed my eyes again and listened to my heart beating in my chest, a disconcertingly strong thud.

For a brief moment I entertained the fantastical notion that today could be the day that I joined the gym, as I had been meaning to for months, and pictured myself dressed in sportswear and a light sweat, moving gracefully between gleaming machinery. Although gyms were horrible places, really, temples to the meaningless expenditure of energy. All the rows of people pedalling furiously, as if they were hoping to take off and go somewhere more interesting, the joggers on their running machines pounding their way to nowhere, when they could have walked halfway across London in the time it took to burn off the desired amount of calories.

Casting the idea aside, I tried half-heartedly to focus on something more practical, like where to find lubricant for my parched throat, and returned briefly again to the question of what music to choose as an anchor in the shifting seas of nausea. Something epic, maybe, to suit the scope of the hangover, the breadth of the pain and its over-compensation for the total lack of epicness in my own life. Although once you reached a certain age it was impossible even to wallow in your own sense of failure, because you couldn't help but know that your entire generation was having a bad day. Every time you turned on the telly or listened to the radio or played a record, some fucker was having a worse time than you were. No one's pain was special any more, least of all mine, just predictable. After an adolescence spent laboriously copying out other people's lyrics into exercise books and singing along to a thousand songs about twentieth-century torpor, it simply wasn't enough to identify with other people's catalogues of discontent. But what were you supposed to do when the only thing that elevated you from the masses was the ability to express your dissatisfaction in an artistic way?

There was a time when music had made me angry, passionate, punchy with ambition, when I still nurtured the same childish fantasy of becoming a rock and roll star before I was thirty, despite the fact I'd never learned to play an instrument and could barely hold a tune. Over the years, however, my disillusionment had grown in tandem with my record collection, both of them threatening to overwhelm me at times. Deep down I still couldn't quite let go of the belief that musicians were the people who made you feel fully human, both in your longings and your despair. There were literally hundreds of life-changing moments in my own musical discoveries, encapsulated not only in whole songs or albums, but instants, fragments that had affected my psyche more than any amount of drugs or sex or spiritual instruction seemed to have done. The little strangled moan that Ian Brown gave in 'Ten Story Love Song' just before the guitar solo. The way Lou Reed's voice broke over the word 'shoes' in 'Oh! Sweet Nuthin''. Even those almost unbearably optimistic fucking sleighbells in 'God Only Knows' had made me want to be part of the human race in ways that books or lectures or parental advice never had. Now, of course, I knew that these things were a trap just as much as a salvation, because if you weren't careful you grew up into a person who had to rely on records to communicate your deepest feelings. But I just . . . couldn't . . . help it.

It also didn't help matters that my chosen profession involved writing about the musicians whose talents I coveted so much. I'd interviewed reams of bands in my years as a journalist, and the experience nearly always left me with a bitter taste in my mouth, whether they were gifted or supremely ordinary. Not least because there seemed to be more and more of them, younger and younger each day, who managed to sell their musical wares and become rich, hip and luxuriously wasted, leaving their suburban bedrooms far behind for large houses in Hampstead and leading lives of media-fed, drug-sated adoration. Whereas I was still a music hack with nothing but a growing realization that I should perhaps have produced more from over a decade of soul coughing than a good record collection. Even that was hardly a consolation, either, because you could never get on top, never catch up; there was too much music to listen to, too many musicians and bands both alive and dead, and it was enough to make you panic, just contemplating the losing battle that you faced every day when confronted with the thought of the mountain of music that you were compelled to scale in your short life, and *what parts of it you might miss along the way*.

Painfully I turned over on to all fours, crawled off my mattress and stood up. I remained stooped, head bowed to fight the dizziness for a count of five, then stepped over the detritus on the bedroom floor and padded into the bathroom. Under the vicious strip-light I ran a hand over my jaw like the men with chins do in the ads, and regarded myself in the mirror. Beneath the pathetic four-day-old growth pretending to be stubble, I had rough blotches on my face, my lips were chapped and my eyes a sunset of red veins and purple shadows. And I smelled. I could smell myself just standing still on the bathroom mat. Tobacco, alcohol, sleep, sweat. I didn't mind it that much, it reminded me I was alive. Just. But I didn't look like a man on the threshold of greatness.

Naked, head throbbing, I entered the kitchen, where I was greeted by a ranker odour. Something, somewhere, was definitely rotting. I swore and opened the fridge door, taking another futile look inside to see if anything on the shelves could be causing the stink, but they were occupied desolately by an empty salsa jar, two onions, a green-furred half-lemon, a foil container of ancient Indian food, a can of Guinness and a bottle of carbonated water which did not sparkle as its label would have had me believe, but merely tasted flat and sour when I took a swig. Shivering, wiping off my chin, I stood by the window, looking out on to the Camden Road through a vista of bare black branches. Outside it was grey and flat. A generic London day; April, cold, traffic roar. There was a photo of Marlon Brando blu-tacked to the glass, torn from a Sunday supplement. He looked moody and glorious. Surely pain would be more acceptable if you looked like that while you were suffering.

I took a deep breath. The foul smell was fainter over at the window and I began to pace around the kitchen, suddenly determined to uncover its source and get rid of it. Whatever it was, it was definitely located somewhere in the far corner, near the cooker. I came to a halt and knelt on the lino before the oven door. Sniffed again, and gagged slightly as my nostrils were assailed by an odorous wave. There was a four-inch gap between the cooker and gas boiler, gilded with a rusty scattering of crumbs. Peering into the dark crack I saw fossilized crusts and silver foil and a piece of dirty string which disappeared into shadow and looked horribly like . . . oh no. Oh *fuck*.

Cold with shock, I pulled the oven a few inches away from the wall, and followed the piece of string with my eyes until I reached its unmistakable conclusion. The rear end of a rat. A dead, grey-brown rat. A rat, shrouded in darkness behind my cooker. I leaned forward gingerly and saw further grim rodent portions: a haunch and a stiff hind leg, curled mid-air in rigor mortis. It was the leg that did it for me. Unable to stop myself I let out a schoolboy yelp of repulsion, and backed away to the other side of the kitchen, shaking with horror and rage.

I snatched up the kitchen broom and approached the oven, poking it into the gap and tracing my way up the tail with the up-ended broom handle. Slowly I dragged the corpse along the side of the boiler until it lay only inches from my feet, a fat rat, in my flat. I stepped away from it again, chanting this mantra over and over in my head, *A fat rat, in my flat, how about that*, like some nightmare nursery rhyme. Suddenly aware of my own nakedness and out of ideas, I threw down the broom and stormed out of the kitchen.

By the time I'd reached the living room, the anger had been replaced by nausea, and I collapsed on to the sofa. Somehow the dismal sight of the rat lying dead on my kitchen floor flanked by the overflowing rubbish bags, the sink stacked high with dirty plates, the dust-covered surfaces, seemed to sum up my whole sorry existence. The kitchen alone was clearly a buffet for rats, an eat-all-you-can special offer for the more discerning rodent palate. Picking up the ragged half-cigarette lying on the coffee table, I sparked it up, and stared at the phone, hacking over the first inhale. Then, impulsively but without much hope, I picked it up and dialled Lovell's number. It rang, once, twice, three times, and on the fourth ring there was a click and a soft inhale of breath.

'Lovell!' I said with relief, surprised to find him up so early, and already puffing. 'When did you get back?'

There was a pause. ''Lo?' said a child's voice huskily.

'Oh,' I said. 'Who's that?'

Another pause. 'Kid.'

'Who?'

9

'Kid,' the kid said again in its throaty voice.

'Er, I'm looking for Lovell. Is he around?'

'Yes,' said the voice. I could hear the child's amplified breathing in my ear.

'Can I speak to him then?'

'Yes.'

'Cheers.'

'Get Lovell I will,' the voice stated oddly. I took a bitter drag on my cigarette. There was a muffled clunk as the receiver was laid down, then voices and footsteps, then the creaking of the phone as it was picked up again.

'Yow.'

'Lovell, it's me.'

'Hello Me.'

'It's Ted.'

'*Easy* Teddy.'

'Who was that . . . kid?'

'That's a real kid. That's Kiddie, my nephew. Lisa's son. You know?'

'Oh yeah,' I said. 'Well, how was it, anyway? Did you get your balls tanned?'

'Uh?'

'Brazil. When did you get back?'

'Didn't go,' Lovell said placidly. 'Well, I went away. But I never made it as far as South America.'

'Where did you go?'

'See my sister.'

'Doesn't she live in Croydon?'

'Uh huh.'

'Oh. Nice?'

'Less wearing on the wallet than Brazil, man. Not to mention my balls.'

I wondered if this meant I could salvage some of my two hundred quid, but dismissed the idea in the same breath. No doubt he'd be sporting some new piece of gear when I saw him.

'So what's been goin' on, Teddy-boy?'

I let out a lungful of smoke and stale air, dropping ash on my bare legs. 'I got completely lashed last night . . .' I began.

'Where d'you go?' Lovell said in the offhand manner he used when receiving information about social events he had somehow unforgivably managed to miss.

'Everywhere. I was with Mick and some of his mates. We tried to get hold of you, actually, to see if you were up for a pint.'

'Why, what was happening?'

'Mick's band,' I said yawning, 'they just signed their publishing deal yesterday, so they were out on a bender. I mean, I was only going to stay for one, I'm absolutely broke . . .' There was a slight snuffle of laughter at this, but I carried on gamely, 'Then Mick started buying everyone tequila slammers . . . Went on from there, really.'

'Where d'you end up?'

'The last bit I remember well, we were in the Edinburgh Castle, playing pool. There was this girl . . .'

'Yeah?'

'She was with these guys who took us on at the pool table. We got talking about David Bowie . . .' I tailed off, remembering the conversation with sickly embarrassment. I didn't even *like* David Bowie.

'And is she in the kitchen right now, making you a fry-up in her knickers?'

'The only thing in my kitchen right now is a dead rat.'

'You what?'

'And Mick ended up taking her back to Clapham with him,' I added.

'Yes, man!' Lovell said joyfully. 'Another victory for South London. What the fuck was that about a rat?'

'I just found one behind my cooker.'

'Jokin'? What a place to die,' he said in a thoughtful voice. 'I seen behind your cooker. Got to say, Teddy, it ain't really that surprising, considering.'

'What, the girl, or the rat?' I said weakly.

'The rat, man, the rat. The state of your place, you should be glad they haven't moved in and opened a theme park by now.'

11

'Well, what am I supposed to do?'

'I dunno, do I? Get someone in to take it away.'

'Who though? The council?'

'Councillor, I'd like to report a vermin suicide.'

'It's not funny.'

'Keep your hair on, darlin',' Lovell said. 'I'm not laughing. Ring the council then.'

'Who at the council?'

'Uh, the rat people. Pest control. Exterminators. You know? Only have a tidy up before they come round if you don't want 'em to laugh in your face.'

'I *don't* know,' I croaked. 'I just want the thing out of my fucking flat now.' I shivered and looked down at my shrivelled nakedness.

'Oh c'mon, don't be such a pussy.' There was a pause, then he said, 'You around this morning? I might swing by in a bit.'

'Yeah, if you want,' I said. 'I'm not going anywhere.'

'Good. I been playing Monopoly since half seven, and Kiddie's just shafted me with three hotels on Park Lane, so I'm ready to roll.'

'What time is it?'

'About nine. Wednesday morning, April 7th, the year of our Lord nineteen . . .'

'Jesus, no wonder I feel so ill,' I said, burying the fag butt in the pot of my long-suffering rubber plant.

'Listen, I'm looking after Kiddie today, he's off school, so I'll have to bring him with me. Alright?'

'I don't care. As long as he's not frightened of dead rodents.'

'If he ain't now, he soon will be,' Lovell said. 'But you probably only count as half dead. Sit tight, sunshine.'

So I put some clothes on my body, the Beta Band on the stereo, and sat tight. Lovell lived in Chelsea, a good forty minutes away in morning traffic, and there was nothing to do except smoke and brood, listening to the singer serenely intoning, '*This is the definition of my life, lying in bed in the sunlight,*' and wishing it was mine too. I'd spent a good proportion of the years I had known Lovell anticipating his arrival from some distant corner of the city where people seemed to occupy a higher plane of existence. Lovell had pages of phone numbers, friends in every borough, a network of contacts spread across the city who connected telepathically when there was a good party, a football game, a gig, a pub session, whatever. Lovell did nothing and everything himself, although he was constantly involved in some kind of Project – with a film producer, with a bar owner, with a fashion wholesaler, with a club promoter, doing something for someone, somewhere, although God knew what.

With Lovell you never really knew anything, partly because he had his own self-constructed mythology, seeming to have erased all the parts of his personal history that weren't useful or interesting to him. I'd met lots of his mates over the years and they all had the same timeless quality to them, like urban changelings. They reinvented themselves as it suited against the backdrop of London scenes both legendary and brand new, from bar to shop to club, Portobello, Chelsea, Camden, Soho; adapting a look, a crowd, a pub, a sound to fit whatever the next layer of London scene was destined to be; always one step ahead of everybody else and with the other foot deep in the mythical past that bound them all together.

Lovell didn't look just like anybody else, either. He had a toasted complexion dotted with dark freckles, a close fuzz of imitation gold hair with dark roots cultivated to show the artifice, and a crack-up grin. Women adored him, blokes stood him drinks. He also had a doubtful pedigree claimed from Trinidadian, Scottish and South London stock, was a purveyor of bars and pool rooms, an entrepreneur and unintentional poet, a believer in the purity of his own spirit and defender of the right to try anything once and live to tell the story himself. He seemed to have managed to do everything I'd ever wanted to, only first, and with far more style.

We met on a landing in Holloway in 1989. I was a first-year bed-sitting student, the old-fashioned kind who should be preserved in Newcastle Brown Ale and displayed to the nation as an historical relic. Acid house parties were happening all over town, students and poll-tax objectors were rioting and people were dropping pills and chewing each other's faces off all night. And there I was in the middle of it all, the eager zeitgeist-disciple who seemed to manage to miss all the important events as they happened and only heard about them afterwards from other people or read about them in magazines.

Being at university was a time of great confusion for me, fresh from my Home Counties grammar school. Contrary to my expectations, intellect counted for very little to most students, whereas a basic sex appeal was still the most valuable asset, just as it had been back at home. And while I was awash in cutting-edge feminist and post-modern theories, being able to quote Lacan didn't help me get laid (girls still wanted to have sex with pop stars even if they realized they were phallocentric manifestations of a patriarchal society). Being a student also meant you were expected to coordinate a healthy radicalism with your desire for the latest in Sony hi-fi, and over time you learned to personally despise the various minority factions who trailed around campus in wounded groups while you exhausted yourself fighting theoretical battles on their behalf in seminars.

Nothing was as it seemed. University was full of crack-pots, therapists, college drunks, Christian preachers with acoustic guitars, rugby players, Socialist Worker Party canvassers, ethnic-jewellery-sellers, modern dancers who wore leotards in the refectory, vague professors who missed their own lectures, rich kids from European exchange programmes, drug-dealers and student-union officials on permanent sabbatical. I had a few friendships born through bouts of drinking and revision, but as most of the other kids on my course lived in halls of residence, I missed out on the real bonding which went on after-hours and off campus, in rooms along institutional corridors smelling of beer and disinfectant. I was proud that I lived in a proper rented flat, but never entertained many guests there, despite the fact that I had my own colour TV.

Back then I had carefully preserved copies of *The Face* stacked in my bed-sitting room and revolutionary Russian posters on the walls with slogans I didn't understand. I had a throwback sixties haircut and had recently crossed the great student sartorial divide from Dr Martens to Adidas, swapping the predictable Oxfam chic along the way for what I perceived to be a more suitably streetwise look. This look was based mainly around a pair of secondhand Adidas sweatpants, blue with a green stripe (purchased furtively at Camden Market and worn as often as hygiene allowed), a pair of grey Gazelles, and a selection of faded T-shirts advertising bands I'd never seen.

Lovell, in stark contrast, looked as if he knew his onions, sartorially speaking. At the time we met he was shacked up in the flat below mine with a girl called Helen, who worked as a barmaid in the King's Head on Essex Road, but I never saw much of her. I used to bump into Lovell in the hallway quite often and we'd nod to each other; or rather, I'd nod, and Lovell would flash me one of his Cheshire cat grins as he bounced in or out of the door, his pre-peroxide ringlets springing jauntily. I always noted what he was wearing with envy and took mental notes, but deep down I knew that he was in a different league from me, and always would be. Lovell had true style, the real deal, the kind promised by a thousand different magazines but which you knew you could never simply buy (at a price) off the peg. You had to be born with it.

The range and breadth of his wardrobe was astonishing. His basic and most frequent look when I first met him was a kind of Urban Terrorist: army surplus, American sportswear, Redwings, bomber jacket, accessorized with expensive sunglasses, and surely one of the earliest and largest mobile phones ever seen on the streets (this was the end of the eighties, remember, when most kids thought BT Phonecards were pretty fucking cool). But this was only one of his many disguises. Lovell was the first person I'd ever met who managed to mix and match, amongst other memorable garments, real Harley Davidson leathers, crumpled linen suits with Greenflash tennis shoes (no socks), Hawaiian shirts, sarongs, jeans with five-inch turn-ups, camouflage army-surplus boilersuits, pale-pink cashmere jumpers, fur coats, cowboy hats and orthopaedic-looking sandals (and who wasn't a religious fanatic, a freak or a devotee of an underground cult band).

We never really spoke, but aside from his amazing outfits, I got to know a little about Lovell in the usual way of those whose lives are separated by sheets of plywood in old London houses. Over time I discovered, for example, that he argued a lot with Helen, lived off Chinese takeaways, had a lot of hip-hop records, burned coconut incense sticks and had a frustratingly robust sex life despite his rocky relationship; its symphonies were played out daily and drifted up through the floorboards into my stubbornly bachelor bolt-hole.

While I signed on for my miserly grant cheques and attended lectures on anthropology and semiotics, Lovell apparently played pool in our local, the Castle, conducted mysterious business deals on his walkie-talkie and pretended to be a freelance graphic designer in between breakfast in Mo's Café on Holloway Road and evening drinks in the Slug and Lettuce on Upper Street. The extent of his design activity seemed to be the production of cheap-looking flyers advertising raves in places like Lambeth and Tottenham, which were always littered around our shared hallway. I think Helen must have kept him in beer and Calvin Klein underpants (she hung their smalls out to dry in the square foot of patio outside their living-room door), because he certainly didn't keep regular hours, and therefore, I assumed, didn't have a regular pay packet.

Just where he got all his clothes was a mystery to me. He didn't look more than twenty-three or -four, and in those innocent days, I could distinguish only two kinds of young people – students and under-thirty career-heads. Those of us in the first group, busily deferring our gratification in the name of further education, derided the latter for having joined the rat-race so young, and yet envied them for their access to all the things we hankered after – clothes, holidays, CDs, computer equipment, good-quality drugs and decent accommodation.

Lovell, who didn't fit neatly into either of these categories, gave me my first introduction to the existence of London's many floating underclasses which circumvented normal nine-to-five city life, and were mythical, universally acknowledged and yet impossible to locate or join. He belonged in the most desirable slipstream – he was a Face. For him, life was a thing of leisure, to be enjoyed at the expense of others wherever possible. As far as I understood it, these enviable types maintained an elusive survival working here and there, by knowing people who could get them something for free, or cheaper than in any high-street shop, by pulling favours, hustling, having the occasional windfall, and above all by being popular, a quality Lovell seemed to have in spades.

Of course, I found all this out later. Holed up in my room writing laborious essays, listening to Manchester bands and pretending I was a full participant in the throbbing metropolis (the nearest to which I got was blagging into crap gigs at the Garage on Holloway Road, or an occasionally worthwhile one at the Shepherds Bush Empire, for review in the college magazine), I noted Lovell's comings and goings somewhat wistfully, but was too shy to try and make friends with him. It wasn't until I'd studied, stoned and solidly drunk my way through the three terms of my first year that I made his acquaintance properly, a few weeks into my long, impoverished summer holiday.

One night, he and Helen had an almighty bust-up after *EastEnders*. As far as I could make out, it had something to do with Helen's goldfish having died from neglect, but after half an hour or so of listening to Helen shout and Lovell make disconcerting animal noises, I turned up the TV and tuned out the droning voices which rose and fell like the soundtrack to a blue movie. I heard the familiar sound of Helen slamming the front door a little while later, but didn't pay too much attention, except to note that I probably wouldn't be subjected to the athletic sexual soundtrack that usually followed their bigger rows. Some time after this I vaguely registered a few distant thumps issuing from their room below, but I was deeply involved in a *Hill Street Blues* re-run, and didn't think about it.

Around midnight I turned the telly off and lay back on my bed. The flat was oddly silent downstairs and I drifted into sleep. Afterwards I found out that at this time, Lovell was sitting on his living-room floor and quietly drinking himself into oblivion. Over the three hours following Helen's departure, and in defiance of her vow never to return until he got a grip and did some growing up, Lovell had apparently drunk six cans of Red Stripe, half a litre of Jack Daniels, and some vintage port which happened to be (inappropriately) in the fridge.

The quantity and combination of alcohol made him quite volatile, and after some half-hearted attempts to throw furniture around the flat, he dialled 999 and asked the police to come and arrest him as he didn't feel he could be held responsible for his actions. When they refused, Lovell, desperate for company and someone to share the drama with, came blundering upstairs, moaning and banging on my door.

I awoke with a jolt to hammering sounds and muffled cries, went to the door and stood behind it anxiously in my second-hand Paisley dressing-gown, debating whether to open it or not. Whoever was outside was spluttering very badly and I couldn't make sense of any of it, until an isolated 'Help me, man,' inspired me finally to undo the chain and turn the handle. I opened the door and gasped theatrically, not recognizing the contorted face that lunged at me, gibbering. I automatically stepped backwards and raised both arms in defence. Lovell fell straight through my doorway and on to the linoleum, where he lay on his side and stared up at me with swollen eyes. I stared back at him, perplexed. He was wearing a red, ruffle-fronted dinner shirt, believe it or not. Like Richard Gere in *Breathless*, but with old Levi's, not sky-blue tuxedo pants, and though I was pissed out of my skull I could still see that this skinny white kid was gawking at me like he'd never seen anyone wearing a red ruffle-fronted dinner shirt collapsed on his floor before. I didn't quite get what I was doing down there, and I tried to stand up, but I must've just groped blindly about, because he gave me his arm and helped me to my feet.

The minute I was off the floor I knew I'd had it. I was about to throw up, with force. I gazed at him mutely, and all credit to the guy, he must have interpreted my look of dread, because he propelled me towards his bathroom without a word. Perhaps it was the knowledge that I was gonna feel better as soon as I'd puked, but I suddenly felt sober as a pike. I knelt down before the toilet, undid a few buttons on my shirt, took a deep breath, and projected a stream of pure alcohol into the bowl.

It must have gone on for a full five minutes, but the kid didn't move. He just stood there by the sink and watched in silence. Once he said, 'Alright there?' after a particularly strenuous heave, but other than that, we didn't get much of a chance to talk. I did think it was quite cool of him at the time, not to flinch or moan or anything, but I was concentrating hard on getting it all out while I had the chance and didn't get round to telling him.

When the last wave had passed, I stayed slumped on the floor for a while, recovering my strength, and then I got up, swilled my gob out in the sink and splashed some water on my face. The guy handed me a towel and I dried myself off, and then I shook his hand and gave him a smile of sorts to show him thanks. He looked at me very seriously and said, 'My name's Ted.' Nice one, man, I was thinking, but I couldn't speak because my teeth were chattering to fuck. Luckily I didn't have to, because next thing I knew I was following him back into his room. He sat me down on the sofa and dragged a blanket off his bed to put round my shoulders. I was so grateful I almost started bawling, but instead I lay down on the sofa and passed right out.

It was my stomach that woke me the next morning, screaming with that hangover emptiness you get after a good night at it. I didn't know where the fuck I was, and I lay there for a bit staring at the back of the sofa and wondering what I'd gone and done, but then I turned over and saw him asleep in his bed, his face only a couple of feet from mine. I had a good gander at him. His mouth was wide open and he was drooling into the sheet like a mental patient. He had this fair hair chopped into a terrible bowl-cut and he was wearing a proper pyjama top – he looked about twelve. I was surprised he didn't have a teddy in there with him. That's when I remembered his name, Ted. Anyway, just seeing him lying there all milky-skinned made me feel about a hundred years old and twice as pikey.

I got up quietly so as not to wake him and tiptoed into the kitchenette to raid his fridge. I was in luck again, he must have just done his weekly shopping because the fridge was packed with student food. I slung together an evil sandwich – fuck knows what I put in it – then I went back into his room and sat on the sofa, trying to piece together what had happened the night before, eating my sarnie with one hand and holding my head in the other.

I remembered the anniversary dinner I'd cooked for Helen (bangers, mash and red cabbage), although we hadn't eaten none of it, because we'd started scrapping before I'd even dished it up. Helen had bad PMT (as in Permanent Menstrual Tension), and started in on me when I was still pouring out the wine. I wasn't in the mood for a row, specially since I'd done the decent thing and was trying to woo her into a night of shagging with a six-month-anniversary dinner and a big bag of grass. Only she'd gone and found her goldfish floating in the toilet, hadn't she, after she'd got home from work. I was gonna break it to her gently that I'd discovered the fish had snuffed it earlier that day – it'd been looking peaky for ages – but of course I didn't get the chance, and she went ballistic when she found it there, hanging around like a persistent turd. The fish was just an excuse really, because it wasn't as if I'd killed it or nothing, but she started going off about how it was symbolic of our decaying relationship and my lack of responsibility, blah, blah. I didn't stand a fucking chance. When Helen wanted a barney, she got it, and she won it and all. By the time she'd stormed out of the house, well, I had the hump, big time. I'd just spent hours burning things in pans and making the flat look nice, and it was all for nothing. So I had a drink, and dived into the bag of weed, and had another drink, and after the fourth or fifth beer there was no stopping me. I passed on into that twilight zone where you think you're invincible and everything you're doing's got some demented logic to it. I must have wasted about three hours just lumbering around the flat bashing myself on all the furniture and shouting out filthy curses.

As for the consequences of the boozing, it all came back to me eventually, sitting on Ted's lumpy sofa and listening to him snoring in the background. I did feel like a bit of a cunt, having unloaded myself on a total stranger, which is what he was, more or less, but I told myself I'd make it up to him. Then I let myself out and staggered back downstairs. My place was trashed, Helen hadn't been home, and there were sausages and beer stains everywhere. The first thing I did was wash out my red ruffle-fronted shirt. Luckily the damage wasn't too bad.

Later on, when I'd tidied up a bit, I went out and bought a bottle of champers to give to Ted (I got a discount from Harry at the Threshers on Upper Street for sorting him out gear occasionally). 'Voove or Mowett?' Harry said, pointing to the two bottles. I went for the Voove. I remember because Ted kept it in his room for ages. He said he was saving it for a special occasion, although when he ever had one to celebrate was news to me.

Anyway, when he found the bottle sitting on the landing outside his door that afternoon, he came down to my flat with a big sheepish grin on his face to say thanks, and I invited him in. We shared a spliff and some cold sausages, and that was that – I spent a lot of that summer hanging out with him and getting him stoned out of his gourd. By the time he went back to college, we'd become good mates, although it took me a while to get his number. For a start he never had any girls round his place, and for a while I thought he might be playing the B-side, though I soon found out it was just that he was unbelievably crap at pulling. His idea of a good chat-up line was to ask a girl to tell him about her favourite seven-inch. Which, let's face it, is open to interpretation. Anyway, even though he didn't know his arse from his armpit, we used to have some pretty interesting conversations, he was no doughnut, old Ted. And it was a laugh taking him around and showing him stuff, like having your kid brother in town. I managed to convince him to get his barnet cut, too; my friend Juliette who owned a salon in Soho did it for free. So at least I can say he looked a lot better after we met, even though his marks might have suffered a bit.

I was thinking about all this in the car on the way to Camden, after I'd dragged Kiddie away from the Monopoly board, and chuckling to myself, because I was remembering what a scum-hole that place in Holloway was, and how crap Ted was at dealing with any of the little visitors that take up residence in cheap, damp flats: the spiders in the bath, the slugs in the hallway, even the pigeons which sat and sculpted their own shit every day on his window-sill gave Ted the creeps. Sometimes he left his bed-sit window open when he went out and there'd be feathers on the carpet when he returned. It used to really freak him, he thought there were pigeon monsters hiding in his wardrobe and waiting to pounce on him in his sleep.

I never really minded any of that stuff, or maybe I just stopped noticing it. When you've lived in London all your life and done your fair share of moving about, you get immune to some of the particular human indignities that come from sharing places that should have been blitzed back in the war. Ted probably never even saw anyone throw up before he met me. I remember once his mum came up from Surrey to the flat for a day, and I heard her up on the first-floor landing by the bog, saying in a shocked voice, 'Teddy, there's only *newspaper* in here.' I never shared a bathroom in any house where there wasn't a permanent shortage of toilet paper. People hoard it, it's a black-market commodity in bed-sit land.

She was nice actually, his old lady, looked a lot like Ted, only with this soft Irish accent from growing up in Dublin. She drove up to town in her little Mini Metro with a cardboard box of food on the back seat for Ted, and I met them in the hall as they were carrying it in. Ted introduced us. 'This is my mum,' he said, with his arm around her shoulder; not embarrassed like most eighteen-year-old kids would've been, but proud. We shook hands. 'Do you go to the college too?' she asked, smiling at me, and I said, 'No, I'm a . . . chef,' and then actually went red as I saw Ted give me a look of total disbelief.

'Oh, lovely,' Ted's ma said, and I could tell she was about to ask me a whole load of questions so I made my excuses and legged it into the flat. I felt so humiliated that I had to play a Beastie Boys record twice in a row and stomp around the room yelling the lyrics out until I felt better. I realized afterwards that while this was going on, the two of them must have been in Ted's room above mine, unpacking the cans of Heinz soup and cornflakes and listening through the floorboards to me shouting that I mixed business and pleasure far too much, and going on about wine and women and song and such, which probably told his mum just about all she needed to know about the real me.

Ted, bless him, never asked me why I'd lied to his old lady, and I probably couldn't have come up with a decent explanation if he had. Maybe it was just the earnest look on her face when she asked me. For once in my life I couldn't face coming up with some flaky bullshit answer. 'Oh, this and that, Mrs P. I sign on, do a bit of petty drug dealing here and there, DJ a little. You know, your average wide-boy hustle. Care for a cocktail in my lodgings?'

She was sweet, though. When I met her, I thought, lucky Teddy. It must be nice to have a mum with big brown eyes who brings you cereal variety packs and new tea-towels. My mum had died a while back, and I never knew my dad, not that I remember, anyway. Me and Lisa my older sister, my half-sister really, we both drew short straws on the dad front. She got Vic from Catford who did a runner with her teenage babysitter when Lise was still in nappies, I got the sulky West Indian who hung around in London long enough to spawn me and create a few major rows, then fucked off to Germany en route to permanent obscurity. At least we both had a few years of their successor, good old Bob from Streatham, who married my mum when I was a nipper and really went to pieces when she died. I don't see him too much these days. It's a shame, really.

Ted's mum used to buy him clothes too, which I couldn't quite get my head round. I mean, she actually picked things out for him and he wore them without complaining or anything. Then again, I been dressing myself since I was four, so I'm bound to think it was a bit sick. Another time she bought Ted this leather jacket he was so proud of. He thought it made him look well hard, although of course it screamed Camden Market, but it was an improvement on his duffel coat, let me tell you. It should have been illegal for students to own duffels in the nineties, British Home Stores ones, anyway.

I suppose you can't blame her for looking after her little Teddy. Buying clothes for kids is wicked, especially if you got taste, like me. Take Kiddie here. He's such a great-looking kid, or he would be if Lisa didn't insist on shaving his skull within an inch of his life. But she dresses him in clothes from Woolworths. I try and redress the balance, so to speak, but then again, Kid probably don't give a damn about any of that, despite the fact all his little friends are doing the toddler strut in Nikes and Polo sportswear. All he really cares about are his *Star Wars* characters.

*

24

'Where we going?' Kiddie piped up suddenly as we drove down the Westway. He was strapped into the passenger seat, fiddling with the buttons on the stereo.

'I told you darlin', we're going to see my friend Ted in Camden. Don't do that Kid, you'll break it.'

'Why we going to see Ted in Camden?'

'Because he wants to see us.'

'Will I be bored?'

'Nah.'

'How d'you know?'

'Well, he's got *Star Wars* on video.'

'Just *Star Wars*? What about the others?'

'I dunno, Kid. We'll have to ask him.'

'The second one's the best.'

'Yeah.'

Kiddie started muttering under his breath in Yoda talk. I caught, faintly, 'Second one the best, it is,' and glanced over at him. He was hunched over in his seat, picking at the stitching on his tracksuit bottoms with a little brown paw. I'd just brought Kid back to mine for a few days because Lisa was under the weather again, and after so many days on the trot we'd tuned right into each other. I could always read Kiddie like a book, and right now, we were on the sensitive page. I'd taken him away from Lisa and Croydon to give her an extra break, and even though he was skiving school, which he hated, he knew damn well that he'd be chanting his times tables right now if his mum wasn't in such a bad way. Kids really need their routines and shit to keep them going, because as soon as the familiar patterns stop, they know for sure something's up. This Kid was bearing up pretty good so far, and it was OK when we were just hanging out at my flat, but as soon as we went out, the fact of being away from home sort of kicked in, and he tended to go all quiet on me. It was a shame, because I loved our little day trips round London together, and I wanted him to get to know the city, too. I wanted him to have the same excitement of going up West that I did years ago, roaming around town, all of that.

As we passed over the Paddington flyover, Kiddie said, 'Hmm soon Star Wars I will watch, earned it I have.'

I said, 'OK, Kid?'

He nodded with inward-looking eyes. I let him ramble on. Kiddie's obsessed, really and truly. It's been going on for well over two years now and it still shows no sign of letting up. I suppose I'm to blame actually. I mean, I'm a fan too, but not in the same league as Kiddie, not by a long stretch. I was babysitting him one evening at my flat when he was about five, and he wouldn't go to sleep, he kept sneaking back into the living room and prodding me from behind the sofa. It was pretty late, and I was lying there, smoking a joint and watching *The Empire Strikes Back*, and every ten minutes or so I'd feel this finger poking my head or in my ear, and I'd jump and look up to see him standing there gazing at me silently. 'What's up?' I kept asking, but he played dumb. I'd take him by the hand and tuck him back into bed next door, and then a little while later he'd be standing next to me again like a little troll in his baggy pyjamas.

In the end I gave up hauling him back into the bedroom and let him sit on my lap and watch TV, thinking it would send him off to sleep. It almost worked, too. I knew he was gonna drop off because he started to get heavier and heavier. My legs were going numb but I was sitting very still so as not to disturb him, engrossed in the movie and resting my chin on his head. Suddenly his whole body went rigid and he jerked upwards. My jaw clicked on his skull, it's a miracle I didn't bite my tongue off, but before I had time to even swear he was off my knees and crouching down by the TV, inches from the screen. I went and knelt next to him, and put my hand on the back of his neck. 'Kid?' I said, a few times, but he ignored me and carried on staring at the telly. So I stared too.

It was fairly intense, both of us huddled there in silence, squinting at the screen in the semi-dark. It was the scene in the swamp, where Luke's just run into Yoda but he ain't having it that Yoda's the legendary Jedi Knight, blah, blah. I'd seen it all a million times before. Only Kiddie was having some kind of epiphany. Every time Yoda said something in his ridiculous strangled voice, he twitched. Now and then he'd let out this little sigh, like a lovesick puppy, and he didn't take his eyes from the TV screen once. I swear I'd never seen anything like it, especially not from Kiddie, who was normally quite a subdued kid and didn't go in for infant dramatics. Although if I'd known then just how insane things were gonna get between Kiddie and Yoda, I wouldn't have been surprised at all.

After five minutes or so of this, I went and lay back down on the sofa and just watched Kiddie watching the film. I suppose I was worried he might flip out or something and thought I should keep guard, but he just kept on staring at the telly. And then, like the great babysitter I was, I fell asleep.

The next thing I know I'm lying face-down on the settee with my feet in the ashtray and the sound of galactic warfare in my ears. It was early morning, and Kiddie was sitting right there in front of the TV in exactly the same position, eyes glued to it, remote control in his lap. I figured he must have gone to sleep at some point during the night, but he wouldn't, or couldn't say anything about it when I asked him. He was lost in a galaxy far, far away.

I managed to get him washed, but only by keeping the film running with the sound turned right up so he could hear it from the bathroom. The whole time I was sluicing him down, he was straining towards the door with his ears pricked. I tried talking to him, but every time I spoke he'd just glance at me blankly and turn his head towards the sound of the TV. I got his clothes on, and then I sat him back down on the sofa and forced some cornflakes down his throat before my sister came to pick him up at ten. I had to more or less feed him myself. When Lisa arrived I turned the TV off and braced myself for a tantrum, but Kid just threw me a sort of stunned look, and let Lisa put his coat on. Then he trotted off with her, back to Croydon.

My sister called me later that day to tell me that he'd hardly said a word all afternoon and asked me what I'd done to him, not that she was complaining. I didn't bother going into it too much. Lisa was never into *Star Wars*, she was more your *Mary Poppins* kind of girl. But Kiddie was hooked from then on. I bought him the videos and within a few months he could pretty much recite all Yoda's dialogue in both films and quite a lot of other stuff from all three of them.

Kid repeated Yoda's lines so often that after a while he actually started to sound like him. After a while I got used to him spouting out lines of Yoda-speak when you asked him a question, but it did other people's heads in, especially Lisa. I think she reckoned he was developing a satanic streak like that kid in *The Shining*. Actually I once won a nice bet with a mate's brother, who didn't believe that my five-year-old nephew could quote the whole of Yoda's death scene from *Return of the Jedi* without missing a word. Mind you, you should have seen this guy's own kids, they weren't exactly the brightest boys you ever met. The closest they'd ever got to education was watching their old man's lips move when he read the *News of the World*. I bought Kiddie a Darth Vader helmet when he passed the test, as a reward, though I think it scared him a bit more than he fancied wearing it.

Of course, sometimes I think it would be better if he was interested in other things besides *Star Wars*, but Kiddie ain't had much of a childhood really so far, what with Lisa being ill a lot of the time, and not having a dad around. Lisa's a good mum and that, but she'd rather have Kiddie acting like a junior member of *The Cosby Show* than a shrunken alien. She loves him to death, but you can tell she's mystified by him. Poor Lisa. She's not had much of a time of it either. Apart from her health being bad, she's got a tosser of a husband (when he puts in an appearance) and never enough cash, and an endless list of problems that come sailing into the bay on a boat called *Victim*.

I know all about the victim complex, trust me – I was brought up around women who expected more than they got out of life and who were always disappointed. Which meant they ended up sort of addicted to suffering. My sister must have learned it from my mum, I suppose, because they both suffered like it was sort of holy, like it was a dying art. Once certain women get a taste for pain, their own ain't enough, you see, they start to fancy other people's as well. Classic example: my mum and my sister each fell in love with a black man. Nothing wrong with that, except in both cases the men happened to be carrying massive plantain chips on their shoulders. So the ladies ended up labouring away with the Black Man's Burden too, because they'd managed to convince themselves it was bigger and better and more *worthy* than any of their own problems. Never mind the fact that it was plain to everyone else that both these cunts had evil tempers and liked their rum too much to be in the running for husband of the year, regardless of what colour they were. I seen it all happen a million times before with nice white girls, girls who think it's some sort of privilege to be a tourist travelling on the visa of a black guy from the Republic of the Great Oppressed.

'We all have our cross,' Ma used to say, except she must have used most of the trees from Battersea Park to make hers, it was that fucking heavy. The funny thing about it is that I always reckoned my old lady loved my dad more than she loved good old Bob from Streatham, who made her cups of tea and bought her flowers and did the ironing on Sundays. I dunno why. She never talked about him that much. But she gave me his name, almost like a premonition he wasn't gonna be around for too long. And she let me get away with murder, too, once he was out the picture.

Anyway, it can't have been that bad, because I managed to get through the suffering circus OK. But I do worry about Kiddie. As soon as Lisa had her own baby, see, and a little brown baby at that, the kid was like a loaded gun. Because he's her vindication, right? Lisa's gonna make sure Kid don't suffer like *she* has, even more so because he's got brown skin, which is probably going to get hurt a bit more than the common or garden pink variety. So she's done the only thing she can within her means – she's tried to make her little boy into a model of caramel cuteness, so perfect and adorable that nobody in their right minds would want to knock him down.

Course, Kiddie went and ruined everything by growing up weird. He's a bit too serious, a bit too awkward to be a proper catalogue kid, he talks in a strange language no one can understand, and most of all, he knows he's different. Not just because of what happened with his dad and all the crazy shit that followed, although that helped set him even further apart from the ideal. Because he's a true loner, Kid is. So, all in all, I understand the appeal of *Star Wars*, the fantasy. It's full of misfits, for one thing.

Kiddie had stopped mumbling to himself and was gazing out the window. I glanced at him and turned on the radio to GLR. Stevie Wonder was singing 'Superstition'. It always makes me think of Lisa, that song. She's well superstitious. And she was the one who first got me into Stevie, although I remember driving myself fucking crazy trying to work out the lyrics, since her albums were strictly out of bounds when I was a kid. I sang along now while Kiddie watched me.

'Who is it?' he said carelessly, which made me chuckle.

'Stevie Wonder.'

'What's supers−?'

'Superstitious? It's when you believe something bad's gonna happen if you do something else. Like if you walk under a ladder.'

'I don't walk under a ladder.'

'See, that's being superstitious. What d'you do when you spill some salt?'

'Sweep it up?'

I laughed. 'Nah, if you were superstitious, you'd throw some over your shoulder. It's hard to explain. It don't really make sense, Kid.'

'Why not?'

''Cos it's a pretty stupid way of looking at things.'

'Are you supers−?'

'Everyone is, a bit, probably.'

'How?'

I thought about it. I am. But not in the old wives' tales kind of way. I've invented my own laws of superstition. It's all about probability. Walk under a ladder and something might fall on your head. Break a mirror and something bad might happen to you. Or it might not. It's the 'might' that's the interesting part, if you ask me. If I finish eating this McDonald's before I hear another police siren in the street, if I make it in my car from King's Cross to Baker Street station down the Marylebone Road without hitting a single red light, if I flip a cigarette up into the air and manage to catch it in my mouth . . . then maybe something I want to happen will happen. See? It's quite a good system. If it don't work, never mind, put it down to probability. If the thing you want to happen does happen, then it's like believing in magic again. I been doing it for years. Makes more sense when you're a kid, because you got nothing to lose then. When you're a kid, wishing hard for things seems like a logical way to go about getting them.

'What do you wish for, Kiddie?'

'Uh?'

'If you had three wishes, what would they be?'

I glanced at him. He seemed amazed by the question and went very quiet, so I didn't push it, and concentrated on looking out for girls on the street – the MTV offices were just round the corner and lots of media chicks went slumming it for breakfast in the Parkway Diner. Not today, though – everyone was hiding inside and waiting for the downpour. In the end I took out the Lovell Line and made a few calls – fucking waste of time, really, as no one I knew was gonna be up for hours. But one of the few advantages to having missed out on a bender was being able to call the wankers up nice and early while they were still sleeping it off, and let their hangovers get an early start.

I left a few rude messages on answerphones which were each trying to outcool the other – why was finding the best bit of music to play on your outgoing message still such an ongoing fucking obsession? One mate of mine actually recorded his own eight-second track in his home studio – he probably thought it was going to get him a record deal. I'd worked my way through all the best options, though, over the years. You name it, Beethoven to Johnny Cash. The opening bars of that Nina Simone track, 'I Wish I Knew How It Would Feel to be Free' lasted the longest ever, partly because I got a big kick out the fact that there was never a shortage of birds asking, 'What *is* that song?' as if it had been keeping them awake at night for years. And the posh ones thought I was well cultured for having the music to old Barry Norman's film show on my machine. Nowadays though I just let Kiddie speak for me.

Five minutes later, as I pulled up outside Ted's house and turned the engine off, Kiddie said in his Yoda voice, 'One. Mummy get better will she. Two. No school there will be. Three. Star Wars.'

'Star Wars what?'

'*Star* Wars.'

We looked at each other for a few seconds and I nodded. Kiddie nodded back. Then I nudged him in the ribs.

'Come on,' I said. 'Let's go and see what Rat Man's up to.'

'Hungry I am,' he said, as we got out of the car.

'I'm not surprised, building three hotels before breakfast.' I locked the car door and went round to the passenger side to take his hand.

'Quick, Kid,' I said, looking up at the clouds massed over our heads. As we reached Ted's front door the sky inched a shade darker and the rain

3

began to come down in slanting grey sheets, misting the ground where it fell. I stood by the window, staring down at the wet, darkening pavements and the tops of the cherry trees above them, trees that had bloomed so early this year, and which were now shaking under the onslaught of rain. 'Unseasonably mild' was the phrase that everyone had been using to describe the weather, the budding plants, the blanket of green which had started to cover London's winter scars. And here I was on this cool, wet spring morning, clutching a little plastic wand with a thin blue line in its window that somehow signified a baby. Unseasonably pregnant.

It seemed like too big a truth somehow, it didn't fit into the scope of a weekday morning, here in the kitchen with the radio droning away and the cup of tea I'd made going cold on the table in front of me, and my nose full of the antiseptic sweetness rising from the pot of hyacinths next to it. I kept glancing around the room, taking a sort of mental inventory of all the familiar things surrounding me, as if their ordinariness might give me some logical answer to all the questions hiding just underneath the strange, blinking denial. My eyes would rest for a minute on something – the jumble of cookery books and medical encyclopaedias on the shelf, the half-raised blinds with their mirrored edges, the row of clean white knickers drying over the radiator – and I'd feel reassured again for a split second. Then there'd be another little hot surge of consciousness in my stomach reminding me that although things might look exactly the same as they had a few minutes ago, they were changed for ever from this point on. Giving up all pretences, my head would repeat its one clear thought: *you poor silly bitch*.

I looked for the hundredth time at the plastic wand in my hand. After I'd seen, disbelieving, the blue line emerge out of its pure, white blankness, and checked the test instructions, and checked them again to make sure I hadn't got it all wrong, and whispered, almost tenderly, my first, quiet '*fuck*' – the next thing I'd done was go downstairs and call up the shop and tell them I wouldn't be coming in this morning. Feigning a migraine, I'd guiltily accepted Jo's clucks of concern at the other end of the line, knowing that deliveries were particularly heavy at the moment. It was spring. People kept on getting married, inconsiderately, and the orders for wedding florals had been steadily trickling in. Everyone bought more flowers when there were things growing on the streets, too – it reminded them they were alive.

The stupid thing was, now I wished I hadn't bothered to lie in the first place, because at least if I'd gone into work I'd have something to do with myself other than skulk around the house, brooding. It was only half past ten now, still over two hours before I was supposed to meet Richard at his hotel. After I'd put the phone down, I'd mechanically made myself breakfast, and got dressed, and wandered through every room in the flat trying to reason with myself. Now there was nothing left to do except ponder the bigger question that had emerged during my meandering attempts at self-reconciliation, in whose shadow all the competing emotions were now merely frolicking. *How was I going to tell him?*

I knew that my lips would have to form the words 'I'm pregnant' and then, hopefully, issue them forth with ladylike control, low but firm-voiced, no wailing or quavering. What came after that, though, was left to the realms of my imagination, which had been wantonly flirting with the variety of possible outcomes that might greet this statement. Such as, the Happy Ending: side by side on the hotel bed in tearful accepting embrace, Richard's head pressed against my miraculously swelling stomach. The Blank Denial: Richard standing by the window, his long, stooped back towards me, gripping the window-sill in silent fury. Then there was the version where my opening knock on the hotel-room door was answered by Richard's wife Claudia, her hair long and loose, wearing a snowy dressing-gown and an expression of blank, enquiring politeness. As I'd never met her, I was almost impressed with this particular scenario's fabrication of detail.

Despite its potential as a setting for high drama, the fact that the revelation of my first pregnancy revolved entirely around a nondescript hotel room wasn't doing much to cheer me up, either. I mean, it would have been fine in fantasies about the *sex* that preceded the pregnancy; I'd had plenty of those myself. Earlier that very morning I'd been lying in the bath imagining the afternoon of physical indulgence that lay ahead of me, and feeling smug. Anyone else would have called it happiness, but I knew better than to tempt fate. I always got that way on Wednesdays, which were Richard days, when even the moments before waking were suffused with a sort of drowsy pleasure, like a kid asleep on Christmas morning who already knows that the luxurious weight on her feet at the end of the bed means something wonderful is going to happen as soon as she opens her eyes.

On this particular morning, having drifted off in a haze of steam and voluptuous thoughts, I'd managed to gouge my knee open with a disposable razor while I was shaving my legs, cutting the reveries painfully short. I'd pulled the plug, moaning with pain, and hopped out of the bath to look for a plaster in the cupboard under the sink, leaving a bloody trail. And that was when I saw the pregnancy kit, crammed in with all the junk. The box had been sitting there primly among the curdled suntan lotions and homeopathic remedies and gluey bottles of old nail varnish for a year and a half, in the panicked aftermath of a one-night-stand that eventually resolved itself before I'd summoned the nerve to use the test. Somehow, after I'd stuck a Band Aid on my knee, I found myself taking out the box and unwrapping the parts and fitting them together and climbing back into the bath to hold it underneath me while I blithely took aim over it into the disappearing bath water. I did all of this without really thinking about what it meant, that there could be a real consequence attached to my actions. There was only the vaguest thought in my head that my period was a bit late, and I might as well just rule out the worst possible scenario while I was at it . . .

Suddenly, slumped over the side of the bath, my feet anointed with water and blood and wee, I was confronted with the sight of the thin blue line in its supposedly empty window. I just held the piece of plastic and stared at it, thinking that the thinness of the thin and the blueness of the blue contained within that line seemed like the most absolute and undeniable properties of anything I'd ever seen, more certain of their purpose and their place in the universe than anyone, with the possible exception of Richard.

Shit. Richard.

Still crouching in the bath, I had a flashback to the first time we'd ever met, making him a temporary stranger again. It was when I was a teenager having lunch with Ben, my dad, in a restaurant in Holland Park. During the pasta and the second glass of wine, which had already softened the edges of his usual mixture of courtly solicitousness and gentle, paternal exasperation, I'd seen a tall man approach our table from the bar. He loomed over us, pointing at my dad accusingly. 'Benjamin,' he said, knitting his eyebrows together and stabbing his forefinger towards Ben menacingly as he pronounced the word in measured, slightly northern tones, pulling apart the syllables of my father's name with a treacly slowness. I was thrilled. No one ever pointed things at my dad, who was an accountant and seemed to inhabit a neutral adult world undisturbed by strong emotions or sudden physical gestures. Ben, who'd just taken a sizeable mouthful of food, turned red, and started waving his hands and chewing fast and trying to speak at the same time in a bizarre display of agitation. I wondered if some sort of fight was about to break out, but the other man said nothing, just held his pose magnificently, finger cocked triggerlike towards my dad, who continued to work his jaws and splutter and flap his wrists about in a very unfamiliar way. I found myself leaning towards him and willing him to finish his mouthful so that the exchange could proceed. At last he made a final swallow and croaked out, 'Richard, God!'

'You flatter me, Ben,' the man said, and winked. Then my dad was up out of his seat and the two of them were shaking hands and grasping each other's shoulders and doing all the tweedy reined-in things that middle-aged men do to show they're happy to see each other. I was a bit disappointed, as I was still half hoping for some kind of duel outside the restaurant, but I sat and waited to be introduced.

'Sara, this is Richard,' Ben said, turning to me after the shoulder-grasping was over. 'You've heard me talk about him, haven't you? We were at university together.' I nodded, because I *had* heard about Richard over the years, his name had a nursery-rhyme familiarity about it. Before I was born, he'd lived with Ben in Leeds, a town peopled with various friends and relatives and dogs and cats that I'd never known, which over the years had acquired a sort of mythical resonance.

Richard had a firm handshake and an air of mild dishevelment which somehow made me acutely aware of how conventional Ben and I must look sitting there together, and I felt suddenly shy, letting my own hand fall back into my lap. Unlike most of my dad's friends – weekend golfers who were getting politely fat around the middle and carefully averted their eyes from my tits whenever I saw them – it was hard to pin Richard down just by looking at him. His impressive length was topped with a wiry brush of stiff, dark, greying hair, the face hosting a large, stern nose with an amused mouth below it, framed by sprouting eyebrows and prodigious ears. He wore a drooping corduroy jacket over a green shirt, and a packet of cigars poked out of a pocket near his lapel. I remember wondering what he did – whether he was an artist or a university lecturer or a gentleman farmer.

Of course I'm overplaying it now – his most significant characteristic to me at the time was probably that he was the same age as my dad. I was seventeen then and thought my boyfriend of the time, Nick, who was twenty-four, the height of mature sophistication. Anyone much older was irrelevant. Anyway, I didn't get more than a brief nod and a handshake before Richard turned back to Ben. I noticed that Ben himself was acting rather oddly – he kept grinning stupidly at Richard one minute, then giving him these slightly furtive looks as if he was unsure what to say next. It didn't really matter, because Richard did most of the talking. He asked after my mum, Estelle, and told Ben he'd been having lunch with his lawyer, who my dad also knew, and rattled on about living in the country and being out of touch with London and the old set, and how long it had been . . . Eventually I switched off, bored, and went back to trying to eat my spaghetti without making too much of a mess.

At one point, Ben finally managed to get a word in, and said, 'And *you*, Richard, you're . . . OK?' Something in the way he said it made me look up from my food, and Richard grinned at him and said, 'They haven't got me yet.' Ben fiddled with his glasses and said, 'Yes, yes, I can see that. Good for you,' and smiled almost shyly. After another few minutes Richard said he was running late, and they shook hands again. I received another smile before he turned and left our table as abruptly as he'd arrived. Then I asked my dad why it was that old people never swapped phone numbers when they bumped into each other, if they were supposed to be such great friends.

Ben had answered that when you were his age, you didn't bother making the same pretences you once had for purely social reasons.

'But I thought you and Richard used to be best mates, or something?' I said.

'Yes, we did,' he said rather wistfully. 'But it's like first love, sometimes. It'll be the same for you, you'll see. In ten years' time you'll have completely lost touch with certain friends that you can't imagine life without at this point in time.'

Then he attacked his food again and began to tell me stories I'd never heard about the student Existentialist Society that they'd founded at university, and how Richard had been their year's *enfant terrible* and brightest hope.

'Oh yeah? What does he do now?' I'd asked, and Ben stopped mid-anecdote and said in a puzzled voice, 'I can't actually remember. He used to teach, years ago. These days, I think he's a . . . *carpenter*?' Sipping wine, I scoffed to myself for imagining there had been anything remotely romantic-looking about him, and we went back to arguing about the size of my bank overdraft.

I didn't see Richard again for nearly eleven years, and Ben was right – by then there were plenty of people I'd known as a teenager who I would have ducked into a doorway to avoid saying hello to. Richard might easily have been one of them, too, if I'd been anything close to the kind of self-absorbed, successfully intentioned person that I'd once imagined I'd naturally turn out to be, unaided. Only over the years away at art college in Glasgow, then back in London on the dole pretending to be an artist, and the summers spent working at the Edinburgh Festival toying with the idea of becoming an actress – followed by the inevitable attempts at serious jobs, once the resulting disillusionment had set in – that vague but persistent belief that I could still do anything I wanted if I really set my mind to it had been slowly worn away to nothing. By then my parents had been divorced for over a decade, and I was more rootless than ever, sent spinning off in different directions like a sycamore key on gusts of inspiration or boredom or love. After Nick, in whose company I stumbled drunk and politically deluded over the threshold of adolescence, there was Stuart in Glasgow, with the big grin and the VW camper van and the driving ambition to dreadlock his red, Celtic hair; and then Julian the art dealer, who rinsed out the remaining dregs of my studenthood by instilling in me a self-motivating jealousy of his loft in Old Street and his weekends in New York and his Lifestyle with the capital L. All of them left me sticky with their own residues – musical tastes and sets of friends and holiday photos, as well as the emotional scars – but none of them took me any nearer to a place that felt, unequivocally, like home.

I ended up selling flowers in Westbourne Park; an over-educated Eliza, as Ben liked to call me. The shop was famous for its exquisite blooms, expensively dressed and seductively displayed, destined for cut glass and polished dining-room tables and marquees and extravagant gestures. I actually liked the work a lot, and there was the hyper-village of West London to keep me distracted with its pubs and shops and gossip and faces, as well as my friends, and the flat I had in Queen's Park. I kept on trying to paint pictures too, starting them in fits of enthusiasm then abandoning them for a good novel or a TV show or a complicated recipe. Maybe under the surface of it all I still had some elusive notion that happiness was floating around in the London air along with the soot and the smoke and the beer-fug, just waiting to be caught one-handed, like thistledown. But I might not have thought about any of this, until one Sunday in early autumn.

I was strolling through Kensington Gardens with my best friend Chloe when I saw Richard walking towards us. The memory of him sprang from nowhere into my head, and I stopped dead in my tracks. Chloe asked me what was wrong and I said, 'Nothing' unconvincingly, because I found myself standing there, watching him get nearer and nearer and panicking about what I should say to him. He was alone, hands in his pockets, walking along briskly, and when we were within about ten or twelve feet of each other, he raised his head as if he'd known all along I was waiting for him, and our eyes met.

There should have been music playing somewhere in the background. An opera, maybe, something sweeping and grandiose, because the moment seemed so staged that it forced a nervous giggle out of me. I glanced around, thinking everyone in the park must be watching us, and almost expecting my dad to come trotting out, beaming, but Richard just kept walking towards me, knitting his brows and then smiling, and I thought, at least he recognizes me. When we were finally standing opposite each other, I asked him if he remembered me from the restaurant all those years ago. 'Ah, *yes*!' he said in a pleased voice, as if my identity was a conundrum that had been puzzling him for ages. I introduced him to Chloe and we talked about polite things like the weather and how quickly the summer had gone, and what we did in London, while he glanced between the two of us and worked his eyebrows around our responses.

All the time we were talking I was covertly studying him, absorbing him as if he was a painting in a gallery, trying him out from every angle. He looked almost the same as I remembered, although baggier around the eyes and with greyer hair. It was my take on him that had changed, and I found myself shaking my head at the teenager I'd once been for mishandling the details of him all those years ago. He was wearing a faded old blue open-necked shirt and I looked at the silvery-black hair at the top of his chest and the brown of his forearms, and felt a sense of amazement at my proximity to these small things.

Eventually he said he'd better get going or he'd be late, and I imagined him going to have dinner with some intelligent older woman in a dark-red restaurant. He shook hands with us in turn, and he looked at me very directly when he said goodbye, in that amused, intimate way he had, and said he'd drop into the shop sometime.

'I'm in your area at least once a week,' he said pleasantly. 'You can instruct me on the art of choosing flowers for women, I've never really mastered it.' He winked as he took off, leaving me standing there dazedly in the late-afternoon sunshine. As soon as he was out of earshot, Chloe said, 'Who was *that*?'

I gave her a sideways look. 'He's an old family friend,' I said, thinking how strange it was to flank him mentally with Ben and Estelle.

'He must have been a killer twenty years ago,' she went on, and then took in my face. 'Although I can see there's no need to tell you that. You've already got the word MINE stamped across your forehead.'

'Have not,' I said. 'Anyway, I've only met him once.'

'Well,' Chloe said, 'you'd better wash your apron and brush up your flower-selling skills, just in case. How old is he? Probably just about the perfect age for seducing a plump young maiden like yourself. Was he wearing a ring?'

'I wasn't *looking*,' I said. 'I'm a plump young maiden, remember, not some kind of desperate spinster like you are.' We walked on into the park. The idea of it clung on stubbornly, though, to the underbelly of the laughter.

Over the next few days, while I idled with the question of whether to tell Ben or Estelle I'd seen Richard (I didn't in the end, knowing the temptation to interrogate them both for details about him would probably give me away), I exhausted our conversation in my head on replay, and the pictures of him I'd stored up became indistinct with over-use. He was so present in my thoughts that I was slightly confused by the fact that he wasn't actually there in reality. It couldn't last though; having nothing to feed off, the crush eventually became thin and listless, and I stopped illogically looking out for him every time I drove past the park.

Things crept along in their seasonal way, the temperature dropped, and I even went out a few times with a man called Roman – a sculptor I'd met whose name I'd fallen for helplessly. These days my liaisons with men seemed to be kick-started by an ever-arbitrary range of stimuli: a poetic name, an artistic talent, nice handwriting, a pair of Clarks shoes. Unfortunately for this guy, his artefacts turned out to be even worse than he was in bed. Anyway, about three weeks later I was at work in the shop one afternoon, and turned around from tying a bouquet with twine to see Richard standing right behind me with his nose deep in a vase of lilies. As I gaped at him, he straightened up. 'How lovely,' he said, directing his comment to the flowers in my hands. For a horrible moment I thought he didn't remember who I was, but then I saw that he was smiling, and I blushed, as if he'd been referring to me directly. I glanced down at the bouquet and nodded, tongue-tied, and I noticed that he had a tiny smear of orange pollen on the end of his nose, and that my hands were shaking.

When I looked up again, he was regarding me with a speculative air. 'You look like a pirate,' he said, and I automatically put a hand to my head, over which I'd tied a scarf to hide my new, too-short haircut. 'A very attractive pirate,' he added kindly, and I dropped the hand and fiddled with the flowers again. His expression changed slightly. 'Actually, you look very much like your mother. Quite amazing, really. Can I buy you lunch?'

We went to the Portobello Gold. He started off by buying us both a glass of wine, and we took them over to the window. I thought I caught him looking at me in a slightly hungry way across the table, but I wasn't sure whether it was a sign of passion or his appetite. Then, when our sandwiches arrived, he took a tearing bite out of his, swallowed it and began tossing questions at me, quite casually, but with an intent that reminded me of the market-research questionnaires I'd once been paid to ask people at the Ideal Home Exhibition. They'd told us how to woo the consumer. *Be interested, but never pushy. Be sincere, but not too personal. Smile!* In between sips of Bordeaux and mouthfuls of food, I relaxed into the even more delicious activity of talking about myself, although part of me was wondering if he'd hold up a scorecard at the end of it all.

'What do you really want to *do*, though?' he said at one point, having established that my job in the shop wasn't a rung on a career ladder to becoming some sort of floral mogul. I almost choked on a sun-dried tomato. No one had asked me that particular million-dollar question for as long as I could remember. I looked at his large, expressive hands holding his glass, and thought, mechanically, *Have a love affair with an older man . . .*

'You know what your problem is?' he said, swirling the last inch of his wine. 'I bet you never got the chance to rebel when you were a kid, did you?'

'*Yes*, I did,' I said, thrown, indignant as the kid I wasn't supposed to be any more.

'Come on, I know your mum and dad, remember,' he said. 'They were never going to produce an anarchic baby. You've probably never had the opportunity to actually break away from anything fundamental in your life, and therefore deep down you're still looking for a way to prove yourself. Which is why you're still drifting, I expect.'

While I was wavering between rebuffal and the desire to put my head in his lap, he winked at me. 'Don't look so affronted. I'm still drifting, and you've got years on me. I just know the signs, that's all.' Then he started reminiscing about Ben and Estelle and the time they'd all been at university together. Had I heard the story about my dad and the ice-cream van they'd stolen in Leeds? No, I hadn't. Did I know that Richard had met my grandparents on Ben's side, who both died before I was born? Well, no. What about the fact that my parents' pet names for each other at college had been 'Ratty' and 'Mole'. *No.* As the details emerged I was filled with pleasure as well as a wincing kind of fascination. I suddenly thought, *He's showing me my life.* Unexpectedly, it seemed to be something that was rich with humour and history, and I was full of grateful tenderness. I wanted to return the compliment but didn't know how.

He was married, of course. He didn't wear a ring, which I stored up to tell Chloe, and he didn't live in London either, but somewhere near Cambridge. He drove in for a day or two every week to teach philosophy in a West London college. He was writing a book, too, 'About my years in the wilderness,' he said, draining his glass cryptically, and looking as if he expected me to press him for further details. But I didn't, I was too jumpy with adrenalin by then to think about asking him anything remotely intelligent.

When he'd run out of questions for me, he took out a slim cigar and lit it. I sat there and bathed in the rich smoke that enveloped both of us, watching him roll it around his mouth with evident pleasure. After a few minutes I asked, gauchely, if I could try a puff. He held it out to me, and as I took it from him my fingers rested on his for a second or two. In that split second the balance between us shifted, and I experienced a moment of absolute feminine certainty in my own power to seduce him. I didn't understand where it came from – it just rose up like a sea monster, and before I could decide whether it was real or not, it had disappeared again into the murk.

He asked for the bill. When it came, he stubbed his cigar out and said, smiling, but somehow serious, 'And are you going to tell Ben and Estelle about our lunch today?' I shrugged, casually, although a voice echoed briefly from somewhere in the depths, *That means he doesn't want you to, stupid.* I took it as another sighting. Maybe that was all the mysterious creature was – the conviction that if you believed in something enough, it *would* become real.

Outside, I thanked him for lunch, and we went our separate ways, but not before he'd told me he'd stop in again sometime to see me. I meandered back to the shop with the bitter taste of tobacco on my tongue, giddy from the wine and the cross-examination, and proceeded to cut my hands to ribbons all afternoon on the thorny stems of indifferent flowers.

The week after, he did stop in again. And the week after that. When he was in town he usually stayed in a hotel in Paddington, and depending on what he was doing that week, he nearly always made time to see me in between his teaching and the odd meeting with publishers or his agent. He never phoned me or anything like that – he'd just show up at the shop on Wednesdays, after his early class, and we'd go and do something together on my lunchbreak. I even switched my schedule without telling him so I could work the first shift at the shop and have the afternoons off.

It was a slow education for me. We graduated gently over the weeks from sitting in cafés to other neutral activities: walks, window-shopping, a photography exhibition once, we even saw a couple of films. Through all the talking and the ever-flowing stream of questions, some kind of intimacy began to seep through the layers of fascination and nervous covetousness that possessed me whenever I saw his steely head bending over the flower pails. And yet there was always some unspoken agreement between the two of us not to discuss exactly what it was that we were doing.

I knew we were doing *something*. In between contemplating whether to ask him what it was decorously, or merely throw myself on him indecorously, I was holding my breath and waiting for another swift glimpse of the sea monster, a certainty that would tell me to act, *now*. I kept on waiting, breathless. Nobody seemed to be able to give me much advice about what to do. The friends I told about him were split into two camps: those who egged me on in their assumption that I was having some sort of frivolous suspenders-and-champagne affair, and the more sensible ones who were constantly droning on about my incipient disaster, since Richard was married and older and generally not for sale. All of them were united in their constant and morbid curiosity about what it was like having sex with an older man, as if he was already a corpse – despite the fact that I kept telling them we hadn't even exchanged so much as a peck on the lips.

One afternoon we were leaving a Turkish café Richard liked on the Edgeware Road and heading to where his car was parked when the skies opened on us. Exhilarated and soaked to the skin, we got in the car, squelching, and decided to drive to his hotel, the Lansdowne, to get dry. I'd never been up to his room before. Once we were through the door, the pressure of being in such an intimate space with him made me shy. I was towelling my hair and studiously trying to avoid looking at the double bed, which seemed to fill every corner of my vision, when he came up behind me and asked me if I was OK. While I was trying to frame my answer, he gently took the towel away from me.

I was so nervous I was shivering inside my damp clothes, but once his hands were on me, I was suddenly calm. It was such a relief to finally be physically close to him, stripped down and unable to hide, that I wavered between the impulse to fight hysterics or burst into tears. Luckily my mouth was occupied and I did neither. Lying there under Richard's heavy, smooth body, with the bleached afternoon light filtering through the net curtains, and my nose full of his skin and hair and the familiar smell of him magnified full strength, I remember thinking, *This is the most intentional sex you've ever had*. It was terrifying and magnificent. All the time he was above me, so close that I could see the change in the size of his pupils when our eyes locked, I was marvelling at the fact that I seemed to be coping perfectly without the veil of darkness and alcohol I was used to. It occurred to me that probably this was what people meant when they talked about sexual maturity.

When it was finally over we lay silently beached in the big white bed, my head on his arm, with the dim traffic noises drifting up from the street, and the closer sound of his stomach gurgling like a drain. I listened to it raptly, as if it was a secret message being transmitted from his body to mine. It struck me that my own body's capacity for pleasure was actually quite separate from that of my brain's for fear, pain, or embarrassment – all the things I generally associated with having feelings for men. It was like having a surplus of chocolate or coffee or cigarettes, with no thought in my head about them being bad for me, and it seemed both deeply wrong and deeply exciting. I thought, this is my biological instinct taking over from all the years of wrongful socialization. And then, I'm not going to move until he does.

Eventually he sighed and reached around to stroke my hair with his free hand, while his arm creaked out from under me. I looked at the red mark my head had made on his skin, silently thrilled at the sight of it. *Sara woz ere.* When we'd put our clothes back on, we sat on the edge of the bed, doing our shoes up side by side. I was so demoralized by the absolute physical satisfaction I was feeling, which I thought must be visible, surrounding me like some glowing Ready-Brek aura, that I couldn't actually look him in the eye. I just sat there staring at my feet and trying not to grin out loud.

Then he took my hand. We faced each other, and my heart sank as I braced myself for his words. *Here it comes*, I thought, *the disavowal.*

'Well, my love,' he began in an almost fatherly tone, and then stopped and peered at me. 'Are you all right?' he said. 'You look sort of . . . stricken. Do you feel ill?' I looked down, hot-cheeked.

'Hey, what's wrong?' he asked, putting his arm around me. 'Was I that bad?'

I laughed through my nose and shook my head, suddenly terrified again.

'This was never my plan, you know, you and me, like this,' Richard said in an absent-minded voice, massaging my hand with his own. I looked at his face with helpless affection, at his eyebrows and his stupid ears and all the things that had become so familiar to me. 'Not that I didn't want it.'

'What are we going to do?' I ventured in a squeaky voice. I was so worried that he was going to tell me we shouldn't see each other any more that I actually felt a bit sick.

He sighed. 'I don't know, flower.'

His uncertainty made me brave for a moment, and I said, 'But I don't want to lose any of . . . this.'

He gave me a quick, rueful smile. 'Sometimes it seems as though nothing has any real value until you realize you might lose it.' I was still pondering this when he turned and looked me right in the eyes. 'Are you ready for it, though? Whatever this is?' I was frightened for a minute by the warning in his voice. Then he went on, 'Are you ready to take the consequences of this wonderful freedom we have?'

I relaxed then – it seemed like such a helpless Richardism. 'Is that a line from your book?' I said, and he laughed, and gave me a smiling kiss. As I returned the kiss I thought to myself, *I'm having an affair with a married man. When the hell did this happen?*

Soon after the first time, Richard was staying in the hotel every week and we were spending most of our afternoons in his room. In over twelve weeks we only missed three or four Wednesdays: twice over Christmas, once when he was in Ireland with his wife, and once when I was in bed with a bad cold. I had inadvertently become someone's mistress. It sounded hilarious and horrible, an indelible word. Chloe put it into my head, half-joking, but it lingered, conjuring up polished images of perfect womanhood – of silky, predatory creatures who mixed cocktails in private rooms while their men rolled up their shirtsleeves and lay back on divans, smoking cigars. Then there was me, Sara of the mid-priced Paddington hotel. I was about as far removed from this imaginary twilight *femme fatale* as was possible. When I was younger I'd always been the girl with the bra-strap hanging down, the laddered tights, and a tendency to burst out of my clothes at inopportune moments. It was only after years of practising that I was able to control the impulses of my body and present a united front, but underneath I knew it was only an illusion that all my elements were held together, and that they could fly apart at any moment.

Over the months with Richard I'd bled on the white hotel sheets and left pairs of knickers forgotten on the carpet. I lost an earring once in bed and made him search for it on the floor, naked on his hands and knees. Once I bit his hand in experimental passion so hard that he yelled out, and a passing chambermaid came knocking anxiously and jabbering in Portuguese-accented English until Richard poked his head around the door and assured her no one had been murdered. Not that any of it seemed to bother him. 'Imperfections are what make us all human. So to love imperfection is to love humanity,' he once said to me in bed, after I'd pointed out the various scars on my body left over from childhood illnesses and my general physical ineptitude. At the time I'd mock-swooned all over him. Only now, in my living room, with the rain beating down outside, I was left wondering exactly what Richard was going to make of this great big perfect flaw that now existed in my belly.

The hyacinths trembled delicately as I got up from the table, which was covered with the tiny half-moons of silver nail polish that I'd been chewing off my fingertips over the last hour. Looking at the clock, I realized that Justine, my flatmate, was due to arrive home from her nightshift at Hammersmith hospital quite soon, so I went upstairs into my bedroom, still holding the test wand aloft like some doomed fairy. I found a tissue, wrapped it up and shoved it in my bag, out of sight. As I turned, I caught sight of myself in my bedroom mirror, and stopped, my mouth slightly agape. When I'd got dressed earlier in my shocked half-daydream, I must have been subconsciously striving for some sort of vision of purity, because I was a whiter shade of pale, right down to my shoes. White T-shirt, washed-out pale-beige combat trousers, the white rubber clogs I always wore when it was wet, and my one concession to luxury – a long, cream, cashmere cardigan which had been a present from Ben. Only combined with my hair, which was sticking up in dark tufts, I looked not unlike some kind of pregnant Eskimo. Either that or a particularly ruffled white duck.

I closed my mouth, slightly stunned, and thought about ripping everything off and starting from scratch, but instead I picked up a bottle from the dresser and sprayed perfume on my neck and wrists. There was no point pretending everything was OK, in or out of my clothes. Richard was just going to have to deal with it, like I was, I announced to myself with false but hearty militancy. And then suddenly, out of nowhere, I was charged with adrenalin. Or maybe I was high on perfume. Either way, I thought dizzily, my nose full of fumes, it was impossible to really prepare yourself for the surprise of what might be. After all, ten years ago Richard was a strange, hairy man in a restaurant. If someone had suggested then that I might end up having a baby with him, it couldn't have sounded more outlandish if they'd told me that ted eats worms.

this is what lovell tells me after i rung the doorbell on teds door and we re waitin for him to open it, and the rains comin down pitter patter on our heads.

lovell says, ok KIDDIE, you ready for the rat attack?

whats that?

lovell goes, we re here to help ted out with his rat problem.

uh?

lovell says, teds got a rat fatality in his kitchen, KID. meaning, its dead. so we ve gotta help him get rid of it.

its dead?

yeah.

will there be worms?

worms? shouldnt think so. why, you scared of worms?

worms are dirty. and wriggly. arent they?

yeah, but most people prefer em to rats, lovell says, specially ted. in fact, teds really into worms, i think he makes em into pies. so if he offers you anything to eat upstairs, better say ta but no ta.

i look at lovell and he aint even smilin or nothin. just then the front door opens and out comes a man wearin shorts and a sweatshirt and theres a picture of mickey mouse on the sweatshirt and theres a stain on mickeys head. *worm juice*.

yuk, the stain man says, lookin up at the sky and squintin at us.

i look at lovell again and he winks at me and goes, remember what i told you, KID. then he gives ted a hug.

you look terrible, man, lovell says. by the way, this is KIDDIE. and this is ted, he goes to me.

ted says hello and shows me his hand.

shake it, KID, lovell tells me, so i shake teds hand, and then we turn round and follow him inside the house.

what happened to his head? i hear ted say to lovell as we climb up the stairs.

who, KIDDIE? oh, his mum trimmed his hair with a razor on the wrong setting, shes trainin to be a hairdresser.

but hes practically bald, goes ted, whisper whisper.

it ll grow, lovell says, puttin his hand on my head, all warm, and he goes, now take us to the scene of the crime.

teds house is right up the top. theres eighteen steps to climb, and i look at teds skinny white legs steppin in front of me, and im whisperin, practickly ball, practickly ball as my feet hit each stair, and holdin on to lovells hand.

we follow him down the hall, and into the kitchen. im a bit scared of what we might see but i dont say nothin, just look around me, and theres books and newspapers everywhere and its cold and theres a mouse lyin down in the middle of the floor.

after a minute lovell says, it aint that big, is it?

ted says, its still a fucking rat, and then his face goes red and he looks at me and says, sorry, and lovell laughs and says, i wouldnt worry, man, KIDDIE knows every curse in the book.

ted looks at me and goes, all jolly, what do you think of mister rat, KIDDIE?

if it is a rat, that is, lovell says, winkin at me.

its alright, i say and put my hands in my pockets.

lovell says, dont worry, KID, its a hundred per cent dead, it cant bite you. no worms neither.

can you smell it? ted asks lovell, and lovell nods, pulls a face, and i want to smell it too and i take a sniff, and i cant smell nothin but i pull the same face as lovell.

yuk, i go.

lovell and ted laugh and then ted says, what now?

we re standin in a line in front of the rat, lookin down at it, and its got little tiny fingers, all curled up.

lovell says, throw it away man, and then get the council in to check there aint a nest.

ted goes, oh christ. well what do i do with this one?

wrap it up and bin it, man. what you supposed to do, stuff it?

what if they need it for reference or something? the pest control people. they might need to, you know, log it.

it aint a homin pigeon, teddy boy, its a dead rat. lets just get rid of it quick.

then the phone starts ringin next door, and teddy boy says, hang on, and goes out of the kitchen. the ringin stops, and he starts talkin. me and lovell stand there just lookin at the rat.

what we doin now? i go.

i think we should give it a decent burial at the very least, lovell says, scratchin.

whats that?

well, lovell goes, remember when darth vader dies?

uh.

they pile him up on a stack of wood and set fire to it, right?

yeah.

well there you go, thats a pretty decent burial.

lovell picks up a newspaper from the kitchen table and throws it over the rat, hidin it.

see, thats more decent already, innit?

thirsty i am.

ok, lets see what hes got, lovell says, and goes over to the fridge, and i follow him.

not much in the way of drinks, KID. water, and thats about it, unless you re in the mood for a guinness. then lovell takes out a silver box from the fridge and lifts the lid and peeks inside.

but look what we have here, he goes.

i take a breath. worms?

lovell looks at me sideways, holdin the box up high so i cant see, and he says, whatcha reckon?

is it?

lovell waits a second and then he yells WORMS and shoves the box into my face.

aaaeeegggh!

i run backwards to the corner of the kitchen, and at the same time ted runs through the door and nearly knocks me over, shoutin, jesus christ, did it move?

lovell comes towards me still holdin the silver box. i take a step back.

its alright, KIDDIE, dont cry, he goes. im only messin, darlin, its not worms, its just rice, look.

i aint cryin.

i know, KID. lovell holds the silver box out in front of me and i look at the rice, all yellow and dried up.

ted goes, why on earth did he think there were worms in my fridge?

me and lovell look at each other and we start

5

laughing, the two of them, like maniacs, while I stood there dumbly, still winded in the aftershock of my sprint into the kitchen. Lovell was holding a carton containing the desiccated remains of a two-day-old biriani, while Kiddie stood next to him like a miniature henchman in his sweatshirt and trainers. Both of them were shaking with mirth.

'*What?*' I said. 'For Christ's sake.'

''Kin' 'ell,' Lovell said eventually, coughing. 'Woah. Sorry. Little misunderstanding.' He winked at Kiddie, who was still vibrating with laughter in shrill, hiccupping little waves which were surprisingly piercing for someone so small. I glanced at him with dislike. There was something oddly forced about Kiddie, he was like a grown-up dwarf disguised as a child, one who had all the right gestures and mannerisms down a bit too perfectly for them to be convincingly real. It was unnerving, especially when you spoke to him. He'd just look up at you with solemn blankness, as if he was secretly marvelling at what a huge lumbering mess this adult before him was. Then he'd usually start muttering to himself under his breath.

Lovell seemed to manage to ignore all this. He'd told me all the stories about Kiddie's thing for *Star Wars* and various other peculiarities which had made me laugh in the past, but now I'd finally met Kiddie I found him more irritating than entertaining. Although I suppose if Lovell's accounts of his sister, the hairdresser from hell, were anything to go by, then it was no wonder Kiddie was a little unbalanced. It would explain his ridiculous haircut anyway.

While I was gazing down at the shorn and fuzzy top of Kiddie's head, he gave a final hiccup and stopped laughing, pointing to the floor where the rat lay, now covered by yesterday's *Standard*. The front page bore a photo of the Queen flashing her fixed grimace, the displeased mouth stretched tight around neat dentures. South of her chin, where her neck disappeared into the fold of the newspaper, an inch or two of greyish rat tail protruded.

'Buried him we did,' Kiddie said, 'decently.'

Suddenly I was overcome by a great nauseous wave of exhaustion, and sank to the floor beside him. Kiddie looked alarmed but stayed where he was, bouncing at the knees as if he might skitter away across the kitchen floor any moment. I listened absently to his whispering monologue, catching a disjointed phrase about having trained Jedi for eight hundred years. He smelled fragrantly of soap and freshly washed clothes. I wondered if I'd ever smelled as clean when I was a small boy. It didn't seem possible.

'Ted?' Lovell was saying. 'You all right, son?'

'No,' I said. 'I feel like shit. And I've just found out that I've got to go to work in about an hour's time.'

'Work where?'

'I just got a call from the editor at *Fisch*.'

'Fish?'

'*Fisch*, it's a magazine I write for sometimes.'

'*Fish?*'

'Yes,' I said impatiently. 'You wouldn't have read it. Anyway, I've said I'll cover for their staff writer who's just called in sick and go to Paddington to interview someone this afternoon.'

'Who?'

'Richard Shaw,' I mumbled.

'Who is he?'

'He's a pop philosopher. And before –'

'What the fuck's a pop philosopher?'

'– you ask me, I have no idea what it means. He's some new

writer, he's supposed to be hot stuff. Oh, Jesus,' I said, as the implications of it all hit me, 'why did I say I'd do it? If I'm going anywhere it should be back to bed.'

'Well, why *did* ya say you'd do it, then?' Lovell said, walking over to the bin and depositing the take-away box in it. Kiddie followed him.

'Possibly because I'm sitting on the kitchen floor next to a dead rat and the thought of even standing up again is enough to make me want to puke? Please don't ask me to be fucking logical,' I said bitterly, watching him as he removed a pile of *NME*s and a full ashtray from the only chair and sat down on it, crossing one immaculate denim leg over the other. Blue Argyle socks. Hygienically clean trainers, imported from New York.

'Well, tell 'em you changed your mind. Can't be all that important, this fish thing, can it? Not if I've never heard of it,' he added, brushing off his knee. Kiddie had assumed a position by the window next to Lovell's chair. In the wan daylight both their brown skins seemed to glow with a uniform burnished warmth. The two sets of dark eyes regarded me steadily and under their twin gaze I felt myself retreating further into my morning filth, hunched on the floor like a kitchen dog.

'I can't,' I said.

'Why not?'

'Because I've said I'll do it now.'

'Well then, say you don't wanna do it any more. Tell 'em you're ill. You *look* fucking ill.'

'Can't,' I said childishly. 'You can't fuck editors around like that, otherwise they never give you any work, and I need the work.'

'Then, fucksake, you're gonna have to grin and bear it, aren't you? Swallow some headache pills and drink some coffee or whatever. I'll even drive you to the interview, right? Only stop whining.'

'Yes Mum,' I said, after a pause. Lovell flashed me one of his pure grins, which it was impossible to receive ungraciously.

'Go on then, Teddy, and get up off that filthy floor,' he said in a passable imitation of my mother. I didn't really want to move, even though the cold lino was pushing a deep ache into my buttocks. 'I should go and have a shower,' I said feebly.

'Yeah, you should, you reek.'

'Cheers.'

'What's a reek?' said Kiddie. He stood with his hands in his pockets, staring down at me from across the kitchen as if I was some biological specimen on the slab.

'That,' said Lovell, pointing at me and holding his nose with his other hand.

'Yuk,' Kiddie said, and for some reason this was enough to set the two of them off again. While they cackled, I rose to my feet and stood there swaying and hanging my head, which felt as if it might crack open at any moment and spatter my addled brains on to the floor.

'I'm going to throw up,' I announced, and left the room.

In the bathroom, I locked the door unnecessarily and sat down on the toilet seat, slouching over my knees and waiting for the nausea to pass with closed eyes. After a few minutes of silence I heard Lovell and Kiddie start singing next door. I lifted my head and listened, wishing I had a cigarette. It took them a couple of rounds to get it right, but the words seemed to be, inspirationally: 'Yuk, yuk, covered in muck, Ted is throwing up,' sung to the rhythmic monotone of 'This Is Radio Clash'.

At least Kiddie was getting a better musical education than I'd ever had, I thought, heaving myself upright and turning on the taps. When I was a kid my music collection was made up of clumsily edited cassettes recorded from the Top 40 Chart Rundown on Sunday afternoons. Since I had no older brothers and sisters to help me out, and the most exciting record owned by my mum was an LP of Greek myths and legends narrated by Arthur C. Clarke, I didn't have much chance of being pointed in any kind of reasonable musical direction when I was younger. It wasn't until I was well into my teens that I got into regularly stalking the local Our Price in my secondhand trenchcoat, searching through the racks of albums for something to alleviate my perpetual adolescent fog of boredom and despair.

After I met Lovell, he became the lucky person upon whose shoulders it fell to fill in some of the gaps after all those solitary years of Joy Division and The Smiths and bleakly tender heroin rock. He was responsible for showing me, quite unintentionally, that music could lend itself to feelings of euphoria other than the kind I had experienced in my headphones during woeful stoned reveries or long bouts of masturbation on winter nights. Lovell liked music that actually made you feel good about yourself, that was about dancing and feeling up girls and general elevation. His idea of a good tune wasn't one that was akin to wallowing down a well full of manic depressives, as he instructed me after walking in on me a few times in Holloway listening to John Martyn.

I knew a bit about elevation from a few sessions with magic mushrooms and Pink Floyd, but it was hard for me to get what Lovell was on about. Basically, I didn't trust dance music. Of course, I understood something about the polarity between the black and white musical traditions of our own cultural backgrounds – soul versus intellect, hope versus despair, pleasure versus life-affirming pain – but the real difference in our musical tastes was much simpler. Lovell could dance. He was *brilliant* at it. Whereas although I had spent plenty of hours in front of my bedroom mirror crooning to an imaginary, spellbound audience of a few thousand or so, holding it down as Lou Reed was nothing compared to the horror of the thought of being on an actual dance floor with girls watching you. You couldn't really dance to any of my favourite albums anyway, not unless you counted a bit of stationary head-nodding and the odd spurt of air-guitar.

Lovell wasn't having any of it, though. Not long after meeting him, I found myself being crushed on dance floors all over London, watching him effortlessly take command of the space under his feet and the women who lined the bar. I skanked next to him under towering speaker stacks at Notting Hill Carnival, I drank Red Stripe with him in a tiny basement club in Hoxton where old West Indian men in pork-pie hats two-stepped with young white girls, I got dishonourably wasted at hip-hop parties in Camden squats where kids with blonde dreadlocks and flower pendants handed out glasses of spiked punch, and I lost a Shell-toe at a rave in Hounslow. But although I found all this interesting in a sort of anthropological way, I was a reluctant convert to Lovell's cause, despite his well-meaning perseverance. This was partly because I was probably one of the few people in London under twenty-five at the time who didn't like pills. They made me angry, not euphoric. I couldn't bear all the gum-chewing and manic grinning and saucer-eyed conversations while you shuffled about on the dance floor – the raves reminded me of nothing more than the assembly-hall school discos I'd had to attend as a pre-pubescent, where you were forced to have a good time under the eyes of fascistic dinner-ladies.

Eventually Lovell gave up on the club indoctrination and tried me with live music. This was more successful, although the first-ever gig he took me to in London was a Ska revival at the Camden Palace, where I nearly got beaten up by a skinhead after I accidentally knocked a can of lager from his tattooed fist. Lovell managed to get me out of it by talking the guy down, but it was enough to steer me towards the jazz-funk scene for a while, where the stoners with their goatees thought everyone was beautiful. As long as you shopped at Duffer. Luckily Lovell knew someone who worked there and got a discount. I got his cast-offs.

I undressed, shivering, and stepped into the shower. After a few minutes under the hot water, I began to feel marginally better. I opened my mouth and let the spray wash in. I guessed it was elevenish now, time to get some breakfast. Or maybe not, depending on the reaction of my stomach to the thought of food. I spat the mouthful of water out. Well, at any rate, get a lift from Lovell down to the hotel where I was scheduled to do the interview, proceed with interview, come back here and spend the afternoon in bed writing it up.

Normally I enjoyed writing for *Fisch*. It wasn't exactly mainstream – one of those small, cultish arts magazines that flourish every couple of years, which are hard to find in newsagents but are racked by trendier London cafés alongside the fanzines and the style glossies. *Fisch* was indulgently élitist in tone and content, and the editor, Daniel, was a shameless trustafarian, but he was also a good writer, had an irreverent sense of humour and a knack for appearing to discover the newest mavericks on the arts scene before anyone else got their hands on them. The key to *Fisch*'s success was in putting its readers at the head of the queue in the cultural baggage claim and letting them know it. The assortment of up-and-coming writers, artists, directors and designers profiled in *Fisch*'s main 'Rising Haddock' section almost always ended up being written about in the Sunday supplements months down the line.

A sense of adventure was always needed when it came to tackling one of these new embryo geniuses, however. As most of them were virtually unknown, and few had agents, publicists or even substantial bodies of work to review for discussion, it was difficult to prepare for an interview in the usual ways. Daniel was usually introduced to his chosen characters at parties or told about them by mutual friends, and would often arrange for them to be profiled in his magazine with only the sketchiest notion of their worthiness as subjects other than a supposedly winsome eccentricity. Coupled with the general lack of information available to the assigned interviewer, it was wise to accept a commission from *Fisch* with a certain amount of caution. I'd heard plenty of stories from unfortunate *Fisch* writers about their efforts to make good copy from various alcoholic ravings, jargon-steeped diatribes, and vengeful monologues about artistic rivals, not forgetting one famously belligerent Scottish film-maker with a taste for Newcastle Brown Ale and a voice so hoarse that every word recorded on the luckless journalist's cassette was practically untranslatable.

I'd done quite a few reviews and minor articles for Daniel, but only one proper interview before. It was with a female chef who'd renovated a pie and mash restaurant in Ladbroke Grove, and liked to exhibit the paintings of local reformed drug dealers who'd formed an artists' support group. One of the dealers went on to become briefly famous for his pictures constructed from empty cocaine wraps. I still got free pie and mash whenever I visited. However, on a bad hangover day, a blind interview with an unknown subject who'd happened to catch Daniel's attention for some reason or other was a daunting prospect.

Of course, there were some genuinely talented people who made it into *Fisch* as well as the phonies. You just never really knew in advance which you were going to be landed with. I'd actually already heard a few things about Richard Shaw, who I was due to interview, both from Daniel and from Jerry, a friend of mine who organized literary events at a working men's club in Shepherd's Bush and had invited this guy to read his work a couple of times. From what I'd picked up, my subject was just the type of person Daniel loved to feature in *Fisch*, a middle-aged, middle-class pseudo-radical who may have shared a joint with John Lennon sometime in the sixties and was therefore deemed to be a cultural authority on anything from ecstasy to sexual politics to the Royal Family, despite the fact that he was probably married with three kids and a house in Essex and knocked his wife around on Saturday nights. But at this point I didn't really care too much. I just wanted to get through the interview, come home, and collapse legitimately for once with an afternoon's work under my belt.

'You got a fax,' Lovell said as I emerged from the bathroom in my ratty old dressing-gown, towelling my hair. The two of them were sitting in the living room on my broken futon, watching cartoons.

I picked the sheet up from the fax machine and scanned through it. It was from Daniel, hurriedly written in his appalling unpunctuated scrawl, and gave the hotel details where I was to meet the writer, plus the following helpful outline:

> *Richard Shaw met once nice guy going to be BIG intellectual flavour when book comes this first ever interview so get as much background from him as poss also get him to spell out pop phil (his term ask for definitions) & remember to ask him about the forth-coming book about lepers thanks for covering at such short notice can you turn round by weekend & call me if*

you want to come Patsys party at the Cobden Club Friday.

I read over the sheet again, cursing Daniel's inevitable cryptic style and the fact that this Richard character was obviously a complete freak, if he was writing a book on lepers, unless it was some clever-arse socio-political metaphor for something or other. Folding the fax in half instead of crumpling it into a ball, which is what my fingers itched to do, I slumped down with Lovell and Kiddie on the futon.

'What are you watching?' I said, following their gaze towards the TV, where various brightly coloured animal characters were bashing each other with what appeared to be other, smaller mammals. They both ignored me, intent on their viewing. I watched with them for a few minutes. A cartoon bear was chasing another bear around a tree while whirling a squirrel around its head by the tail like a club, and trying to whack the other bear with it. The second bear retaliated by catapulting a rabbit at its tormentor with a huge sling. During this activity both squirrel and rabbit kept up a conversational dialogue about the stupidity of the bears. The whole thing was crude and moronic, but Lovell and Kiddie sat transfixed, intently taking it all in.

'Did cartoons always used to be this violent?' I remarked, as the rabbit hit a tree trunk with a loud thwack and slid to the ground.

My words were met with silence.

'It's not exactly *Bagpuss*, is it?' I continued. 'Jesus.'

'Shut it, Grandad,' Lovell said, without taking his eyes off the screen.

'What's Bagpoos?' Kiddie asked, without moving his eyes from the moronic bears.

'Ask Grandad.'

'Don't tell me you never saw *Bagpuss*, Lovell,' I said. 'I bet you loved it, really. The singing mice . . .' I fell silent. I had certain other friends with whom I'd spent entire, stoned afternoons delving for remembered fragments from our childhoods, those sudden and precisely illuminated details from the past which seemed to acquire a mystical significance when recalled collectively, as if a mutual consensus over something we'd seen or read or heard or worn as children confirmed a strange truth: that we were all once small and full of innocent wonder, and believed that cats could talk.

From the sofa I heard Lovell belch.

'What you sighing about, Teddy?'

'Nothing. Jesus,' I said again in disgust, as the cartoon terrorism continued on-screen and various mammals were pounded into the ground.

'It's American, innit. What d'you expect?'

'No, I'm serious,' I persisted. 'This kind of stuff is what turns kids into homicidal maniacs later in life, it sanctifies violence, it . . . it decontextualizes mindless whacking, and . . .'

Lovell turned to me with an incredulous beam. 'Come again? No, say that last bit again for me, will ya? Decontextualized whacking . . . what was it? I want to learn it off by heart so I can pop it out next time I'm cuddled up on the sofa with a bird watching *Tom and Jerry*.'

'It's *true*,' I said. 'I did this at college, there's plenty of conclusive proof from research which shows that if you subject children to –'

'Hey, Kiddie,' Lovell interrupted, turning to the kid, who was still staring resolutely at the television, 'you know this cartoon we're watching?'

Kiddie nodded.

'Does it make you want to bash Ted's head in?'

Kiddie slid me a look and rearranged his mouth uncertainly. 'No?' he asked, directing the question at Lovell. His voice was husky and soft, an innocent growl.

'There you go,' Lovell said, turning to me and winking. 'Conclusive proof from tomorrow's youth – hey, that rhymed – that cartoons do *not* make you violent. Now stick the kettle on, will ya? I'm dying of thirst here.' They both turned their attention back to the screen.

*

I went into the kitchen to wash some cups up, my dressing-gown trailing behind me dismally. The Fairy bottle was empty, so I used Flash. It didn't seem to work very well, the china still felt greasy when I'd finished rinsing, but I made the tea and then looked in the fridge and remembered there was no milk left either. At this point I swore and sat down at the table. Everywhere I looked there were imperfections. The mould at the bottom of the fridge door, the fine crack which ran from ceiling to floor on the far wall, the sharp crumbs on the lino underneath my bare feet. And in the middle of the floor, the rat, fetid beneath its paper shroud. Taking it all in, my hangover seemed to shift into tighter focus, a stocking cap of pain stretched across my entire head.

I sat there, sipping the black tea which tasted faintly of detergent, clutching my dressing-gown to my chest like an old man. From next door I could hear the tin-pot blare of the cartoon, and I found myself thinking again of Bagpuss the sleepy old cat and the ticking quiet of that fictional living room where Emily and her friends played delicately together, and I felt an almost unbearable rush of nostalgia for the safety and calm of childhood, for an age when the most important internal questioning lay over such matters as giving your vote to *Bagpuss* or *The Clangers*. Teddy or Action Man, the *Beano* or *Dandy*, strawberry or chocolate, Liverpool or Man. United, Maths or English, hamsters or guinea pigs. All the things you remembered once you grew up with a golden-hued fondness because of the uncomplicated happiness they gave you back then.

Having a favourite toy or TV programme was an act of unselfconscious purity when you were a child, I was thinking, when you were too young to be even faintly aware of the looming cloud of decisions massing on the horizon, decisions which would make you an adult and change you for ever. Now, as I looked down at my bony feet on the dirty lino and thought jealously of Lovell's new trainers, of Nike or Adidas, and which was best, I wondered if the same question had occurred to Kiddie yet. Did he lie awake at night, suffused with longing for designer sunglasses or whatever the current trend was at his school among groups of seven-year-olds more conversant than I was in the relative merits of street fashions? Had he experienced yet the full crushing weight of that limitless, divisive breadth of choice that seemed like freedom but really just damned you to a place in the hierarchy of lifestyle?

Nike or Adidas, vinyl or CD, the *Guardian* or the *Independent*, Ibiza or Goa, Marlboro Lights or Camel Lights, Cellnet or Vodafone, cocaine or ecstasy, hip-hop or house, the Beatles or the Stones, and on and on and on, right up to the final choices – which song to be played at your funeral; which single piece of music to summarize your whole life with all its loaded preferences, each preference contributing to a transient summation of selfhood, each summation saying more about you than you would ever be able to put into words. And you were powerless to stop choosing, to opt out, because it was hinted all along that there was always the possibility that if you shuffled and juggled and wiggled all these different chosen elements of your life together you might emerge with a finished picture, a composite whole, developed and perfect, and you could breathe a deep sigh of relief, and think, 'Ah, so *that's* who I'm supposed to be.'

'Lovell says where's the tea.'

I looked up foggily at Kiddie, who was standing before me as if he'd just alighted from a train and was waiting for his luggage to be handed down. Before I could answer he pivoted his whole body in the direction of the newspaper-rat construction. I imagined his twitchy urge to inch further and further towards it, to poke under the paper and confront the horror beneath.

'Here,' I said, getting up and handing him a lukewarm mug. 'Tell Lovell there's no milk so he'll have to drink it as it is. I'm going to get dressed.'

Kiddie took the cup from me gingerly and held it with both hands, but stayed standing where he was. Then, fixing his eyes straight ahead of him, he stated loudly, 'Can we watch *Star Wars* Lovell says you got it.'

'Sure,' I said, after a second, surprised at his determined tone.

'Lovell knows where the videos are. Ask him to find it for you, OK?'

He nodded in a businesslike fashion and marched back into the living room where I heard him parrot to Lovell, 'There's no milk you'll have to drink it as it is,' and caught the sibilance of Lovell's faint rejoinder, '*Shit*,' followed by a loud and indignant, 'We're not in Holloway any more, you cheap scumbag!' Smiling, I went to get dressed in my bedroom.

While I was burrowing through the laundry bag for a relatively clean T-shirt, like a mole in the half-curtained murk, Lovell came to the door and flicked the light switch on. I winced at the instant glare from the bare bulb and at Lovell's wry expression, crowned by an eloquently arched eyebrow, as he took in the state of the room and the ripped green tartan boxers I was wearing.

'Falling behind with the washing, are we?' he said, stepping across piles of clothing and sitting down on the unmade bed. I ignored this and pulled out a crumpled Playboy T-shirt, sniffing it before pulling it over my head.

'Someone's happy next door, anyway,' Lovell said, lounging on the bed in isolated style, bright-faced above the surrounding carpet squalor.

'Who?'

'Kiddie, you doughnut. He's off skywalking again.'

I nodded, spraying anti-perspirant on to the cotton under my arms.

'He knows practically the whole of that fucking film off by heart. Did I ever tell you about the bet . . .'

'Yes,' I said, 'several times. Kiddie's a child prodigy and you're an unscrupulous bastard who'll put money on anything. Chuck me those socks down there on the floor, will you?'

Lovell threw me the balled-up socks and wiped his hands on my duvet cover.

'Fuck, Ted,' he said, lifting his nose. 'It smells like a hamster cage in here. No wonder that rat copped it. Should open a window, man.'

I grunted and stood up. 'Don't you worry that he'll turn into a freak?' I asked, turning my back and stepping into three-weeks-unwashed clammy Levi's with distaste.

'What, Kiddie?'

'Yeah. I mean it's a bit over-zealous, isn't it, this *Star Wars* fascination? All the muttering and everything, seems a bit abnormal to me. Don't you think he must be desperate for attention or something?'

'Nah,' Lovell said, propping himself up comfortably on the pillows. 'It's just a phase. He's just bang into it, that's all. I bet you had all the *Star Wars* toys and shit when you were a kid, right?'

'No, but I'm not saying it's bad to be into *Star Wars*. I'm just saying there are *levels* of interest, you know. Normal and . . . not so normal. Kiddie might grow up into one of those weirdos who go to *Star Trek* conferences in school-assembly halls dressed up as Klingons. And probably make their wives talk Klingon to them in bed.'

'*Nah*, man. First off, *Star Wars* and *Star Trek* are in totally different leagues, right, you can't compare them. *Star Wars* is like . . . fucking high *art* compared to *Star Trek*.'

'Oh God,' I said, stuffing my feet into unlaced Converses, 'there is absolutely no fucking way I'm getting into a row about the merits of *Star Wars* versus *Star Trek*, not now. Anyway, you're missing the whole point. It doesn't have to be *Star Wars* he's into, it could be anything. It's the fact that he's so obsessive, the *way* he's obsessive that's weird.'

'So what, man?' Lovell said. 'All kids get obsessed. I was as obsessed when I was his age.'

'With what?'

'Jeannie Clarkson. We were in the same primary school, I used to follow her home. Loads of shit. Football. Don't tell me that ain't obsessive. And what about you, you fucking trainspotter? You were probably in the shed wanking over your collection of 45s when you were Kiddie's age.'

'Yeah, but at least we grew up with some grip on reality, didn't we? Kiddie's on another planet altogether. It seems to me,' I ended lamely, wondering if I'd sounded too critical. If there was only one thing in the world Lovell could be slightly touchy about, it was opinions about his family that he didn't personally volunteer. I threw a quick glance at him where he sat, head bowed, fiddling with the stitching on the hem of his sweatshirt.

'Yeah, well, whatever,' Lovell said after a moment, and the corners of his mouth quirked down a fraction. 'Kid's doing all right in my book. Could be a lot worse, considering what he's been through. I ain't gonna be the one that tells him to stop watching *Star Wars* 'cos it's bad for his health, not until he starts really losing the plot or some child-shrink tells me it's time.' He picked up a magazine from the bedside floor and began to leaf through it.

Guiltily, I glanced at my watch. 'Listen, are you still on for taking me to do this interview?' I asked.

Lovell shrugged, turning a page. 'Said I would, didn't I?'

'Great. OK, well it's half eleven now. I've got to be there at one. Want to go for breakfast?'

'Parkway Diner?' Lovell said, brightening. 'Yeah. If we can tear Kiddie away from you know what. Let's get some scran and then I'll drop you off. In fact, if this interview ain't gonna take too long, I'll wait for you and all. Not gonna be more than an hour, is it? What's the hotel again?'

'Uh, the Lansdowne. Paddington.'

'The Lansdowne,' he repeated, eyes narrowed. 'Don't think I know it.'

'Why should you?'

'Spent a lot of time in London hotels over the years,' he said, winking mysteriously. 'Mainly in hotel bars. Management days, you know.'

'Oh, yeah,' I said. Lovell had once apparently managed a couple of bands years ago, back when girls with big hair and small voices were teaming up with college dropouts newly versed in the art of programming house beats. As the story went, Lovell's main achievement was to effect the management of both female lead singers into his bed simultaneously, an undertaking which lasted until his supply of meetings with friends at record companies was exhausted, as was, by then, his own stamina.

Lovell had a faraway look in his eyes, lips curled around a faint grin. 'OK, the Lansdowne it is,' he said after a minute, standing up and smoothing himself down. 'It's always good to check out a new hotel. Hotels are

6

great places to pick up women. But that ain't the only reason I love hanging about in hotels. They're such unreal places, if you think about it. There's something sort of wild about them under that show of order that they have, these huge great houses full of strangers living side by side, eating, drinking, fucking and misbehaving in their little rooms, like lab rats in cages. Hotel rooms just ask to be trashed, because whatever you do to them, they always get cleaned up when you're not looking, like an Etch-A-Sketch. And I reckon this makes normally civilized people flip out. Where else but in hotel rooms would sane adults bother going to the effort of hurling TV sets out of windows? I always fancied myself as a concierge in a good hotel, actually, tight-lipped over hushed acres of carpeting. All concierges look as if they know the secrets of the universe. Some of them even get to wear fairly good suits.

Meanwhile, back in Rodentsville, it was taking forever to get old Ted out the door. By the time he'd finished getting dressed and dried his hair and hunted for a blank cassette for his tape recorder and snailed around looking for his keys and his coat and his extra painkillers, and I'd prised Kiddie away from the telly and we'd all piled into the motor, I was already over the whole freak trip, tell the truth.

It was well past twelve when we stopped for what was supposed to be a quick bite at the Parkway, but the caff was crowded with people who'd come in out the rain, and there was a

71

big wait on for food. I was fucking Hank by the time it finally arrived, but Ted went white and refused to eat his eggs because he said they were so undercooked that he'd throw up if he put them anywhere near his mouth. He waited for a new order, looking about as peckish as a sickly chicken, while I got stuck into my own breakfast and managed to plug Kiddie's mouth with Marmite soldiers. Of course Kid'd got all psyched up watching *Star Wars* so he was babbling on more than usual, and I could tell it was winding Ted up something chronic – he kept on giving Kiddie the evil eye over the ketchup bottle.

Ted did seem to perk up a bit after he'd got some food down his gullet, but back in the car it was worse than ever. I knew he was in one of his pussy moods because he made a big rebel statement out of not wearing his seatbelt, after I'd buckled Kiddie in, and kept looking at me out of the corner of his eye, as if he thought I was gonna challenge him over it. Then we got stuck in traffic for over fifteen minutes near St John's Wood and he went all quiet and twitchy. He kept glancing at his watch and sighing and biting his lip. At the same time, Kiddie was droning on in the back seat about Luke and Princess Leia, and in the end it drove me so mad, what with all the mumbling and the smoke and the steamed-up windows, that I told Kid to shut up for a bit, glaring at Ted to let him know he had it coming as well. He knew it too, because he gave me a nasty look and took stabbing puffs of his cigarette. Kiddie, of course, stopped talking instantly like a radio being switched off. It wasn't his fault, but there's something about kids when they're around grown-ups who are seriously hanging over. They're like wolves who can smell fear – they just seem to *know* when you're about to lose the plot and your nerves are frayed to pieces, and they hone in on it until you want to throttle them. I felt bad for having a go at him, though, because it ain't like me to lose my temper. So when Ted said under his breath, 'Thank God for that,' as the car went quiet, I wasn't about to let him get away with it.

'You can be a right pain in the arse when you're hungover, you know that?' I said. Ted looked shocked for a second, then shrugged and exhaled a thin stream of smoke.

'Jesus,' I said, winding down my window another inch. 'You know, you wouldn't feel half as bad as you do if you stopped chain-smoking for about one damn minute.'

'It's hardly going to make me feel worse, is it?' he muttered. 'You've got absolutely no idea how terrible I'm . . .'

'Yeah, yeah,' I said, bored with the invalid routine. 'Maybe you should've thought of that before you ladled all that booze down your neck last night. How much did you put away, anyhow, fucksake?'

Straight away Ted mashed out his cigarette in the ashtray and folded his arms tight. 'In case you've forgotten, I didn't know I was going to have to go out to work today, did I? Or, in fact, that I was going to have to start my day face to face with a dead rat,' he said, all sniffily, as if that was the reason for the ills of the world. 'I've had better mornings.'

'Yeah? Me too,' I said, looking in the rear mirror at Kiddie, who was moving his lips soundlessly. 'I didn't know I was gonna spend my morning dealing with the rat as well as your hangover,' I said. 'Not sure which is worse, neither.' I glanced at Ted's sulky chops and almost laughed, he looked so stupid, but I didn't really feel much like laughing. It seemed he was always hungover when I saw him these days. Bit ironic really, considering how we met, that Ted would end up being the piss-head, but that's what he'd become, and some part of me had only got a handle on it recently. It's kind of depressing when you suddenly realize something important about someone you know really well, something you never spotted before. Like you weren't paying as much attention as you should have been all along. Or you read their personality manual years ago but you skipped a section because you thought you knew everything you needed to know and didn't bother doing your homework. And it turns out that the section you missed was the really essential one, the one which explained how everything hangs together in that person.

No one spoke much for the rest of the journey. When we got to Paddington we spent over five minutes cruising around looking for a place to park, and in the end I stuck the car half up on the pavement right at the end of a cul-de-sac off of Queen's Gardens, just to put Ted out of his misery. I was almost willing to pay for a fucking parking ticket by then, anything to stop him twitching. I locked up and we legged it round the corner to the hotel following Ted's directions. It wasn't far but it was still raining quite hard and everyone on the streets around us looked almost as pissed off as the three of us did, except most of them had umbrellas so at least they were pissed off and not pissed on into the bargain. I took Kiddie's hand and he trotted alongside me, blinking off raindrops, while Ted scurried in front of us, head down. Occasionally he turned and gave me a slit-eyed, anguished look. By then I didn't feel angry any more, just wet and sort of sorry for Ted, who really did look like he was in bad shape, panting down the street with his shoelaces undone and flopping about in the puddles like a kid's.

We found the Lansdowne. As soon as we were through the revolving doors Ted went running off to make his apologies. I sat down in the lobby with Kiddie and dried him off as best I could with my sweatshirt, then we both sat back and had a good look around us. It was pretty dull as far as hotels go, one of those nondescript refurbished townhouses with plastic potted plants and a smell of freshly hoovered carpets. But you can always judge a hotel best on the quality of the women in the lobby or the bar, and the birds in this hotel weren't up to much. No high-class brass in this one. Only a few middle-aged business-types in imitation Chanel suits, and some Arab women all in black, huddled together like a gaggle of dark geese. Some of them were wearing those weird gold nose-shields that look like beaks. Imagine lying in bed and seeing your mother bending over you for a goodnight peck with a fucking great beak on. You'd have nightmares all your life.

I glanced at Kiddie, who was perched on the sofa next to me with his legs dangling. He was watching a group of plump little boys dressed up in suits and shiny shoes who were chattering to each other in Arabic and clowning around by the front desk, where Ted stood talking to the receptionist.

'Alright, Kid?' I said, nudging him.

74

'Are we in their house?' he whispered, still gazing at the Arab kids.

'Nah,' I said. 'They're visiting. Like us.'

'Who we visiting?'

'A man Ted has to interview.'

'What for?'

'So he can write about him in a magazine.'

'Why?'

'I dunno, Kid. Don't think Ted does either.'

Just then Ted came back and stood in front of us, looking ill under the tasteful lighting.

'How you doing?' I asked.

'God knows how I'm going to get through this.'

'Why don't you have a drink before you go up?'

'No fucking way.'

'Come on, it ain't that bad.'

'Yes it is. I'm not prepared for this fucking interview. I hate it when I'm not prepared.'

'You'll be alright, mate,' I said. 'Just let him talk. Ask him about his childhood, they all love that, don't they?'

'Yeah,' he said despondently. 'Anyway, I'm going to go up now, he's waiting for me in his room. You'll stay here, yeah? I shouldn't be more than an hour at the very most.'

'We'll sit in the bar. I should probably move the car at some point, so don't get your knickers in a twist if I'm not here when you come out, alright?'

Ted nodded and looked down at Kiddie, who was kicking his feet against the sofa and whispering to himself.

'Is he OK?'

'Yeah,' I said. 'Aren't you, Kid?'

'May the Force be with you,' Kiddie said, looking straight at Ted, who grinned, despite himself.

'Good luck,' I said, as he ambled off in the direction of the lifts, but he didn't hear me. 'Right then, sunshine,' I said to Kiddie, 'let's go and have a drink, shall we?'

'Lemonade?' he asked, looking up at me so soulfully that I had to laugh.

'You can have whatever you want, darling,' I said grandly, taking him by the hand and leading him towards the bar area at the back of the room. There's something amazing about walking around holding a kid's hand. It's like you're somehow connected to their world while they're gripping you with their fingers, like they're zapping you full of child vibes.

We took a blue plush booth in the far corner with a good view of the lobby. Kiddie scrambled in next to the wall and eyed me expectantly.

'Lemonade then, huh Kid?' He made like one of those nodding dogs people put on their dashboards, his tongue practically hanging out. 'Sit tight then.' I walked over to the bar. Funny thing was, I really fancied a drink by then, I mean a proper drink. That's another thing about hotels, they demand the consumption of booze. Maybe it was the cosiness of the bar after battling with the rain, and just maybe it was thinking about Ted being a lush that put me in the mood, too, but when I got to the bar I ordered coffee first, and then a Jamesons to go with it.

As I watched the barman squeeze the optic I thought that if Ted could see me now he'd probably go nuts, after the pasting I gave him for being hungover. But there was a big difference in the way we handled a drink, though it was something I could never have explained to him. Some people have a feel for booze like they might do about wearing a good whistle or about a nice car or something – they *respect* it. They know how to use it with a bit of style. It don't always have to be about going on a bender, you know? Gin and tonics on hot afternoons, a few cold beers over a game of pool, a really good Bloody Mary. Taste. Whereas Ted was an undiscriminating drinker – it was all the same to him, had the same effect, anyway. He was the kind of guy who'd raid the kitchen cupboard at a party for the cooking sherry once the Red Stripe had run out, no bother.

I inhaled a deep breath of Jamesons. It was pretty stupid that I couldn't sit in a hotel bar and have a whiskey or two for the hell of it and because it was a shitty day and I felt like something to mellow me out, without feeling guilty about Ted. But I wouldn't have been drinking at all if he'd been there with me, because he wouldn't have stopped at one or two, and I knew it. Sometimes I thought it would almost be better if he was into packing his beak or something instead of getting pissed all the time – coke wouldn't have been such a bad habit on Ted, it made him a bit more mouthy, but it gave him an edge. Everyone's a wanker on coke, anyway. But that rambling, red-faced, shouty drunkenness – that don't sit well on anyone, specially not someone as clever as Ted. There was no edge with him when he was drunk, that was the problem. His edge had been worn smooth, rubbed away by booze.

I necked the Jamesons and took Kiddie over his lemonade and some peanuts, which seemed to thrill him to bits. I watched him get busy. First he took a cautious sip of his drink through the straw, then when I'd opened up the peanuts, he reached over and shook out a fistful. Holding them in his hand, he took another sip. After that he allowed himself a single nut. Then another sip. Another nut. He was totally absorbed, and watching him, I had a sudden pang. Everything about Kiddie is so careful, like he's expecting the worst and doing his best to postpone the inevitable. He's more like a little old man than a kid, though considering what he's been through, and the distances he's travelled, so to speak, I suppose it ain't really that surprising.

Just being around him is a reminder of how fucked up my family is. Every time I look at him I realize how loaded the gun is when it comes to inheriting a family. You either strike it lucky or you don't. I didn't, and nor has Kiddie, and I suppose that's why we're good for each other. At the end of the day, you got to learn to recognize the people who are good for you, even if they only come up to your waist.

Ted's another good one, despite the hangovers. I suppose deep down the reason I've never tackled him over the boozing is because I've always been pretty sure that one day he'll just get bored of being pissed. Oh, he'd never admit it, but he's living in a fantasy world, and one day he'll leave it, and me, behind. It'll happen slowly and in stages but it'll happen all the same. First thing to go will be the fancy freelance thing. He'll get bored of being skint, he'll give in to temptation and get a job, a proper one. Then when he's got used to having cash in his pocket, he'll buy a place, and stuff it full of secondhand sofas and dodgy stereo equipment. Then he'll find a girlfriend and set up shop, start breeding. And then he'll start wearing his seatbelt and lecturing his kids about wearing theirs, and finally he'll have somewhere proper to hang that executive expression that he tries on for size occasionally, this furrow-browed, weary-eyed, weighed-down look which he was born to wear. Not that there's nothing wrong with any of it. It's just that Ted don't realize yet that he actually wants all those things. He thinks he wants adventures, but he doesn't really, he just wants to believe he's not wasting his life on normality. But there's nothing wasteful about a family. Trust me. It's a good way to spend your life, if you got a bit of luck on your side.

Kiddie had saved enough lemonade to blow bubbles with in the bottom of his glass through his straw, and I looked down at him as he hunched over his glass gurgling away. The sound cut right through the empty bar. For a split second I thought about telling him to pack it in, but I didn't. One of the things I did remember about being a kid was wondering how come it was the simplest things that were the most fun, and why doing them seemed to piss grown-ups off no end. If I'd blown bubbles in my drink when I was little, guaranteed my mum or someone else would have taken my glass away.

I went out with a psychology student once who told me that all behaviour is basically inherited patterns which we are doomed to repeat. Not me, I said at the time. I meant it. She didn't like this answer and we ended up having a big fight about it, with her screaming about why I thought I was so different from everybody else and what made me immune from scientifically grounded human rules. I choose to be different, I said at the time, there ain't no way I would ever end up being like my parents, I'm too smart for that. This made her even more mad, and she started banging on about the basic arrogance of all men, blah, blah. At which point I got my coat, metaphorically speaking. It was a shame really, because although she was a pain in the arse, she was filthy in bed, she had a mouth like a tart's handbag.

Ted can be a bit like her sometimes, not in terms of his sex appeal, but I'm sure he don't really believe in half the crap he spouts out when he gets in one of his righteous moods, whether it's about kid's cartoons or the price of lager. He just gets a kick out of pontificating, it makes him feel like he's got a grip on the world. Not that it's fooling me or anything. Actually I don't mind the pontification as much as all the endless nitpicking. That's what the psychology student was like, what the fuck was her name? Sophie. No, *Sophia*, that's right. Jesus. Sophia was the queen of analysis, and it drove me up the wall. She was one of those girls who think that as long as you *share* everything together, you're having a successful relationship. Of course what birds mostly mean by 'sharing' is knowing exactly where you are and what you're up to twenty-four seven. My last girlfriend Trudy would've wanted to know if I'd scratched my arse on the way from the kitchen to the living-room, just so she could feel like she was participating fully in my seedy little life.

You can't fucking win, though, because the more you share your bullshit with women, the more they want – they shovel it in like Häagen Dazs on a hot day and then complain when they get a bellyache. Specially once you've got them in the sack. You can almost see them making mental notes so they can write up an essay afterwards to read to all their friends about the fact that you only held them for three minutes afterwards, and what it means. Thing is, of course, there ain't no great meaning to most of the things people do, not outside their own heads. Sometimes it's better to just get on with it all, without endlessly searching for reasons why. I tried to explain some of this to Sophia the student one night when I was really stoned, and guess what she said? 'That's really Zen.' Serves me right for trying to be deep.

'Want another one?' I said, when Kid'd drained every last drop from the glass. He nodded and gave a small burp, looking pleased with himself, so I went to the bar to order another round. Sitting in hotel bars in the middle of the day gives me a feeling of infinity. Time seems to stand still. People come and then they go. Nothing to do but drink and watch.

As I stood there waiting for the barman to bring them over, and idly wondering how Ted was getting on upstairs, a girl appeared from the back of the lobby where the lifts were and made her way past the bar and towards the front desk. I wasn't even sure if it was a girl or not at first because she had short hair and you couldn't see her legs or nothing, but halfway between the front desk and the door, as if in answer to some silent call, she stopped dead in her tracks, then turned on her heel and made a bee-line straight for the bar, and me.

It was so sharply executed that it was sort of comical, and I watched, interested. She was on the petite side, nice little tits under her T-shirt, but wearing this strange get-up like she'd just been to a martial-arts class or something, all in white. She walked like she meant business, trotting across the hotel carpet with her head down. I shifted position, leaning against the bar slightly, and waited. Seemed like a good omen, somehow. Anyone who wears all white on a dismal day like today's got to be saying something.

As she came to stand next to me at the bar, my drinks were placed before me. I handed some cash over to the barman and took a quick look over my shoulder at Kiddie, who had his eyes fixed on the girl too, which tickled me. I winked at him and turned back to the bar towards her. We were a few feet apart. Up close, she was quite pretty in a no-make-up kind of way. Big brown eyes, very dark straight eyebrows, which gave her a bit of a stern look, or maybe she was just having a bad morning. Her mouth turned down at the corners; a naturally red mouth, no lipstick, which asked to be appreciated for the fact. Which I did. I'm a sucker for a nice mouth.

The barman returned with my change, then turned to the girl. 'Yes, ma'am?' he said. I liked his gallantry although I noted the bastard hadn't practised it on me when he took my order. But she didn't react, just stared straight ahead at the rows of bottles behind him. I studied the smooth side of the cheek nearest to me, a small mole high on her cheekbone.

'I'd like a drink, please,' she said eventually. Her voice was good too, deeper than I expected, a Marlboro Light voice. Faint London accent by way of posh girls' school, a bit husky.

The barman, a balding guy with a landlord's paunch under his white shirt, laughed at her answer in a friendly way. 'Any particular kind of drink?' He caught my eye, seemed to raise his eyebrow a fraction.

The girl narrowed her own eyes and seemed to consider. I was about to ask her if she wanted to try my whiskey for inspiration, when she cleared her throat and said, 'Gin.'

'Tonic? Ice and lemon?' the barman asked, patiently. She shook her head without looking at him, seeming to concentrate on the beer mat on the bar in front of her. She still hadn't clocked me. I took a sip of my drink, replaced it on the bar. While I carried on pretending not to look at her, she raised an arm and rubbed her head slowly with one hand, massaging the crown, which made her cropped hair stand up like cat fur. Then I noticed her fingers – bitten-down nails with chipped silver nail varnish. They seemed a bit out of place somehow with her voice and the nice cashmere cardy she was wearing.

After a second I also realized she was wearing a perfume I didn't recognize, a very clean, expensive smell which wasn't flowers and wasn't musk. By then I was a little bit intrigued. The challenge of new people, it gets me every time. You see a pretty girl, and you know nothing about her, and next thing you know, there she is, right next to you, sleeves almost touching. Anything could happen. As she moved the heel of her hand across her brow she turned her head to the side and glanced at me across her shoulder. It was a tiny connection, like brushing past someone in a corridor, but it charged me. I was ready for the anything.

When the barman put the glass in front of her she gazed at it for a few seconds before picking it up. Then she downed the shot in one, tipping her head back, and put the empty glass down smartly. I exchanged impressed glances with the barman, though she ruined the effect a bit by making a choking noise straight after she'd swallowed it.

'That's three pounds, please,' the barman said. The girl seemed to slump suddenly, and made groping movements towards her bag on the top of the bar next to the gin glass.

'Here, let me get this,' I said, nodding sideways at the barman. He shrugged and I quickly gave him a fiver before she had a chance to say no. Then she looked at me fully for the first time. I gave her a measured smile and for a second the corners of her mouth turned up slightly, but she cut her eyes away, though not before I'd had a chance to see she'd been crying, or was just about to; the eyes had that glassy look which I recognized from years of experience.

'Thanks,' she said to me then, glancing at me sideways. 'I was really thirsty.'

I laughed at this, didn't mean to, but it sounded funny. 'My pleasure,' I said.

Our eyes locked for a second longer, then she smiled briefly, and in one movement she turned away from me, picked up her bag and walked away from the bar towards the revolving doors. I watched her go dumbly, feeling like a bit of a cunt.

'Nice try, mate,' the barman said, putting my change down.

'Yeah, yeah,' I said and took another mouthful of whiskey. 'Shame. I was getting quite into the mystery act.'

'Nah, not worth it,' the guy said. Then he linked his hands across his belly and spent five minutes telling me an elaborate story about a woman who'd come into the bar one evening pleading a stolen handbag and ponced drinks off all and sundry before passing out in the lift and puking on some businessman's shoes. I watched his face as he spoke, the little red broken veins on his cheeks, the thinning hair, thinking, I bet you tried it on enough times yourself. Port and lemon for the lady, all on her lonesome.

'Women who drink on their own are always trouble,' he went on, wiping the bar down.

'Yeah, and men who buy drinks for women who drink on their own are always fools,' I said, nodding at the empty gin glass which was still sitting there. He laughed and took it away. I left the two quid on the bar for him, picked up my Jamesons and the glass of lemonade and turned around to take it over to Kiddie.

But Kiddie had gone.

part two

7

Sometimes I get a kick out of imagining my mother, Estelle, thrown into awkward social situations. In daydreams I watch her from a secret vantage point, struggling with her bait like an elegant fish, arching and twisting on wet sand. Say, being seated at a dinner party next to a charming and talkative Rastafarian of whom she can't understand a single word. Or confronted by a store detective in Harvey Nichols linen department and loudly accused of shoplifting before the entire floor. I see her so clearly, mascaraed eyes blinking, mouth clamped shut in shock at being lifted clean out of the safe waters of civilized behaviour and suddenly finding herself stranded on an unfamiliar shore.

Of course, it would never happen. I am her daughter, her only child, and I have still yet to witness my mother lose control. I have never seen her cry. I have never heard her fart. I've barely seen her without make-up in the last twenty years or so, and I can't remember much about her before that. Next to Estelle – perfumed, colour-coordinated, hormonally adjusted – it was generally hard not to feel imperfect and askew, nor to envy her groomed serenity. With her cigarettes and her ice-tinkling drinks and her archly humorous asides, she was like some glamour comedy actress from an old film who emerges unscathed and immaculate from every scrape, with an outfit and a parting shot to die for.

My favourite fantasy when I was a kid was running away from

our manicured household to join the circus, to live barefoot and dressed in ragged sequins among the animals and freaks. This was more to astound Estelle at my daring than from any wild desire for adventure – the daydreams always ended with her begging me to come home. The furthest I ever got in reality was boarding school, a progressive institution that I insisted on attending at thirteen in the belief that it would allow me the artistic independence I'd decided was my right. I lasted two terms before I came home, desperate to escape the lack of rules and the group therapy and the exhausting attempts to keep up with all the indolently wealthy kids there, whose terrifying world-weariness seemed to promise that adult life would be just as much of a drag as being a teenager, only with the advantages of more sex and drugs.

Years later, my imagination was still pitting me, the intrepid adventurer, against my mother. The most recent daydreams involved Estelle walking in on me and Richard in bed together: her ex-husband's old university pal with her little girl. I derived a certain sadistic enjoyment from these visions, the kind you get watching ordinary people humiliate themselves on TV game shows, where every nuance of their normality is magnified to almost tragic proportions. Some childish part of my psyche obviously still wanted to see Estelle stripped down through shock and chagrin to be revealed as messily, stupidly human as I was.

In my head, Richard and I are in each other's arms, lost to each other, when I open my eyes and over his shoulder I see my mother's face at the end of the quaking bed, every feature rounded in an O of outrage. In the instant that our eyes meet we become equal as women, the generational line between us pulled taut by pure female understanding. Triumphant, delighting in my wickedness, I lock my arms around him more tightly.

Right now, however, this confident imaginary self was nowhere to be seen. As I walked out of the hotel and on to the wet London street, my mouth tasting of gin and my eyes blurred, I thought painfully of the real Estelle, and imagined her familiarly righteous, wrapped in her blue kimono and shaking her head sadly as she ticked off the list of unforgivable mistakes I had just made up in Room 48. The tears. The cursing, including the use of the C word. The complete loss of composure that is required in order to walk away from a man you care about with dignity intact.

The rain on my face mingled with tears, hot and cold on my skin as I walked blindly towards Paddington. There was a distant roaring in my ears, punctured every now and then by the blare of a car horn passing me on the road. The rain intensified as I walked, and on Praed Street I stopped at the first bus-stop and stepped underneath it. Taxis kept passing on the street, but I couldn't seem to gather my wits enough even to raise my hand and flag one down. Plus the idea of a slow, punishing ride home on a double-decker seemed perversely appealing at this moment, more than the swift privacy of a cab.

I found a space on the bench under the bus-shelter, surrounded by teenage school kids in navy uniforms eating McDonald's. After a few minutes the sickly smell of their food filtered through to my senses and I lowered my head, swallowing down my nausea. That stupid shot of gin I'd had in the hotel bar, which had seemed like some sort of dramatic necessity at the time, had now bleached its way through my chest and throat like warm detergent. I don't know why the hell I'd decided on gin, especially neat. Maybe, given my time-old female predicament, it had some grim Victorian echo of Mother's Ruin: of hot baths and secrecy and cramping pain. It was a mistake, anyway, especially considering I'd let that guy at the bar buy it for me. I cast my mind back to him, the brown skin and the yellow hair and the wide grin. He'd probably thought I was a cheap hotel tart. Neat gin, for fuck's sake. I'm surprised he didn't try and stuff a tenner down my T-shirt, too.

My eyes welled up with fresh self-pity and I closed them for a few seconds, hoping the tears would crawl back up. It was no good. As soon as my eyelids were shut, I was assaulted with random images from the scene with Richard back in his hotel room. His shock-frozen expression, the toe of his shoe which I'd stared at while he talked, the single yellow rose standing upright and in the first fragrant stage of death in a vase on the bedside table. I forced my eyes open again, although I really wanted just to lean my head against the glass behind me and let the water run down my face along with the rain trickling down the pane into the gutter below.

The traffic kept pouring in and around Paddington station as I sat there gazing into the middle distance. I was aware of all the noise and soot and the kids around me chewing and talking in great gulpfuls of activity, but I felt almost invisible under my coat of misery. A rational part of me said knowledgeably, that's the shock, honey. Meanwhile Richard's response to my big announcement rolled through my head as if on autocue – I actually saw the words as if on screen, glowing green on black, smoothly disappearing as the next line of text appeared, punctuated by spaces left for my disbelieving silences.

Oh Christ, are you sure? Space. *Sara, you didn't . . . plan this, did you?* Space. Clearing of throat. *Look, this is all a bit of a shock.* Space. *There are things you need to know, too, things that I simply can't explain to you right now . . .* Space. No, hold on, that was where I had employed the C word, incredulously.

'What kind of things exactly, Richard? Like what a *cunt* you actually are?'

He'd flinched at that, which made me insanely proud for a second. Then, incomprehensibly, *Look, I've got to do this fish thing now, the journalist should already have come and gone, but he's late – he's only just turned up and he's waiting for me downstairs. I was going to have to ask you to sit in the bar anyway for an hour while I did the interview. Can you come back at two so we can talk about everything? I'm sorry, love, but I've got to do this, it's important.*

Five minutes, that's all it had taken. I'd been in the room with him five minutes, long enough to kiss him hello and shake the rain out of my hair. Then, the two words I'd been practising all morning. Only when they finally came out of my mouth, they didn't sound neutral at all, as I'd planned, but stupidly, loudly hopeful. I think I even grinned as I said them out of sheer nervousness. It didn't last though, not after I'd seen the way his face sagged, and listened to the speech with its dreadful questions, all of which were delivered in such a matter-of-fact voice that I had to remind myself we were talking about me and a baby, not one of Richard's weekly seminar topics. And at the end of all of this, I'd somehow ended up with an orderly appointment at two p.m. for the purposes of calm discussion, as if I was already at some clinic surrounded by pamphlets on contraception and posters of smiling babies who'd made it through, lives intact.

So I'd turned away from him and walked out of the room, with tears of defeat and rage already sliding down my face and with my brain screaming, *What fucking fish thing, Richard? What fish thing? What in the name of FUCK can be more important than what I've just told you?* As soon as I'd shut the door behind me I wished I'd said it to him out loud. But once you've left a room in tears, you can't go back in.

When the Number 23 pulled up, I wiped my face on my sleeve and automatically followed the crowd waiting on the pavement, which was sucked up greedily by the bus in the usual rush for seats. The kids clutching their milkshakes and bags of chips burst up the stairs ahead of me, shouting and elbowing each other. It suddenly seemed like a very bad idea to be wedged in a bus full of strangers gawking at me while I blubbed away, and halfway up the staircase to the top floor I stopped in a panic, wondering whether to push my way back down and jump off while I could.

I glanced down behind me at the impatient faces waiting to ascend. The platform was jammed. Someone, maybe the conductor, muttered, 'Get a move on, lady,' and I thought I felt someone tug at the belt of my coat. A small brown boy with a patchy, shaved skull was standing on the step below me, staring up at me unsmilingly with huge eyes. Then he reached out and gently tugged the belt again. It was an oddly intimate moment.

'OK, OK,' I whispered, and pushed on up to the top of the bus, breathing in the familiar tang of dirt and old tobacco from the ghosts of ancient, outlawed cigarettes. The conductor's cry, 'Tight *please*,' sounded over the grinding engine as I walked unsteadily down the aisle. I slid into an empty seat near the front and hunched against the window, praying no one would sit next to me. As the bus pulled away from the pavement I heard someone settle into the seat behind mine, and a middle-aged woman lowered herself down into the one in front of me with a sigh. I was safe, but as she sat, I caught a waft of her, a sweet, talcy smell, and I had another pang for Estelle. '*Poor* darling,' I could hear her saying.

My head lolled against the window, lost in memory. My mother is talking to me from her favourite position, her hot-seat at the very end of her double bed, which sags slightly from all the hours she's put in there on my behalf. Her bedroom has the smell of female privacy: of old perfume and fresh cigarette smoke, lingerie hidden in drawers, the lotions and paints she uses to construct herself. I am, what, nineteen? Still living at home, and wretched from my recent break-up with Nick, who will forever now be referred to by my mother as Nick the Prick for his failure to appreciate all my apparently obvious and blinding virtues. Which somehow remain invisible to me.

I am sitting on her bedroom floor, long-haired, eating Smarties from the tube. 'He said I wasn't *mature* enough,' I moan through a mouthful of chocolate, embarrassed to be admitting as much, even while I know it's partly true. (Nick is a postgraduate, a militant socialist and a drinker of bitter. He has tired, among other things, of my political apathy, and of taking me to pubs and being forced to order me deplorable glasses of Pernod and black, which is my drink of choice at the time.)

Estelle sits on her white bed, a pair of rolled-up stockings in her hand. Her perfectly plucked eyebrows are narrowed in concentration, or maybe against the smoke spiralling up from the thin liquorice cigarette burning in the ceramic ashtray I made her at school. She picks up the cigarette and takes a puff. She is getting ready to go out somewhere, to a cocktail party, to her life-drawing evening class, to the supermarket for medium-priced red wine? It doesn't matter, she is always poised on the edge of an event.

'Not mature enough, really!' she says chidingly, replacing the cigarette. Smoke drifts in layers above our heads. 'You're not supposed to be mature, darling, you're still a teenager. Anyway,' she adds, 'you said he had a disgusting hairy back. You're better off out of it, if you ask me.'

I sit there, crunching angrily, cheated by the illogical perfection of her arguments. 'Well, he thinks I'm bourgeois, too,' I add with determined self-loathing.

She exhales a little nasal choke of laughter. 'Listen, there's nothing wrong with being a bit bourgeois,' she says, inserting her polished toes into one opaque stocking-foot and smoothing it up her leg in a fragile, practised movement. 'I'd thank your lucky stars you're not going to marry a revolutionary.'

'Why?' I ask defensively, having accompanied Nick on plenty of long, cold demonstration marches through South London and stood on picket lines outside foreign embassies with only Polo Mints for sustenance.

'Oh God, revolutionaries make the *worst* sort of boyfriends. I knew a few at university myself. All the really political ones were terrible at relationships, because everything came second to the Cause, you see, whatever it happened to be. But you can't save the world *and* give women the proper attention they need, can you?' She chortles to herself, and lifts the cigarette from the ashtray to her mouth in a graceful arc. I remind myself that my mother was not one of the original feminists.

'I do wonder sometimes what became of them,' Estelle pauses, lips pursed. 'All those dreadful Marxists with their beards and arguments and wounded girlfriends moping around them.' She glances at me then, sees my mouth half-open, filled with chocolate and indignation.

Her own mouth twitches. 'I don't mean *you*, silly girl. This was all years and years ago. Anyway, they weren't all that bad. I mean, your father was quite political when he was young, but at least he knew how to have *fun*. That's what you should be doing, having some fun,' she adds. 'Not sitting around worrying about whether your IQ's high enough for some hirsute . . .'

I let out a groan, exasperated. My mother stops admiring her gossamer legs and gives me a shrewd look, which is also, for a magical moment, regretful, tender and wholly comforting.

'Oh, darling, I'm sorry,' she says. 'I know it's hard breaking up with your boyfriend. But don't *ever* let yourself be convinced that you're not good enough for anyone. And don't ever think that all your happiness can come from just one person, either. It simply can't. And *that's* the mistake I made with your father, intellectuals be damned.'

I sigh to myself and the moment is lost.

During my parents' divorce the year I turned sixteen, I had temporarily shelved my supposed teenage radicalism and developed in its place a suburban sense of propriety, to combat the fact that both of them had taken to sharing their feelings about the end of their marriage with me. I couldn't bear it, hearing Estelle dissect her relationship with Ben like a carefully skewered newt, or listening to him reminisce about my mother with the same distant nostalgia he employed when talking about Bob Dylan or favourite restaurants of his which had now closed. I wished I was part of a romantic, secretive family who sobbed in private rooms and would sooner have walked through the streets of West Hampstead naked than engage their only child in conversational discussions about the problems of sharing a bedroom after twenty years.

But no, when my parents had decided to separate, Estelle and Ben held a family meeting in the garden, at which I was the guest of honour. The three of us sat in a circle on wicker chairs and I was obliged to dispense the sangria and Marks and Spencer tiramisu while listening, squirming, to both parties tell me exactly why they'd decided to divorce and how they were going to do it. It wasn't unlike an updated version of the lessons they gave me as a toddler; A is for alimony, B is for break-up, and so on. It was all very civilized, and at the time I was so full of embarrassed outrage that I hardly spoke to either of them for days, although now, of course, I'm glad the separation was relatively painless for me, compared to those endured by lots of my friends and their parents.

Compared to the one I was enduring now.

Did it count as a separation, being dismissed from a hotel room by a middle-aged man? I wondered if that was all mistresses were entitled to, if it was equivalent to the break-up of a legitimate relationship with all its wine-drinking and chain-smoking and satisfyingly conclusive rows.

'If I'm your mistress, what does that make you . . . ?' I'd asked Richard once, muffled in the crook of his arm.

He'd spluttered with laughter. 'Ah, so *that's* what you are. I always wondered what you got up to on your days off.'

'Well, aren't I, objectively speaking?'

'Is that a Cartesian question?'

'Stop trying to be clever and answer me,' I'd retorted, moving on to the pillow.

'What exactly is it you're asking me, flower?' Richard had said in an affable voice.

'I'm asking, if I'm your mistress, what does that make you? My master?'

He'd laughed again, slightly more warily.

'Well?' I persisted, 'Why is it only the women who get the job title? Don't you think that's highly suspect?'

'Yes, I suppose it is.'

'Well, why does it happen, then?'

'I don't know. Maybe because men aren't required to be made morally distinct on the grounds of infidelity,' Richard had said thoughtfully, flat on his back, with a sheet draped across his hairy chest. 'I mean, historically, it's always been accepted that men have mistresses. The right of men to possess more than one woman is taken for granted. There's no need to refer to the fact, no need to name him.'

'That's not fair,' I'd said.

'No.' He'd rolled over on to his belly and stretched. 'Actually, you're right, it *is* an interesting point. You have to admit that the English language has always showed a great deal more imagination in depicting the vagaries of female sin than the male equivalent.'

'So you are to remain nameless in the midst of all this female sin?' I'd asked, casually, to disguise myself. It was the closest we'd ever come to discussing the nuts and bolts of our relationship. We'd never talked about his wife. I knew that bringing up the subject would be disappointing, somehow. It would let the side down, even if I wasn't sure whose side I was on.

Richard had moved towards me, smiling. 'Anything that feels this good can't be all that sinful, can it? Whatever you want to call it, or me, or you.' And there the conversation had ended.

Sitting on the bus, now, I was suddenly struck by the thought that I was afraid of disappointing everyone, including my mum – despite all the defiant fantasies. Not because she'd think I was some sort of wayward hussy for having an affair with a married man. But because I was still unable to find a relationship with some sort of real potential – certainly not one with one of her old college friends, and an intellectual, at that. I could imagine Estelle thinking, *how mediocre. Sex with Richard in hotel rooms? You can do better than that, darling*, just as she had when I was nineteen. Because essentially, that was all I had been doing, even though the sex was all it had taken to stop me distantly envying my mother her steady post-divorce flow of boyfriends, those walking cashmere cardigans who were as expensively bland and well-maintained as Richard seemed to be slowly, comfortably unravelling like a favourite sweater.

Estelle's face kept swimming into my head, lipsticked mouth pursed. 'Be honest, now, darling,' she seemed to be saying briskly. 'Why do you think it's so easy for a man like Richard to get involved with a girl like you? It's because he's probably never been committed to anyone or anything in his life, despite the fact he's got a wife. He told you he was still drifting, didn't he – why should he change now, for you? You're not as modern as you think – despite all this nonsense about *freedom* that Richard's always going on about, you're just like everybody else, Sara. You just want to be loved.'

'Not like this!' I wanted to shout back, not seated on a bus with swollen eyes and disillusionment spread across my shoulders like a fucking peasant woman. And then as if in answer, all I could see was Richard's blunt-featured face before me, seconds after I'd barked out my news, wearing an expression I'd never seen before, and yet which was somehow familiar. Resigned yet stoic. Almost as if he'd been expecting news that I'd screwed up, and had prepared himself in advance. It was actually, and I felt a fresh rush of emotion as I made the connection, an expression very like the one my dad used to pull on me when I still lived at home, if I phoned him late at night for a lift home because I had no cash for a taxi, or asked him for money, or made some stupid, hot-headed comment designed purely to provoke an argument.

My eyes were streaming again. I mopped at them ineffectually with the disintegrating wad of sodden tissue in my hand, wanting more than anything to get off this bastard trundling bus so I could bawl without shame. We were nearing the top of the hill, by Sainsbury's. Four more stops, I said to myself, like a kind of promise, four more stops and then you can get off and let it all out. But four stops was a long time to think about one subject. My brain seemed stuck on replay, an endless carousel of tawdry images, flaking gilt and sentimentality. I stared out of the window resolutely as the bus crawled up the upper half of Ladbroke Grove, and I kept noticing abandoned mattresses left out on the pavement. I counted three of them, all doubles, rain-soaked and drooping amid a dismal clutter of black rubbish bags and wet cardboard boxes. They seemed obscene, somehow, soiled expanses of sleep and love, the intimacy of unknown strangers indifferently displayed on the streets.

I thought bitterly of the white hotel beds in which I had come to know Richard, the excitement generated in me automatically by the sight of clean sheets and crisp pillows. I'd become like one of Pavlov's little panting dogs, all hot fur and hanging red tongue. Sitting up and begging with my paws for affection, lying across my master's feet and waiting to be stroked into a state of passive gratitude . . .

Then the conductor's slow, distracting stamp upstairs and his low, singsong 'Anymorefares' as he shuffled down the aisle towards the front of the bus. On his way back up he stopped before the perfumed woman in front of me and she flashed a bus pass at him imperiously. He grunted acknowledgement and as he turned away I caught his eye: a heavy black man with white grizzled hair, whose tufted eyebrows lifted slightly as he took in my red, smeary face. I looked away, embarrassed, and croaked out

8

send luke, please.

she sounds like when you got a cold, all snot, but when i hear her say it i go a bit shivery. *send luke, please.* then i know its got to be her, and my heart starts goin boom bang in my chest. lovell calls a heart a ticker, but it doesnt make a tickin noise. it dont really make a noise at all, except for when you re lyin down or when you get all excited, and then it goes boom bang, just like now.

i look up to see if anyone else heard her, but its only me and the bus ticket man that did. he just goes to her, ninety please, and then she gives him some money and he gives her a ticket and turns his back to talk to someone else and the next thing she blows her nose really loud and i nearly laugh because it sounds funny but i dont want to scare her so i sit and watch the back of her neck instead.

i can tell shes cryin by the way her necks bendin forwards all sad like a droopy tulip. my teacher says tulips are greedy flowers and you should never give them too much water because they drink it all up and then they feel ill and thats why they bend over in the vase, like they re goin to be sick. i was sick on lovell once, when i drank too much lemonade.

then i think about the lemonade at the hotel place and how lovell started talkin to her at the bar, and how i couldnt hear what they was sayin and i got all cross because i wanted to speak to her too.

i didnt believe it was her at first, but when i saw that she looked all upset, i decided to follow her when she walked away, out the door of the hotel place and down the street. i didnt tell lovell who she was and where i was goin or nothin, and then i got on the bus.

i dunno where the bus is goin, neither.

i feel all worried for a minute but then she turns sideways a bit and leans her head against the window and i can see her nose, her cheek, and the top of her hair, and i forget about being worried and get all excited again, like the time when i went up in the spaceship although lovell said it was a helicopter.

the bus ticket man says loud, any more fares, and i put my hand in my pocket and get the pound coin lovell gave me yesterday to buy chewin gum. i hold it up at the bus ticket man and he stops by my seat and looks down and im a bit scared but he only says, how far you goin?

i dunno the answer so i say, all quiet, im goin the same as her, and point in front of me at her back.

he says, saint lukes church, right? how old are you, son?

eight, i go, which is lyin because i aint, not until next christmas and then he says, you dont want to pay more than a half fare then do you?

i dunno but i shake my head anyway, and he smiles at me and takes my pound coin and gives me a ticket and two 20p coins and one 10p coin and one 5p coin and i hold them in my hand and they get all hot and when i put my hand in my mouth it tastes like metal.

the bus drives for miles and miles and miles. lots of people get off and on, but i just keep watchin her droopy neck with her short hair, which is different to how its meant to look. sometimes she stares out of the window and sometimes she takes a tissue out and wipes her nose. i want to touch her on the shoulder, pat pat, to make her feel better. i want to tell her, stop the cryin, no ones dyin, like lovell does when i hurt my knee, poor princess all alone on the bus.

she tells obi-wan hes her last hope right at the beginning. now im her last hope and im on the bus tryin to think of a plan to save her, but i cant, so i start wishin instead. i wish that the bus stops soon and she gets off, or i might end up far away in manchester or somewhere like where my auntie lynn lives.

just as im wishin it, the bus slows down outside a big church and suddenly she stands up and walks past me towards the stairs. i slide out of my seat and follow after her, and i feel all happy because the wishin worked and i wonder what to wish for next. outside it aint rainin no more and im waitin near her on the pavement at the crossing, and when the green man comes on the traffic lights she crosses the road and i cross it too.

i walk behind her all the way down the street. i have to walk fast because shes a grown up and their legs are longer so its quicker for them to get to places. she turns into a road with trees planted into the pavement and im countin the trees and there are thirteen trees before we get to a house with a yellow door where she stops and walks up the path and gets out a key and fits it in the door while i wait by the hedge.

then i know what to do.

lo, i say.

she stops unlockin the door and turns around. we look at each other and her eyes are all red.

im waitin for her to ask me if im a little short for a stormtrooper like shes supposed to. instead she goes, sorry?

my names luke skywalker, i go. i ve come to rescue you . . . then i wait for her to ask me who i am.

you re who? she says.

she got it right!

. . . come to rescue you, i say, and my ticker is boom bangin again. me and your r2 unit and ben kenobi.

rescue me?

yeah. with r2 and ben keno—

did you say ben?

yeah.

what, you mean ben my dad?

ben aint our dad, silly.

hang on, how do you know ben?

hes a jedi master.

ben? hes not a teacher, luke. i think you must be talking about someone else.

no.

look, she goes, i ve really got to go inside now, so are you sure you re ok? are you visiting carol from downstairs because she wont be home from school yet.

im visitin you.

but we dont know each other.

i know you.

i dont think you do.

yeah.

do you? whats my name, then?

i feel all shy then and i dont want to say it, so i whisper instead because if you dont say wishes out loud they come true (sometimes).

whats that?

i whisper it again.

layla? my names not layla, honey, its sara.

not *layla honey*. just . . .

just what?

then i start to feel all cross. *leia*, i say. *princess. you* know.

she stares at me for a bit with her pinky eyes. *princess?* no, you ve mistaken me for someone else, she goes, smilin.

but, i say, you look like her a *lot*. and i came from the *hotel* place.

what hotel place?

that hotel. with the big green carpet.

she stops smilin and goes, what . . . the *lansdowne* hotel?

lovell gave you a drink at the bar and i had lemonade.

who gave me a drink?

lovells my uncle who gave you a drink at the bar.

your *uncle* was at the bar? at the lansdowne? hang on . . .

she comes towards me and hunches down so her knees stick out. maybe she dont look *exactly* like princess leia close up. but her eyes are big and brown. all of a sudden im all confused.

let me get this straight, she goes. you saw me at the hotel

and you came all the way here because you thought i was a friend
of your uncle?

a friend of *mine*, i say.

but how did you get here?

on the bus. same as you.

oh lord, she says, shakin her head. so wheres your uncle now?

i shake my head too.

does he have any idea where you are?

im sort of cryin now, but i say, no.

dont cry, she goes, lookin worried, its ok. im sure hes not far
away. i ll help you find him, ok?

i aint cryin, i say, puttin my arm over my eyes, just . . . a bit
hot, i am.

hot?

yeah. my face just looks all wet because im sweatin

like a bastard, wringing wet under the arms and still clammy from the rain and the rush to the hotel, but didn't dare take off my jacket and reveal the damp patches of despair that I knew would be visible on my T-shirt. Richard Shaw sat across from me in front of the window, looking like a disgruntled geography teacher in his baggy grey sweater, with glasses askew on top of his head and his impressive eyebrows pulled together into a single line of black foreboding. At least he wasn't looking at me. He was scowling furiously at the carpet before him.

Discovering that he'd been waiting over an hour for me to appear was bad enough, although he'd been fairly friendly about it all when I'd arrived at his room. But while I was fumbling through a mess of excuses about the rain, the traffic, and the problems we'd had parking, ending with a falsely compassionate and unnecessary anecdote about the heavily pregnant woman in the lift who'd needed help with her suitcases, he'd suddenly snapped, 'OK, OK, spare me the details,' and lapsed into a grim silence.

After that, I sat and fiddled with the Dictaphone, although I hardly should have bothered turning the thing on, because Richard hadn't said a word in the few minutes the tape had been rolling. He just continued to glower at the carpet while I issued forth a series of increasingly desperate opening gambits, including a rambling and unasked-for history of *Fisch*, which was met with apparent disinterest. His silence seemed all the more unsettling given the odd intimacy of facing him across a large and virgin expanse of double bed.

Eventually I stopped talking and just sat there, shifting my hands underneath my bum, palms up, and hoping that some of the moisture that was springing from my palms would be absorbed into my jeans. I felt exhausted already. One last attempt to kickstart the interview, I was thinking, before I crumpled. Or threw up, or walked out. I wished I'd told Lovell to find an excuse to come and rescue me after half an hour. I needed the idea of an escape route to get through this almost as much as I was beginning to need a drink.

I took a deep breath. 'So, um, Richard,' I began, after a few more strained seconds had passed, 'let's get going, yeah? Can you tell me a bit about your lepers project?'

After an abstracted pause, he raised his head and looked at me frowningly. 'Lepers?'

'I understand you're writing a book about lepers.'

'A book about lepers,' he repeated. He leant forward in his chair and peered at me, seeming to take me in for the first time. 'Who told you that?'

'Daniel, my editor. He faxed me your, er, details,' I said, thinking of the hastily scrawled fax in my pocket. 'Said you were writing a book about . . . lepers.'

Something in Richard's look made my stomach contract with sudden dread, but he said nothing, only raised one heavy eyebrow. As he did, the corners of his mouth seemed to lift slightly.

'What?' I said hesitantly, encouraged by his look of vague amusement.

'Lepers, eh?' He gave me a brief but startling smile, and I found myself grinning back, stupid with relief.

'I'm afraid I don't know much about leprosy,' he said, and his voice was rich with humour. 'It's a book about *losers*. Which seems all the more apt, given the monumental fuck-up you've made of this interview so far, don't you think?'

There was a hanging moment or two in which I digested these

103

words and felt the grin tremble on my face. 'But Daniel said it was about *lepers*,' I bleated, unable to stop myself, my voice as reedy as a child's. I fumbled in my pocket for the fax, unfolded it, and held it out before me. 'Look,' I said, scanning the page and pointing at the crabbed writing near the bottom. 'It says lepers, look.'

Richard took the thin sheet of paper from my fingers and slid his glasses down on to his nose with a purposeful air. 'Mmm,' he said calmly, holding the fax up before him. 'Interesting. I see what you mean. It's all in the "s", isn't it? An "os" transcribed as an "ep", and an entirely different semantic universe is opened up.' The favoured eyebrow inched upwards again. 'He certainly has appalling handwriting. Is he dyslexic, d'you think?' he went on in a conversational voice. 'I would imagine it's quite a rare trait in a magazine editor.'

Slumped in my chair, I shook my head wordlessly.

'Not dyslexic?' Richard was folding the fax back into an uneven square. 'Well, let's just hope the Sub-Ed hasn't come up with any quirky captions yet about missing limbs for your article.' He gave a quiet snort of laughter and placed the limp paper square on the bedside table next to a vase holding a yellow rose. I watched, mesmerized, as a single yellow petal dislodged itself from the flower head and drifted silently down to rest on the fax with funereal dignity.

'Are you OK?' he said unexpectedly, and I swivelled my gaze towards him. 'You don't look very well.'

'Me?'

'Indeed.'

'Absolutely, yeah,' I said, feeling a fresh prickle of sweat on my forehead.

'Well, you could have fooled me. You're white as a sheet. Do you want some water or something?'

'Er, I'm alright, thanks.'

'How about a drink?'

I paused, confused.

'Well?'

'What, a *drink* drink?'

'Yes,' Richard said patiently, 'a drink drink. You look like you could use it. I could use one myself, it's been a bit of a morning for me, too, all told.'

'Well . . . sure,' I said, stunned. 'If you're having one.'

'Shall we check the mini-bar?' He stood up and squeezed past me, bending down before the veneer sideboard and opening a door. 'I've never used the bar in this room before,' he said, peering into the cavity. 'Beer or whisky, I think. We've no ice, unless we call down for some. Do you fancy anything?'

What I did fancy, more than anything, was a lager top, ice cold. 'Um, what beer have you got in there?' I asked feebly, licking my cracked lips.

'There's Heineken. That do you?'

I nodded.

'I think I'll join you.' He straightened up, holding a couple of beers, nudged the bar door closed with his knee, and grabbed the bottle-opener off the sideboard. With a practised movement he flipped the caps off one by one, then, passing me a bottle, he sat back down opposite me and took a swig.

'Ah,' he said, smacking his lips with some satisfaction. 'Not bad. Well, shall we get started, now that we've cleared up that little misunderstanding?'

I stole a look at him. Then I swallowed a mouthful of beer. It had the smell and taste of drunkenness. Unable to help myself, I let out a deep intestinal sigh as the first sip bloomed into my stomach.

Richard shot me a look. 'Better?'

I nodded my thanks, speechless with gratitude.

'OK, then,' he said decisively, 'let's press on. I've got another appointment here at two.'

'Yeah,' I said, still limp with relief, trying to sit up straighter in my chair. 'Right, so, your book about . . . losers?' I took another tentative sip from my bottle. The glass felt wonderfully cold against my lips.

'Indeed. *The Losers' Manual*.'

'That's the title?' I said, spluttering Heineken.

'Don't choke. My publisher thinks it's a great title. It's a users' manual for the habitual loser.' He raised the bottle in salute.

I followed suit, nodding encouragingly. 'And, er, what's it all about, then?'

He settled back in his chair with a benign expression. 'Well, to begin with, let's say it's about . . . a philosophy of failure.'

'Right.'

He smiled. 'It starts with a simple premise. All humans fail.'

'Oh, OK.'

'You look rather horrified,' he remarked in a pleased voice. 'But it's an important point to make. And a difficult one to fully appreciate, too, given that our society is geared towards fooling us into believing the opposite. You have to look far beyond the cod-psychology which masquerades as wisdom these days in order to grasp the idea in its full magnitude.'

'Cod . . . ?'

'Beyond the words of all the failure-insurance salesmen, as I call them.'

I sipped at my beer, trying to concentrate.

'The self-help experts, the spiritual gurus, the entrepreneurs with their bestselling bibles about the power within, the will to win, blah blah. Right? Users' manuals for everyday existence. They're very persuasive, many of them, but essentially they're just cashing in on everyone's deep-seated anxiety about failure. It's a very specific problem of our age.'

'What, you mean, failing?'

Richard laughed. 'Well, not failing itself – that's not exactly a new phenomenon of human existence, is it? I'm not particularly interested in all the different reasons *why* people fail – leave that to the sociologists and psychologists. No, I'm interested in the paradox of modern experience that lies within our obsessive pursuit of ways to cheat the very things that make us human – the ordinary existence and all its attendant problems. Things that we are con*ditioned* to perceive as failure. Powerlessness, boredom, sickness, ageing. And of course, the ultimate failure: death.'

'Wow,' I said, nodding like some studious undergraduate, and immediately felt myself go red.

He carried on, oblivious. 'Thus a philosophy of failure which attempts to address some very fundamental questions about how we come to classify ourselves existentially as losers or winners. Right?'

'Right.'

'So, how about you? Loser or winner?' Richard said innocently. 'How would you classify yourself?'

'Oh, I don't know,' I mumbled. 'Depends on how you define failure, really, doesn't it?' I stared down at the half-empty bottle in my hand, suddenly embarrassed again, then raised it to my mouth and drank a long and silent toast to failure. The beer trickled down my throat in icy recognition of my own uselessness as I recalled his words from before. *It's a book about losers . . . all the more apt, given the monumental fuck-up you've made of this interview so –*

'Insignificance!' he exclaimed loudly, making me start.

'Wha–?'

'Insignificance is a key component of how we define failure. In fact you could say it is our greatest fear, our greatest failure. Right? In the modern world, culturally speaking, the idea of failure has increasingly come to be based upon the threat of insignificance.'

'I suppose so.'

'Yes! People aren't satisfied with simply being able to lead comfortable lives, to self-consciously and freely consume, to achieve the material and social goals of Western society. We're deeply afraid of disappearing into the backcloth of that everyday existence.'

I nodded and swirled the last few inches around in the bottle.

'In this age, being ordinary is the worst crime,' Richard said. 'Do you agree?'

Yes, I thought, with sudden clarity. Emboldened by the final gulp of beer I opened my mouth to speak, but he swept on.

'I realized this in my own life a few years ago when I hit fifty. Although of course I'd changed over time, essentially I felt exactly the same as I did when I was in my twenties, or younger, even. All the experiences I'd had over the years hadn't amounted to anything in themselves, they seemed as meaningless in the greater scheme of things as *I* still felt, as insignificant as I was at twenty-five. I was certainly no *happier* with all these years of experience behind me.'

I looked at him, a bit startled. It seemed to echo my own fears too precisely for comfort.

'Now, this is no accident. Although we're all encouraged to find meaning in our lives as part of our socialization – personally, culturally, politically – at the same time, our civilization has slowly ceased to value experience as a basis for true knowledge. The greatest faith of the twentieth century is that *technical* knowledge can solve everything. Not wisdom, only information. Facts.'

'Yeah, you're right,' I said, mulling it over. 'But . . .'

'I know I'm right. And yet how can facts help us deal with our insignificance?'

'Well . . .'

'They can't, of course. Only through practical wisdom, through the application of experience, can you ever hope to answer such a great philosophical question as that.' He sat back in his chair with a satisfied air.

I gazed at him helplessly. The beer had worn down the pain in my head to a fuzzy throb but I felt completely muddled. It was too much to take in – lepers, losers, insurance salesmen. At least Richard didn't seem to notice, he was staring, enraptured, at a point above my head.

'The practice of philosophy understands this,' he continued. 'And it seems to me that it's the only way to move forwards from this impasse of unmotivating fear we all seem to be caught in. But people aren't interested in philosophy as a process of disciplined understanding. Especially when it doesn't employ an underdressed celebrity spokeswoman, or guarantee results or your money back.' He grinned at me, and I smiled, wondering if I dared ask him for another beer.

'The thing is,' Richard went on, 'philosophy has to move forwards too, to accommodate these enormous changes in human consciousness. It has to be accessible, or there's no point.

The days of the philosopher in his ivory tower have gone, and that's why I'm arguing for a new, *popular* philosophy, which helps people to battle with their basic human fear of failure and to find *meaning* in that battle. Without recourse to the sort of reductive mysticism hawked by those failure-insurance salesmen,' he said, sounding disgusted.

'Right, right,' I said, encouragingly. I fixed my eyes on the mini-bar, willing the door to swing open.

'Unfortunately, it's easier said than done. Now, many of the salesmen, along with certain modern philosophers, would have us believe that experience, or to put it in philosophical terms, subjective meaning, is in fact our power-base – that it not only counts for something in our lives in itself, but allows us to develop into the people we want to be. There's no doubt that we *want* to believe this. But at the same time, to live in the modern world means we are constantly being reminded of our basic human powerlessness, our macro-insignificance. Thus we are constantly pulled apart, constantly tormented by the conflict between the belief that we are imbued with power as individuals, and our knowledge that we are, essentially, helpless, cosmically speaking. It's no wonder everyone's so confused.' Our eyes met and his narrowed slightly. 'Are you following me?'

I nodded. I was remembering all the university lectures I'd ever sat in, where you slumped, pen in hand, scribbling down disjointed phrases as they emerged from the lecturer's mouth, and tried to string them together afterwards into some semblance of meaning.

'OK, look,' he said, obviously unconvinced, before pulling on his beer bottle and wiping his mouth with his hand. 'I was drawn to philosophy in the first place for the very reason that it deals head on with the fact that all humans are, by nature, insignificant. Forget about horoscopes, chat shows, agony aunts, shrinks, personal-assertiveness training for a moment – all the cultural palliatives that we use to help deal with the pain of our insignificance. Alcohol, too,' he added.

I coughed and put my empty bottle down discreetly.

'Philosophy, by contrast, makes no promises,' he said. 'It

attempts to deal with the great paradox of humanity – the universe is vast and humans are tiny specks. Yet within the vastness, there *is* meaning for individuals and groups. Politically, culturally, personally. Are you following me? By its very *practice*, philosophy declares war on human insignificance. See?'

I nodded again, letting out a belch. 'Sorry.'

''Nother beer?' Richard said, eyebrows aloft.

'Er . . .'

'Do the honours then.'

I liberated another couple of bottles from the mini-bar and handed him one. He cracked the top off his bottle, and motioned for mine. 'A couple of years ago,' he said, as I handed it over and tried not to snatch it back from him, 'I was waiting for a tube and I saw this poster advertising one of those adult-education courses at the LSE, a history of philosophy. It said, in huge letters, "There has never been a greater need for practical philosophers." Something about that really appealed to me, it was like a call to arms.'

'What do you mean?' I said, coming up for air after a long greedy swig.

He smacked his own lips around a mouthful of beer with relish. 'I mean, isn't it ironic, this academic institution trying to rally the crowds on the underground? I studied philosophy at university years ago, and I've taught it in a few different places, with varying degrees of success. But the statement on this poster struck a chord in me. I suppose it reminded me of the very galvanizing mixture of practical action and ideology that was in the air when I was a student – something I seemed to have completely forgotten about. Maybe it was just nostalgia for those days that prompted me, but I wrote down the number and signed up. I suppose I wanted to see if anything had changed in the twenty-odd years since I'd read all those books. I went to a few lectures; it was a funny crowd – middle-class women, some kids about your age with political badges. Lots of head-nodding and note-taking. Vaguely anxious-looking people. Some of the lectures were pretty stuffy, but I liked them. In fact, they were a great blessing, in terms of where my head was at the time.'

I sipped at my beer with inward-looking eyes. 'Where was that, then?'

'Up my arse,' Richard said succinctly. I glanced up, surprised. 'I was having a rotten time, actually,' he went on. 'Bored with my work, drinking too much, feeling very sorry for myself. Your typical mid-life crisis, I suppose, looking back. But I couldn't shake the horror that I was half a century old and to all intents and purposes a loser. Nothing to show for my years but experience and opinions, perhaps a little wisdom, but so what? I had failed to achieve any of the things I'd set out to do, the most important of which was proving my own significance to the world, at least intellectually speaking.'

'Oh,' I said, with a flash of recognition, gazing down into the green eye of my bottle.

'Oh, indeed.' He paused for a minute and added, 'And then, of course, there was my own unique anxiety about why it was I'd never succeeded . . .' He tailed off, staring into space, then shot me a look. 'There's an interesting subtext to my fear of failure, you see, something very personal that's had a profound influence on me all my life.'

'Right,' I said expectantly, while Richard gazed at the ceiling, frowning. There was another, longer pause, then he snapped out of his reverie and added in a brisk voice, 'But more of that later. Let me finish my point.'

'OK,' I said, confused, and a bit disappointed. It sounded like something promising, finally. I was already wondering how I was going to make anything readable out of the interview.

'Anyway,' he went on, 'the point is that the disillusionment I was feeling allowed me to understand for the first time that the whole of philosophy is really a history of losers. And I took great comfort from this, somehow.'

'What, you mean the philosophers themselves were losers?'

'Well, not just the philosophers, although there have been plenty that were fairly repellent human beings. It's quite amazing, when you think about it, that Western civilization is built upon the ideas of various syphilitic manic-depressives and the like. But no, I say a history of losers because philosophy is the very

111

endeavour of human beings battling with their insignificance. Human beings are naturally prone to anxiety about their origins and their meaning, right? And because philosophy allows that experience has value, then there is *also* value to pain and anxiety. You see? Through suffering can come awareness, and through awareness, knowledge. Therefore philosophy validates my experience of loserdom.'

My mind instantly flashed back to the depressive agony of waking up this morning. I applied my mouth to the glass eye, and looked at Richard carefully. It sounded like some sort of philosophical hair-of-the-dog remedy. I just wasn't sure if it was genius or complete and utter bilgewater. Not that I was particularly equipped to tell the difference at this moment.

'This is all pretty standard stuff, of course,' he said. 'But it got me thinking hard in a new way about the possibilities of philosophy as a real, practical method for addressing the kinds of modern problems I've been talking about. It helped that we had a wonderful lecturer, Dr Gardner, who looked like one of the last true Oxbridge scholars. He must have been nearly seventy, very refined, wore a bow-tie and reeked of tobacco, and he sliced through the fundamentals of human existence with great delicacy. Like a roast goose,' Richard added thoughtfully, 'or a rather elegant layer cake.'

I tried to think of an appropriate response and failed.

'The most immediate effect all of this had on me,' he went on, 'was that after a few hours sitting in an overheated lecture room with this weird bunch of people, I realized that I was in a position of strength, compared to a lot of the others. God, some of them were nearly in tears after an hour of Kierkegaard.' He sat back and took an energetic swig from his beer bottle, releasing it from his mouth with a wet pop. 'I was probably better equipped than anyone in that room to deal with the philosophical dissection of our human values, simply because of all the years of experience I'd had of failure and fear. I was over-qualified, in fact.' He smiled at me comfortably from his chair.

'How exactly do you mean?' I asked, fuzzily intrigued. There was something very compelling about his voice, the way he framed his sentences with those thick eyebrows.

'Well, all my life I'd made mistakes, right? Like everyone does. And I battled against the fact that I'd failed – when my first wife left me, when I couldn't get the work I wanted. But I had something bigger to deal with too. I lived with the ever-present threat of losing my mind.'

'Over what?'

'No, I mean literally,' he said, nodding at me. He pressed his lips together for a second, then said, 'That subtext to my fear of failure that I told you about?'

'Yes?' I said, trying to remember.

'I'm going to try and explain it. OK, now. Think back to when you're a child, and you learn about death.'

'Right . . .'

'It's an abstract concept at first, isn't it? Death is ungraspable, although frightening, the kind of fear enshrined in fairy tales. But even when you experience it directly, and someone close to you dies – your grandparent, a pet, whatever – the human loss is always separate from the concept of your *own* death. There's something of that very same fairy-tale quality about it. It's real and yet unimaginable.'

I returned his questioning look with a nod. 'With you so far,' I said.

'Now imagine if you'd never been told the fairy tale,' Richard went on. 'Imagine if you had to grow up accepting that death wasn't that far-off fantasy, but that there was a strong possibility that it would come for you sooner than everybody else. Can you?'

'Well, no, of course not.'

'No,' he said softly. '*Now* try and imagine how this would affect your perception of yourself in the kinds of terms we've been talking about. Your belief in your potential to succeed, for example. How would you even hold on to the fundamental human belief that life was worth living if you were constantly reminded that yours might be about to end?'

For a split second I wondered if this was all something to do with the lepers issue, then I remembered that I'd made that up myself.

'I've been asking myself all these questions for years,' Richard continued. 'I didn't want to, but I had no choice – that was my unique inheritance, you see. And the closer I got to that most overwhelming of all fears – the fear of death – the more I tried to accept it, the more incapable I became of dealing with the simplest of everyday functions. You see?'

I nodded, then said, 'But everyone's afraid of dying, aren't they?' I didn't see what was so unique about it. Put practically anyone in a room and pipe Ian Curtis singing 'Atmosphere' or the Cure's 'The Drowning Man' through the speakers, and they'd be afraid, too. Maybe Leonard Cohen's 'Suzanne' if you actually wanted them to get a head start and top themselves.

'Of course,' he said a little impatiently, 'I'm by no means the first person to get thrown by the issue of his own mortality. But the point is, when I was confronted with all these great big philosophical questions about the nature of human existence, at this point in time, I suddenly felt a great peace. I was liberated from my fear of death by the knowledge of my own insignificance in time and space.' He pushed a hand through his wiry hair and threw me a glance. 'Do you get it, er, what's your name again?'

'Ted,' I said.

'Good, Ted. Look, forget all that, and let's try the theoretical route, you're looking at me like a stuffed fish.'

'Sorry,' I mumbled, automatically. I thought I'd been doing quite well, considering the hangover, as well as the fact that this was the most intellectual stimulation I'd had since I'd watched the entire series of I Claudius in one weekend. Although I had to admit that on top of everything else, I was starting to feel a bit drunk.

'Don't apologize. OK, let's see if I can make things any clearer. The history of philosophy has many important lessons, one of which being that there's a world out there, outside our heads and thoughts, which is knowable, understandable, objective. It exists independently of what I call it and how I perceive it, right?'

'. . . Right.'

114

'Come on, this is basic metaphysical realism. So, in that world, to be blunt, shit happens. We are tiny ants, and our pleasure and pain mean precisely nothing.'

I stared at him, head swimming.

'This is only one way of looking at it, of course. You could call it the loser's way, OK? It's natural for a loser to try and rationalize their lack of achievement in terms of human insignificance,' Richard said matter-of-factly. 'But the evidence of human powerlessness *is* overwhelming. You just have to read the newspapers to see that. The Hubble Telescope has sent back pictures from space, which have exposed the true vastness of the universe. Thank God Nietzsche wasn't around to see it, it would have confirmed all his worst fears.'

'I don't . . .'

'Of course you don't. It's almost impossible to make sense of your life in such nihilistic terms. That if you lose or you win, you fail or you succeed, in the greater scheme of things this doesn't alter the reality of the world – the world just keeps on turning indifferently. However, the trick is to use this idea as a launching pad towards both greater intellectual freedom and power.' He paused. 'Let's have another drink,' he said, standing up abruptly and pushing past me once more. He bent over and rummaged inside the bar for a few seconds before removing a fist that bristled with miniatures.

'Oh God,' I said faintly, accepting a tiny bottle of Johnnie Walker. Richard sat back down and cracked the top off his own drink.

'What was I saying?' he said, sipping ruminatively. 'Mmm. The Greeks knew what they were doing, you know – drinking and philosophizing go hand in hand.'

I wasn't about to argue. The whisky burned a pleasant brambly path down my throat. I just hoped I wasn't going to have to pick up the tab for it all.

'Now, if you take this train of thought to its logical conclusion, then the universe is vast and we are dwarfed by time and space into complete and utter insignificance,' he said, deadpan.

I gulped more whisky.

'Sounds frightening, doesn't it? But that in itself is a statement of faith,' he went on. 'It may not seem like a very positive piece of faith, but it is.'

'What, that the universe is vast and we are dwarves, what was it?'

'We are *dwarfed* by time and space into complete and utter insignificance,' Richard said sternly. 'It's a big piece of knowledge. Right? But the beauty of it is that swallowing that huge big piece of knowledge requires *the smallest possible leap of faith*.' He leant forward and fixed me with his eyes, which were alight with evangelical zeal. I recoiled in my seat slightly. 'And once you *have* swallowed it, you're left with a choice – you can either let your ego be battered constantly by the fact that most humans fail on the cosmic scale, and take drugs to alleviate the pain . . .'

'Drugs?'

'Real drugs or cultural drugs, whatever. Or you can make that leap of faith to a safer place, where you can accept your own powerlessness in existential terms, and then start to allow yourself to be educated by your experiences, by practical wisdom. Pop philosophy, in other words. That in itself is a kind of power, a force.'

A picture of Kiddie immediately came into my head. 'You mean, sort of like using your own nature?'

'What?' Richard said sharply, as if he couldn't believe I'd said something comprehensible. 'Yes, if you like.'

I grinned at him. 'I've been hanging out with someone who's really into *Star Wars*.'

'I see,' he said, raising his eyebrows. 'Well, anyway, the *best* part of this whole equation is that losers are the better equipped to make this leap of faith *because they've got nothing left to lose*. See?'

'Er . . . no. Not really.'

'Oh, come on, use your brain. It's no bloody wonder you kids are all so messed up – you've all been baby-fed such a dreadful diet of soft intellectual non-discrimination. Encouraged to suspend all your judgements in favour of this obsessive PC insistence on relativism and perspective, rhubarb, rhubarb. Yes, it's all very right on, but it doesn't disguise the fact that you and I, we can't control the world, no more than we can control space. It doesn't stop people from suffering, does it? Doesn't stop people struggling to make sense of the world, does it? Kids keep on being born into all this mess, don't they, without any choice in the matter?'

I looked up at him, completely nonplussed. Richard was frowning.

'God,' he said to himself, swigging whisky, then: 'Listen, a few years back, when I was really depressed, I spent a lot of time in bed just being miserable. As I've said, I was drinking too much, I was lonely, and I was frightened about my own fate. At the very lowest point, the greatest philosophical question of my life wasn't about the value of knowledge or the place of humans in the cosmos, it was, why get out of bed in the morning? Now there's a bit of practical wisdom for you. In fact, why get out of bed at all?'

I opened my mouth and closed it again.

'Sound familiar?' he said, studying my face. I nodded dumbly. 'Well, believe me, I really gave it some *serious* thought. And in the end, it liberated me. I mean, after I'd worked through all my personal problems for a good long time, I discovered this kind of freedom in the absoluteness of my failure. I stopped wondering "why me?" because I realized that my suffering didn't alter the reality of the world *one little bit*. And once I'd embraced the fact that I was, to all intents and purposes, another loser in the universe by the very nature of being human, I started to feel happy again. And then I felt able to get out of bed.'

'But *how*?' I blurted out. 'How can you be happy if you know you're a loser?'

Richard passed his hand across his brow. 'Anyone can be happy if they're doing more than just surviving. Surely the point of living is to *flourish*.' He looked at me intently.

'To flourish?' I had a sudden, cold flash of scepticism that he was about to reveal himself as one of those self-made gurus he'd been slagging off before.

'Yes. And if I don't get out of bed, I'll miss out on opportunities to flourish. See? Remarkably simple. I can be both insignificant in the greater scheme of things and valuable in my own corner of the world – my family, my society. It seems terribly easy on the surface, but it's not. I can see how hard it is for your generation. None of you seem to be very good at flourishing.'

'Why?' I said, jumping on the words 'your generation' in the hope that they'd get me back on to some kind of familiar territory.

'I teach students round about your age, you know,' he said, kindly. 'I'm not talking complete rubbish. Your generation is constantly trying to dodge the responsibility of flourishing – it's too much like hard work. It's easier to numb yourselves with pleasure. But hedonism is a relatively easy choice given that pleasure is so easily obtainable. It's a much more conservative way of living than it was back in the sixties.'

Here we go, I thought gloomily. But Richard paused and leaned towards me with deadly sincerity. 'Would you like a cigar?' he said.

'OK,' I answered, thrown by the offer, and could then do nothing but watch helplessly as he whipped a packet of Café Crème out of the jacket hanging over his chair and extended it to me. I extracted a cigar and waited for a light, thankful he wasn't a Havana chewer. When he'd lit both our cigars, he inhaled slowly and leaned back with pursed lips. I managed a tentative puff.

'You see, Ted,' he said, through clouds of bittersweet smoke, 'we're all so deeply frightened by the thought of not leading extraordinary lives that none of us take any intellectual risks.' He looked straight at me. 'The threat of insignificance, once again. But it's something that's particularly crippled your generation, thanks to the advanced state of capitalist consumerism you were born into. Think about the Existentialists . . .'

No, my brain was pleading.

'They accepted their insignificance, they acknowledged the benign indifference of the universe, but they at least explored some notion of what it means to be free, intellectually, and their *responsibility* to make life meaningful. Whereas our society tries to convince us that the universe isn't indifferent to our presence at all, in fact it's constantly showing how deeply it cares about fulfilling both our material needs and our fantasies by supplying us with an endless array of things to buy and devour in the misguided belief it will bring meaning to our lives.' He paused for breath. 'To combat your fears, all you kids seem to have become completely caught up in the relentlessness of the modern search for significance in *everything*. Everything you do, all your lifestyle choices, your opinions, your tastes – it's all so endlessly scrutinized. There's a famous Socratic quote, "The unexamined life is not worth living" – do you know it?'

I shook my head, feeling the cigar wobbling between my fingers.

'Well, it's true to a degree, but he didn't know what life was going to be like towards the end of the twentieth century, did he? The over-examined life isn't worth living either, not when everything has infinite meaning, when everything is endlessly spotlighted and picked apart and put on quiz shows. It's our search for validation and yet it's a form of slow torture. Not what Socrates had in mind when he stated, "Know thyself."'

He caught my eye just as I was inserting the cigar between my lips, and I sucked on it manfully, nodding at him.

'Of course, it's unfair of me to be lecturing you like this, because no one can stand outside their own generation and look at it with any real critical judgement. But just consider what you take on trust from the papers and television and films, and, I don't know, *celebrities*, for God's sake. It's all so bland and insipid and uninspiring. Or if it *is* inspired, it's inspired by self-loathing.'

Automatically, I inhaled the smoke and felt it scorch its way down my throat and into my lungs, before I realized the gravity of my mistake. I held my breath for a few seconds, trying not to cough.

'People are so repulsed by their own flaccidness,' Richard continued, while I expelled the smoke and let its bitterness flow over my tongue, fighting tears, 'so paralysed by their lack of power, that they'll never motivate themselves to flourish outside of their own materialistic parameters. It's a new and very frightening thing to see. Back in the sixties, popular culture was much more politically informed, because there were clear utopias, there was some sense of freedom to be sought, and fought for. Not any more. There are no freedom songs left to be sung. No one's listening, anyway.'

I was busy washing the taste of the cigar away by draining my bottle of whisky. 'Wait,' I managed to croak out. 'You can't just . . . dismiss an entire generation like that. It's not as if people don't want to *believe* in things any more. I mean, talking of freedom songs, just look at music – that's a kind of utopia in itself, isn't it?'

Richard looked puzzled. 'Really? Well, back then music might have been a motivating force, but today? Manufactured pop bands? People with nothing to rebel against? Where's the politics in rock and roll these days?'

'Well, there's plenty,' I said, sitting up in my chair quickly, and feeling suddenly dizzy.

'Listen,' he cut in, 'there was a time when I was a student when it really felt like revolution was in the air. Can you imagine that? Music was a big part of it, of course, but we had the Beatles and Dylan and the Stones and Cat Stevens . . .'

'Cat Stevens?' I said with disgust.

'The point is, Ted, it wasn't necessarily that all the music we listened to was overtly political itself, although of course there were people like Lennon who did evolve into political figures over time. It was what it *represented* as much as anything. The music that came out of those times engineered a complete overhauling of the establishment. Rock and roll stuck its fingers up at acceptable popular culture, at all that our parents had experienced, and it encouraged our generation to want to change the world. You can't tell me it's the same now.'

'Of course it's not the same. People aren't as idealistic as they were then, for a start,' I said, searching for the right words. 'But that doesn't mean they don't have as much to *invest* in music as they used to. Or that it has less intrinsic . . . meaning,' I managed to finish, gripping the arms of my chair. I felt ominously light-headed, unable to believe the unfairness of it, either, just when I was actually getting engaged in the conversation.

'Yes, you're right, of course,' Richard said, looking slightly surprised. 'There *was* a lot of idealism in my coming-of-age, and just as much frivolous escapism as there is now, too, but there was more to it than that. Shall I tell you what it was?' He blinked through another cloud of smoke. 'There was a feeling back then that you could do almost anything, and that there was *no hurry*. Can you imagine? It seems unbelievable now, but it really felt like everything would just go on unfolding in an exciting way for ever and ever.' He laughed softly and relaxed in his chair, crossing his legs. '*But time is running out, Ted.*'

I sat, silenced by the fermented churning of my guts.

'The difference today is that no one asks any big questions any more. For a start, everyone's too distracted by their over-examined lives to look beyond the ends of their noses. *Your* generation is also terrified of big questions because you seem to equate the asking of them with some kind of ideological totalitarianism. So what's left? I mean, historically, philosophers were allowed to ask the big questions, but contemporary philosophy has simply failed to capture the popular imagination. It's not the fault of philosophers, of course, they're having to compete with *EastEnders* and the pub and getting porn over the Internet – so they've joined in the game. Hence the postmodern intellectualization of the everyday world of popular reality.'

I suppressed a shiver at the mention of the word 'postmodern'. Richard raised one finger and held it aloft.

'And due to the lack of people asking big questions, this decade has entered into the same kind of lull that existed in the fifties – everyone's just waiting for an outbreak of radicalism. They may not know it, but it's definitely coming.'

I stubbed out my cigar in the ashtray on the sideboard and pushed it away, the smell of it passing through me on a wave of nausea.

'Think about it, all the things that are piling up – economic insecurity, ecological disaster, unsustainable consumption, international genocide. Everywhere you look, there's threat hovering over your head. Oh, I know how difficult it is for you, Ted,' Richard said intimately, craning his head towards me so that I found myself staring uncomfortably into his eyes, which darted from side to side like dark newts. 'No one knows who the enemy is any more. There are no easy targets, no communists or Charles Mansons or world wars looming, but there's catastrophe everywhere.'

I watched him, mesmerized, clutching my stomach.

'It's not your fault, but it's your generation who will have to clear up the mess of the last four decades, Ted, and you're not equipped – intellectually, politically, or personally. You've inherited the currency of freedom but you don't know how to spend it. And I worry for you. I may not be around to help, either. *What are you going to do?*'

Rising to my feet, I opened my mouth and let out an acidic belch. 'I think,' I said, 'I'm going to have to use your bathroom.'

I made it just in time. On my knees before the toilet I spat out a snarling cocktail of beer, whisky and cigar-flavoured bile. Gasping at the heady fumes, I rested my head against the cold plastic seat for a minute and then rose to my feet and flushed the stuff away. I felt shivery and weak, but the relief was immediate. The sickness had completely gone. The drunkenness, however, hadn't. I'd experienced this kind of hungover vomiting before. Drinking and then throwing up the day after a serious binge sometimes seemed to reactivate the alcohol still lingering in your blood from the previous night, and before you knew it, you were royally pissed again.

At the sink I rinsed my mouth out and wiped the sweat from my forehead. My face was ashen, but I felt better than I looked. I stepped back from my reflection, wondering if Richard had heard me retching, although I didn't think he'd mind, apart from the fact that I'd cut him off in mid-rant. Part of me was still reeling from the attack of his apocalyptic monologue, which had struck fear into my soul. And yet why the fuck should I trust his prophecies, I thought, trying to articulate a counter-attack in my head. *Look Richard, you've got it all wrong. We're the kids, yeah, and we're all right* . . . Fuck it, I couldn't start quoting the Who. Staggering slightly towards the sink again, I drank some more water from the tap and tried to compose my face into some approximation of normality, if not of blooming health. Maybe he was actually on to something. Maybe it was all a piece of cake and I just was too pissed to appreciate it. I gave my reflection a sickly grin and then opened the bathroom door and walked carefully back into the room.

'OK?' Richard said, from his armchair. Was it my imagination, or was he wearing a slight smirk? He was toying with an empty whisky bottle. I cut my eyes away from it and lowered myself into my chair.

'Yeah. Sorry about the, er, interruption. Is the tape still on?' I leant forwards and examined it for something to do, feeling him scrutinizing me.

'It's all right, I left it running. So,' he said placidly, 'am I merely terrifying you, or are you getting your head around some of my ideas?'

'Definitely,' I said as confidently as I could, although the word came out a bit slurred.

'I was thinking about lepers, actually, while you were in there.'

'Oh yeah?' I said, not sure whether I was supposed to be flattered or humiliated.

'Yes. It's funny, but you've hit on something there without actually realizing it. Lepers are a great illustration of my argument, and why I think it's important philosophically.'

'How?' I said, pleased to have contributed at last.

'Well, lepers are such an extreme example of card-carrying losers. They actually lose physically – fingers, toes, limbs. It's much more of an effort for them to flourish in the face of their adversity than it is for ordinary people who are merely grappling with their own insignificance. But in a way they're better off, philosophically speaking.'

'Wha–? Better to be a leper than . . . than not to be able to get out of bed in the morning?' I said, triumphant at actually having retained something from his exposition.

'Ah, but that's the whole point! We have a *choice* whether or not to get out of bed. Unlike the lepers. Or victims of any kind of oppression – racial, sexual, political, whatever. And yet *they* tend to be the groups who manage to find a collective significance, to flourish in their adversity, to create identities for themselves in their battles against losing out. You see? For the rest of us, it's our *choice* that both condemns us to our worst fears, and yet, as I've been trying to show you, gives us such potential freedom at the same time.'

'Yeah, sounds good,' I said, nodding. 'I'm glad you got something out of the monumental fuck-up part of the interview, anyway.'

Richard laughed. After a minute he added thoughtfully. 'The thing about being part of a monumental fuck-up is that sometimes it becomes your personal motivation to grapple with the universe. It was certainly mine, anyway.'

'Oh, yeah,' I said, and hiccupped. 'Sorry. Um, can you tell me about the personal motivation thing? You know, the subtitles to your, er . . . fear of flailing . . . *failing*, I mean. Whatever it was.'

He inclined his head, looking amused. 'You're right,' he said. 'I was sort of saving it till the end. Actually the *subtext* you're referring to is a very important element of the development of my argument.'

'Great,' I said, giving him a thumbs up. 'Fire away.' I cast my eyes around the room to see if there were any open bottles waiting to be started on. I was just about to ask him if he'd mind me having one for the road, when the phone began to ring, a mean electronic squalling which sliced through the thick air of the room.

'Christ,' Richard said, looking round and dropping the empty bottle on the carpet. 'Hold on a minute.' He stood up and moved towards the bedside table, snatched up the receiver and inadvertently smacked himself on the head with it – I heard the slap of plastic and bone. 'Bollocks,' he muttered, turning around and catching me in mid-grin. I tried to make my expression serious and failed. At this point I realized just how much drunker I was than by rights I should have been. And then from nowhere I felt suddenly, absurdly happy, and a great, warm alcoholic flush of exhilaration passed through me.

'Yes?' he was saying curtly into the receiver. 'Yes, yes. Hold on, please.' He muffled the mouthpiece with his hand. 'It's for you,' he said, and the left eyebrow twitched. 'Says it's urgent.'

I hiccupped again with surprise. ''Scuse,' I said, foolishly. 'Are you sure?'

'Of course I'm sure.'

'Sorry about this.' I stood up, then walked over to the phone and sat down on the bed. 'Hello?' I said into the receiver.

'Ted, it's me.'

'Lovell!' I gave Richard another cheery thumbs up and said across the receiver, 'My best mate.' This time both eyebrows did the dance together.

'What?' I heard Lovell say.

'Nothing. Alright?' I said. 'How's it going down there?'

'It ain't,' he said tightly. 'It's Kiddie. Kiddie's done a runner. He's disappeared.'

'Wha—?' Then I looked at the alarm clock on the bedside table and saw that it was nearly two o'clock, and with a burst of inspiration, I realized that Lovell had once again come to my rescue. Probably bored to death of waiting for me.

'He's *disappeared*, Ted. I've been searching the whole fucking building for the last forty minutes with the hotel manager and he ain't here. He's gone.'

'Oh shit!' I said, playing along with delight. 'And you need me to help you look for him?'

'Yeah.' Lovell's voice was a parody of its usual self, full of jagged London threat. 'Can you come down here and wait, while I go and look for him around by the car? In case he comes back inside. OK?'

I sat in drunken silence, clutching the receiver and appreciating the magnitude of Lovell's scheme.

'Ted, you there? Fuck*sake*, Ted, this is fucking *serious*, man.'

'OK,' I said, casting a quick look at Richard. 'I'm coming now. Wait for me down—' Lovell had already hung up. I put the receiver down and turned to Richard. I was so overwhelmed with

125

gratitude at Lovell's gesture that I almost felt sorry I was going now. And saying goodbye to the mini-bar.

He was looking at me expectantly. 'Kiddie's run off,' I said, trying to convey deep disappointment at the news.

'Sorry?'

'My mate's nephew. Gone.'

'What are you talking about?'

I took a deep breath. 'My best friend's nephew's run off. They were waiting for me downstairs. Bit of a nightmare.'

'Your friend's *nephew*,' Richard said incredulously. 'God, what is it with everyone? It's like a bad Ealing comedy.'

'Eh?'

'Forget it.'

'Sorry,' I said, shrugging helplessly. 'I know we haven't finished talking, but Kiddie's run off . . .'

'Don't be ridiculous, of course you should go. It sounds serious. This is a child that's disappeared?'

'Yeah. A little boy,' I said sorrowfully.

'Well, have they called the police?'

'Dunno. But Lovell wants me to help look for him in case he's hiding or something.'

'Well, if your friend needs you, you must go,' he cut in. 'We'll just have to round this up another time. We've covered a fair amount of ground, anyway,' he added with a swift look at me. 'I'll be very interested to see what you make of it all.'

I nodded, wondering if I could scrounge that last drink before I left, although it didn't seem like very responsible behaviour. I didn't want Richard to start guessing that Kiddie's disappearing act was a total scam. It also occurred to me that I didn't want to spoil Lovell's moment of glory. He'd been genius on the phone – you could always trust him to come up with the goods when you needed them. And somehow I couldn't help feeling he'd get all touchy if he found out I'd had a drink or two up here. These days he seemed to get wound up whenever I was the slightest bit

10

toasted. It was obvious. I watched him coming out of the lifts towards where I was sat with the assistant hotel manager, a speccy guy with an edgy smile and a double-barrelled surname I'd already forgotten. As Ted got nearer and nearer I could tell by the sloppy way he was walking – like a puppet being held by a kid with a tired wrist – that he'd managed to crack something or other open upstairs with his writer and get loaded.

It's unbelievable, Ted's talent for sucking booze out of people. Although he looks like he don't know his Tennants from his tonic water, he could always wangle a drink when anyone else would have given up and gone off to bed. He could always get some after-hours corner-shop to sell him a six-pack of Red Stripe under the counter, or find the hidden bottle of Jack at a dry house party, or sniff out a pub lock-in. So I suppose I shouldn't have been all that surprised he'd managed to get a couple in, really, especially not considering how bad he'd complained about his hangover. But it still rankled.

He didn't look at me while he walked over but kept his eyes on the carpet instead, depriving me of the chance to stare him down. I was pissed off enough as it was already: with myself because I'd been thinking with my dick and had let myself get sidetracked by the girl when I should have been minding Kiddie; with Kiddie for even *wanting* to sneak off in the first place. Not to mention with this hotel bloke, Mr Whatever-his-name-was Assistant-Bland-Manager, for having a couple of shaving cuts on his chin and a nasty suit, both of which gave me zero faith in his ability to help me find Kiddie. But seeing Ted doing the drunkard's roll, wearing this faint, apologetic half-smirk he always wears when he's half-cut – as if to say, don't give me a hard time, I know I'm a cunt, but aren't I a character, aren't I the lad? Well, that got up my nose even worse.

It was about as predictable as a fucking missed Spurs penalty shot, and just as useless. It ain't often that I turn to Ted for help, after all, not that he's much cop at anything practical, but at least he's good at making you *feel* better about things when you need it. Only right now I didn't want a load of drunken rhapsodizing, I wanted a show of strength, something to stop me feeling like such a miserable fucking idiot for managing to lose my nephew. Again.

When Ted finally sat down in the chair next to me, he gave me a nervous, cock-eyed grin and leant forward so I could smell the booze on his breath. My own mouth still tasted faintly of whiskey, overlaid with the bad hotel coffee I'd been necking since I'd been looking for Kiddie, but Ted's breath nearly knocked me out. Beer and nicotine, and something else, something sour and nasty. I sat back in my seat, looking at him with barely concealed disgust.

'You're a star, mate,' was the first thing he slurred at me, and I got another blast of devil-tongue.

'You what?' I said, giving him a hard look.

'You've no idea what a headfuck I've just had,' he said. 'You called in the nick of time. It was so bad, I actually puked,' and he gave a bleating little laugh.

I shook my head. He had a sunken-eyed look about him, as well as that blotchy red booze-flush on his neck that certain kinds of thin-skinned birds get after their first white-wine spritzer. Completely fucking toasted.

'Yeah, well, thanks for the moral support,' I said, and glanced at Mr Bland-Manager, who said, 'This is . . . Ted?' looking at him as if he'd been expecting James Bond.

Ted looked a bit puzzled, but nodded at the guy. Then the smile returned to his face. 'Shall we have a drink to celebrate?' he said to me. 'I owe you one.'

'Are you taking the piss?'

'Oh come on, Lovell, you were brilliant, mate. Let's have a quick one before Richard comes down and sees us.'

'Who in the name of holy fuck do you think you are, Teddy?' I said, too surprised to be really angry. 'Kiddie's fucking vanished into thin air, and you just want to keep boozing?'

'But, hang on,' Ted said, looking a bit panicked, 'Kiddie hasn't really run away, has he? I thought . . . I thought . . .' He looked over at Bland-Manager and then back to me. 'Oh shit,' he whispered, and turned beetroot.

I twigged suddenly, and nearly laughed at the sheer fucking nerve of it – it was so like Ted to assume that the world revolved around his hangovers, but I didn't say a word. There was too much to do.

I addressed Bland-Manager. 'Right. Ted's gonna stay here in case Kiddie shows up while I go and see if he's anywhere near the car. Think you can remember what he looks like?' I asked Ted sarcastically. He flicked his eyes away from me and for a moment I felt like a bastard. Then I thought about the closed-in joy on Kiddie's face, poised over his lemonade glass at the bar, and reminded myself that if Ted hadn't made such a big drama about me driving him here for his moronic magazine interview in the first place, I'd still probably be letting Kid beat me at Monopoly and planning a trip to McDonald's back home in Chelsea. Instead of sitting here with a pisshead and someone who hadn't been shaving long enough to be any use to anyone.

'Fuck it!' I said out loud to no one in particular.

Bland-Manager shot me a startled, rabbity look and cleared his throat, then said hurriedly to Ted, 'Er, we've looked pretty much everywhere for Kiddie, all the hotel common rooms and the staff areas and so on, but no luck yet, I'm afraid.'

'Right,' Ted said efficiently, pulling himself up in his chair. He wasn't fooling no one.

'Now, none of the staff have seen him wandering about, or actually leaving the building, so it seems most likely that he's just tucked away somewhere, perhaps in a guest's room. They're still being checked individually. But could he have followed you upstairs, Ted? You were in room forty-eight, I think, is that right? With Mr Shaw?'

Ted nodded. 'I don't really think he would have followed *me*,' he said, looking at me doubtfully. 'Kiddie hardly knows me.'

I shrugged. Hardly likes you neither, I wanted to say, but didn't. I sighed instead. 'Well, if he ain't in here, then he must have got it in his head to go somewhere else.'

'*Where*, though?' Bland-Manager asked, helpfully.

We were interrupted then by a hotel minion who came creeping over in her two-piece polyester and murmured something in Bland-Manager's ear. He stood up. 'I'll be *right* back,' he said and slipped away across the carpet, leaving Ted and me on our own. We didn't look at each other.

'Lovell,' Ted said eventually, 'sorry about that, mate. I thought . . . You alright?'

'Oh yeah, I'm just peachy.'

'Erm, do you think he's hiding? You know, for a joke?'

'Kiddie doesn't do hiding, it ain't his style. Nor's joking, for that matter. I got no fucking idea where he's gone. He could be anywhere in London by now.'

'Well, how?'

'Don't underestimate Kiddie.'

'I'm not. But he's only been gone, what, not even an hour, right? How long was I upstairs?'

'Long enough.'

'Well, maybe he's just poking around somewhere – it's quite a big hotel, isn't it? Lots of places to get lost.' I could tell Ted was trying really hard not to slur, because he'd started to talk in this BBC broadcaster's voice he always takes on when he's pissed and pretending not to be. *Lorts of places to get lorst.* I sort of forgave him then, he sounded so ridiculous.

'Ted, I got a bad feeling about this, man,' I said. 'You've seen Kiddie, he ain't like some little Famous Five tomboy looking for adventures. He sticks close to the grown-ups. The only time he's ever gone off on his own before . . . well.'

'Well what?'

'Well it was no fucking picnic, let's say that much.'

'Right,' he said, sympathetically. Then after a pause, 'Could you use a drink?'

I almost laughed. 'If you want a drink, Ted, have a fucking drink.'

He had the balls to look hurt. 'I asked *you* if you wanted a drink.'

'Well, ta very much, but not right now. Why don't you hop it to the bar though and get yourself a double?' Ted looked as if he was about to cry. 'Look, Jesus,' I went on in a slightly better voice, 'I don't give a shit if you get pissed out of your tiny mind, as long as Kiddie shows up. Alright? Just don't ask me to carry you home, OK, Teddy-boy? Think you can stay upright?'

Just then Bland-Manager came trotting over again and sat down. 'Lovell,' he said carefully, 'we've got some new information for you.' He smiled at me, but his small, worried eyes behind their lenses told a different story, and my stomach began to flip over like a kebab-shop burger in the hands of an over-zealous Greek.

'What?' I said, as sternly as I could.

'I've spoken to Carol, one of our receptionists,' Bland-Manager said, and cleared his throat. 'She's just come back from her lunch break, and she says that before she left the front desk, she *did* see a little boy leaving the hotel, who sounds as if he must have been Kiddie.' He paused.

'Well, go on. What did she say?'

'He was wearing a blue tracksuit, he had very, er, short hair, was about six or seven. This was about forty-five minutes ago,' Bland-Manager went on cautiously. 'Now, Carol *thinks* Kiddie was with a female guardian, but it's possible she was wrong.'

'A *female guardian*?'

'A woman,' Bland-Manager said, clearing his throat again.

'What, he was being taken off somewhere by a woman?'

'Not necessarily. But there was definitely a woman at the door *near* him as he left. Carol remembers Kiddie because he ran through the lobby and she wondered if he'd been left behind by his mum. By mistake,' he added.

'Shit!'

'Now, we shouldn't draw any conclusions from this, but I think now it would be best to call the police with no further . . .'

'Are you saying *kidnapping*?' Ted said incredulously, looking at me with horrified eyes.

I snorted helplessly. 'Who the fuck would want to kidnap Kiddie?' I said, and then looked up at the two serious faces regarding me. 'Jesus,' I muttered, ashamed. 'What was this woman like, anyway? Have they got a description?'

'Carol really can't remember, I'm afraid. She only saw the back of her. She thinks she had dark hair . . .'

'That narrows it down, then,' I said. Bland-Manager gave me an apologetic shrug. 'What time is it now?' I asked him.

'It's just after two,' he said, glancing at his wrist. 'I *really* think it would be best if you spoke to the police . . .'

I stood up. 'I'm gonna look by the car before I do anything else,' I said, with mechanical logic. 'Ted, stay here, in case.' He nodded mutely. I looked at Bland-Manager over my shoulder as I started towards the entrance. 'Do me a favour and get my friend here a large one,' I called back, indicating Ted. 'It's all been a bit of a shock, you know?' Then I turned away.

Once outside, I walked quickly down the street away from the hotel, squinting in the prickling rain. It was weird being outdoors after the artificial warmth of the hotel, unnaturally bright despite the thundery sky. Blinking, I looked around me like I was searching for clues, trying to see what Kiddie might have seen when he'd left the Lansdowne. White and grey buildings, puddles, empty parked cars. What the hell would Kiddie want to be going out into the streets in the rain for? He hated rain.

My head was full of nothing and everything, people's faces kept zooming in and out. Kiddie in the bar chewing a straw, the little black dried spots of blood on the hotel bloke's cheek, Ted's boozy look of concern. Lisa, God – I thought of Lisa's eyes and imagined just how they'd change colour when I called her and told her that her son had done a runner: a white panic spreading out from the pupil and across the pale-blue irises until they were nearly washed away.

My nose started running. I wiped it on the back of my hand like a snot-nosed kid, and kept walking. It felt good somehow to be moving through the rain and the traffic, purposeful, at least, and I kept going for about another three or four minutes, thinking and walking hard, before I had to stop and get my bearings. As I was standing there on Praed Street like a moron, a passing car beeped and I barrelled round to face it, thinking Kiddie might be in the passenger seat and I'd see his little brown hand waving at me through the rainy glass. Then it was gone, and I was trying to remember where the fuck I'd parked *my* car. I saw the sign for Queen's Gardens across the road and stepped out at the zebra crossing, remembering how I'd pulled Kiddie over the same crossing by the hand, not an hour before. I tried to remember the feeling of his hand in mine, but it seemed like too long ago.

The things you tell yourself when you're in a lather about something, they're pretty hilarious really. If you could record what went on in your brain in moments of panic and play it back afterwards, you'd crap yourself. Me, I had a mantra going in time with my footsteps as I headed down Queen's Gardens – *please* Kiddie, *please* Kiddie, *please* man, *come* on; *please* Kiddie, *please* Kiddie, *please* man, *come* on. Meanwhile, I was trying to imagine him sitting on the bonnet of my car waiting for me, talking to himself, happy as a piglet in shit. It was such a clear picture that when I turned the corner of Queen's Gardens and spotted the car at the end of the cul-de-sac, it was almost a jolt that he wasn't there.

I headed towards the car, sick with disappointment. I dunno quite what I was expecting to see, but I just couldn't bear the thought of going straight back to the hotel empty-handed, having to walk back in and everything be the same, no Kiddie, just the yards of empty carpet and discreetly ringing phones and Ted slumped there in his armchair with sweat on his forehead. Nothing but the hollowness of waiting for something to happen. Phone calls and explaining. Shit and shit and more shit.

The funny thing is, although part of me was panicking, somewhere deep down I just didn't believe Kiddie was really in *danger* or anything. The thing about Kiddie is that it all goes way beyond the realms of the threat of physical harm. He's impossible to predict, sometimes, despite all the die-hard habits and that, all the *Star Wars* shit. You never knew what he was thinking when he gazed at you with those eyes. You know, once a mate of mine brought a Superman outfit for his kid back from America, and when the kid first tried it on, they found a label sewn into it that said 'Warning – this suit will not enable you to fly.' I never knew if it was bollocks or not, but it was a great fucking story. Only Kiddie – he was the kind of kid that it would actually be worth spelling it out to. That's what I'm trying to get at.

I was getting close to the car, close enough to see the stretch of empty pavement and the total lack of Kiddieness anywhere around it. And *then* I was near enough to see the ticket on my windshield and the flash of yellow on my front wheel and hearing myself say with almost a little moan of laughter because it seemed just too much, 'Oh, no, no, nah, man, *FUCK*!'

When I got back to the hotel, soaked with sweat and rain and rage, Ted was sitting where I'd left him, deep in conversation with an older guy with glasses and grey hair. For a moment I thought it might be the Filth, but then I noticed they both had what looked like whiskies in their hands. Ted had just taken a sip when he saw me approaching, and straight away he put his glass down on the table in front of them and pushed it to one side, as if he was about to try and convince me that both the drinks belonged to the other guy.

The man followed Ted's gaze and stopped talking, and they both kind of drew back to accommodate me as I arrived and stood in front of them. This bloke had eyebrows like a Muppet, and massive ears, and he gave me an interested look. Ted mumbled, 'Lovell, this is Richard Shaw. You know, the interview for Fish.'

The guy nodded at me and said seriously, 'I'm sorry this has happened. I've just heard the whole story.'

Bet you hear most things with ears that size, mate, I thought, looking down at him and trying to place his accent while he trotted out the anything-I-can-do line and followed it up with a sip of his drink. From Manchester, maybe? City supporter, probably. I dunno what I expected Ted's genius philosopher to look like, but it wasn't this. He looked more like some Stoke Newington pub bore than an intellectual. Or maybe that's the same thing.

'Yeah, you can help, matter of fact,' I said. 'Got a toolbox handy? Fuckers have clamped my car.'

Ted groaned and said moistly, 'You're *joking*?'

I sat down heavily in an armchair. Now I really did want that drink.

'Joking's strictly for jokers,' I said, picking up Ted's glass and taking a big gulp. 'Jesus,' I said, spluttering over the whisky.

'Lovell,' he said, 'don't you think you should tell the police now?'

'What, about my car? Think they'll let me off the clamping fine?'

'But someone saw him *leave* – he could be anywhere. The sooner you call them, the sooner he'll get found.'

'What about his parents?' Richard interjected suddenly. 'Have they been told?'

I glanced at him with dislike. '*I'm* his parents, more or less,' I said, thinking of Lisa's tired face. I really had the jitters now, all the caffeine whizzing round my system, or maybe it was just the thought of making that phone call to Croydon.

'Well, I meant it when I said I'd help. If you need a lift anywhere while your car's down I'd be happy to take you,' Richard said, all matter-of-fact. He glanced at Ted. 'I had another meeting here at two o'clock but the person hasn't shown up, so I've nothing to do. I feel rather implicated in all this, anyway, since I understand it was you that drove Ted here to interview me.'

Nothing to do except muscle in on a bit of drama that ain't your own, I thought cynically. But sitting there in that hotel chair I felt suddenly so drained that it was as much as I could do to pick up Ted's glass and take another sip of whisky. On the other hand, I knew that I was trying to postpone the inevitable. It was just that coppers and questions and phone calls and all that made it seem so definite that Kiddie wasn't about to come back. It was almost like I wanted to give him a chance, you know, to reappear, all proud of himself for scaring the grown-ups. Before we went and filled in forms and made him feel like a criminal, a weirdo, a fucked-up kid who couldn't be trusted.

Still, hanging round in this plywood-and-plush mausoleum wasn't going to do any good. I'd accepted Kiddie wasn't here any more – once I was told he'd been seen leaving it was like I could almost feel the emptiness, the negative of him hanging in the air.

Then Richard said out the blue, 'Has he ever run away before?'

'Why d'you ask?' I said casually, even though I was caught completely off-guard.

He shrugged. 'You just don't seem very surprised, somehow. Some kids are good at disappearing. I used to do it myself – I usually only made it to the end of the garden before I got scared and came back. London's an entirely different place for a kid to get lost in, though.'

'Kiddie's from Croydon,' Ted interjected. Richard gave me a sober look, and said nothing.

'All right, all right,' I said, sighing. 'Let's call the fucking police.'

'Good,' they both said together.

In the end it was Richard who went off to speak to Bland-Manager about calling the cops. Since he was involved in the whole caboodle by now, I thought I might as well get my money's worth. Me and Ted sat there in silence for a bit, then I pulled my mobile out of my jacket pocket and turned it off. Ted gave me a respectful look – he knew this meant things were serious. What he didn't know was that I was anticipating a call from Lisa any moment – she had a sixth sense about Kiddie getting into trouble, and I wasn't about to tell her what was going on. Not yet, anyway.

The hotel was pretty deserted by now. After I'd finished off Ted's drink for him, and he'd finished off Richard's, there was nothing to do but slump on the sofa and stare into space. After a few minutes of this I couldn't bear it any longer. The place was giving me the heebie-jeebies, it was like being at a fucking wake.

'I'm gonna get some air,' I said, standing up. 'I'll be outside for a bit.'

'OK, I'll come with you,' Ted said, hauling himself to his feet.

'You don't have to,' I said, eyeing him. He looked like he could barely walk.

'No, no, I need to go to the shop anyway,' he said. He patted me on the shoulder and went off to tell Big Ears what we were doing, then we traipsed off across the carpet towards the front door, receiving sympathetic smiles from the two receptionists as we passed their desk.

Outside the rain had slacked to a thin drizzle, but the sky above us was still black and dense. Talk about a fucking portent of doom. It was the kind of weather that makes you feel like something's about to happen, and it had given me a bellyful of wriggling fish into the bargain.

Ted went and bought fags and Lucozade from the newsagent and stood there swigging it between sucking in lungfuls of smoke and coughing them out. The booze high was obviously wearing off because he'd gone all white and limp, he looked like a schoolkid having a sneaky smoke at breaktime. We stood there getting slowly wet, and watching the cars swoosh by. I kept looking up and down the street, willing myself to see a small, familiar figure scurrying towards me. But apart from a couple of biddies with plastic headscarves who limped past, giving us a wide berth, the road was pretty much empty.

'You OK?' Ted said eventually, squashing his cigarette butt out on the white hotel wall.

I grunted noncommittally.

'Don't worry, I'm sure he's going to turn up sooner or later.'

'Yeah.'

'As soon as the police are on it, they'll find him.'

'Yeah.'

We both stared into the road. Ted drained his bottle and put it down near his feet.

'What's your friend Richard's story, then?' I said.

'I dunno, really,' he said, straightening up. 'I mean, he's an interesting bloke, very smart, but he's a bit . . . cryptic. It was pretty heavy up there, actually.'

'What d'you mean, heavy? He got you loaded, didn't he? What more could you have asked for?'

Ted sighed. 'We had a couple of beers, that's all.'

'Could have fooled me.'

'Look, you've got no idea what I went through up there, Lovell,' he said wetly, spraying me with alcoholic spit. I took a step back. 'It was like fucking Armageddon. I needed the drink just to stop myself from jumping out of the window after listening to some of the things he said. Tell you what,' he added, 'I hope I'm not like that when I'm his age.'

'Like what?'

'Well, he might be clever and everything, but it was pretty depressing, listening to him go on about what a waste his life had been. More or less the first thing he told me was that he was no wiser, no happier and no less afraid of things *now* than when he was my age. It doesn't exactly give you a lot to look forward to, does it?'

'Yeah, well,' I said, not feeling particularly charitable towards Richard. 'Welcome to the real world, sunshine. That's what most people would have to say about their lives if anyone was interested, isn't it? Only most people don't get the chance to spout off and get it written up in a magazine.'

Ted gave me an unfocused but dirty look. 'Well, he's more articulate than most people are, anyway. And he obviously believes in what he says. I just wasn't in the mood to hear it.' Then he sagged against the wall and gave another great world-weary sigh. 'Things are hard enough, you know, without being told categorically that your future's shot to pieces and that you're about as insignificant as . . . as a *leper*.'

'Eh?'

'Oh, never mind,' he muttered. 'I doubt you'd understand, anyway.'

'Jesus,' I said, starting to get the hump. 'Well, forgive me for asking, but what exactly's so hard about your life, Teddy? You ain't got much to complain about, if you ask me. Other than the frequency of your delightful hangovers.'

'Bollocks,' he shot back. 'Believe it or not, not everyone has it as easy as you, Lovell.'

I was a bit stunned, not least by the way he was rising to the occasion. 'Are you having a laugh? Listen, man, I've had no money to buy food in the past, I've stood out in the rain and wondered who I could crash for the night, I've had to fucking hustle like the next wanker for a crappy job . . .'

'Yeah, right, when you were sixteen, maybe,' Ted said, all hoity-toity. 'And even then I bet you never went without a shag, a new pair of trainers or the latest Public Enemy record, did you?'

I cracked up then. I could never stay angry with Ted for long, specially not after he'd dished up a line like that. He didn't even know he was funny. 'What?' he said, sheepishly, looking at me doubled over laughing.

'Ah, nothing,' I said, coming up for air, and putting my arm around him. Ted took out his fags and lit up again. 'Let's call it quits, yeah? You be as miserable as you want, darlin'. It suits you. Look, shall we go back in? I'm freezing my tits off out here.'

'OK,' he said, with obvious relief, giving me a watery grin. 'Let me just finish this.'

'Fuck the cigarette, it's going to piss it down any minute.'

Ted threw his fag on the ground and followed me inside without a word.

Richard was waiting for us inside with three fresh glasses of whisky on the table.

'On the house,' he said, raising one of them. 'I thought you could do with it.'

'Cheers,' I said, sitting down on the sofa and picking up the drink. Ted sat next to me, cradling his glass to his chest with a dazed look on his face.

'The police are on their way,' Richard said. We all nodded, and then we sat and listened to the muzak that some fool had decided it would be nice to have piped through the speakers in the lobby. Halfway through the whisky, the song changed and Luther Vandross started singing 'Never Too Much'.

'Jesus,' I said.

'What?' Ted looked at me. I shook my head. My spirits suddenly took a nose-dive again. Somehow, sitting there with him next to me, stinking of whisky, and Luther crooning in the background, it reminded me of nothing more than all the minicab rides I've ever shared, pissed in the early hours and squashed in the back with a couple of mates, when there's always some terrible late-night radio station playing on the stereo, and you're guaranteed at some point to hear this very song, and you'll sit there with your head lolling on the back seat while the cab driver's singing along with Luther, completely out of tune, and it's the most depressing fucking end to your night imaginable.

I must have had a really long face by then, because Ted reached out and patted me on the shoulder again. I gave him a nod, and got back such a big wet grin that I would've cracked up again if I'd been in the mood for it. Bless Teddy, I'd never seen him in full-on Samaritan mode before, wasted though he was. Usually it's me scraping him off the floor and telling him to get a life.

'What about you, Ted? Did you ever run away?' I said. 'I bet you didn't have the balls.'

'Not really,' he said through a mouthful of booze. 'My mum tied me to the back door once, though, on a dog leash,' he added.

'You what?'

'Right after my dad moved out, I told her I was going to piss in her bed if she didn't let me go and live with him. It wasn't the right thing to say, really. She was quite upset.' He squinted at me sheepishly.

I tried to picture his nice old lady stringing little Teddy up. 'Well what the fuck did she do to you when she was *really* upset?' I asked. 'Jesus.'

Richard laughed. 'How old were you when it happened?'

'About ten.'

'*Ten!*' Me and Richard said, in stereo.

'Yeah,' Ted said, screwing up his face again.

'You were obviously a well-adjusted kid,' I said, half-impressed. 'And I thought Kiddie had problems.'

'Does he?' Richard said, straight off.

'No,' I said quickly. 'Well, some people might think so. Depends how well you know Kiddie. He's different, I'll give you that. But he ain't . . .'

'What?'

'He ain't stupid,' I said, sighing. 'That's half the problem. And he's got more bottle than you'd think if you met him.'

'How so?'

'Well as it happens, you were right, before.' I paused, wondering if I should spill the beans or not. 'This isn't the first time Kiddie's done this kind of thing.'

'What, gone missing?'

'Yeah. He ran away once before. About a year ago.'

'What happened?' said Ted.

'He was AWOL for nearly a day,' I said. 'It made the news and everything.'

'Where did he go?'

'Long story.'

'Well, are you going to tell us?' Ted said patiently.

I wanted to, now, and all. Just to see the look on their faces when they realized what kind of tricks Kiddie had up his sleeve.

'Lisa's ex, right?' I began. 'Roy. Kiddie's dad. Him and Lisa had a big fight one time, when Roy was still living with them. He had a temper on him, the cunt. Lisa got smacked around pretty bad and Kiddie was right there, he saw the whole thing. So he decided to run away.'

'Poor kid,' Richard said.

'Yeah, poor Kid. Only this wasn't your everyday kind of running away,' I said. 'Kiddie didn't just go to the end of the street and come back for tea. He had a bit of a plan.'

'What was it?'

'It was a pretty full-on plan, actually.'

'Come on,' Ted said.

'Wonder if you can guess what it was about?' I said to him, and threw him a wink. I still got a buzz out of the story. I was fucking proud of Kiddie for it, I can tell you.

Ted looked doubtful. 'What do you mean?'

'Come on, use your loaf. What's the single most important thing in Kiddie World?'

It took him a minute. 'Not *Star Wars*?'

I nodded, grinning.

'What's *Star Wars* got to do with it all?' Richard asked. 'Ted was just talking about that upstairs.'

'Yeah?' I said, ignoring the interruption and glancing between the two of them. 'Well, get ready for this. Kiddie ran away so he could learn how to be a Jedi Knight.'

Ted laughed incredulously. 'You're kidding?'

'It's actually quite logical, if you think about it,' I said, picturing Kiddie in his Vader mask, and swallowing down the lump in my throat that appeared from nowhere. 'You see your mum get beaten up enough times, you'd want to learn a bit of magic too, stop it happening again.'

'So what did he do?' Ted said in a hushed voice.

'He tried to run away to the Dagobah System.'

'Where the fuck's – ?'

'It's the planet Yoda lives on. *Empire Strikes Back*. In the swamp, right? The forest? You know, where he trains Luke Skywalker to be a Jedi, gets him doing all those fancy handstands and keeps on telling him to use his nature, remember?

'Ah, so Kiddie's the one that's been influencing Ted,' Richard interrupted, looking amused.

'You what?'

'Ted used that very phrase when we were discussing some philosophical ideas. He wouldn't disclose his sources, though. I can see I must meet Kiddie.'

I looked at Ted, surprised. 'Well, well,' I said, smirking at him. 'And I can see I'll have to start puntering Kiddie out to all your intellectuals.'

'Go on with the story,' Ted said, blushing like a girl.

'OK,' I said. 'Dagobah System. That's where Kiddie wanted to go, see. He wanted to ask Yoda if he'd teach him the same tricks, make him invincible. Only Kiddie didn't have a spaceship, did he? So he did the next best thing.'

'What?' they both said.

'He went to the airport. Thought he'd try and take a plane instead.'

'Hold on,' Richard said in a puzzled voice. 'When was this, exactly?'

'Gatwick airport, to be precise. Lisa lives right by the train station in Croydon and she'd taken Kiddie to Gatwick a couple of times to see the planes landing and taking off – he loves planes. So anyway, the day after Lisa gets punched, while she's in the hospital with a stitched-up mouth, Kiddie gives his babysitter the slip and he goes down the street to the station and he gets on a –'

'I remember this,' Richard was saying slowly.

'He gets on a train to Gatwick,' I continued. 'And guess what, somehow, all the odds work in Kiddie's favour, just once. He manages to get on the right train, and he don't get spotted by the ticket inspector because he's sitting next to a big family, this black family, right, with lots of kids and suitcases. And as luck would have it, it turns out the family's going to America, to Washington DC, actually, to visit their grandma. Kiddie hears them talking about it on the train, and, as he ain't got *that* much of a clue how to get to the Dagobah System, he figures America's the next best place to find Yoda, *Star Wars* being full of Yanks, right? So he kind of tags along with them . . .'

'Now hang on a minute,' Ted said, suddenly alert.

'He gets off at Gatwick station and he follows this family into the airport, sticks close behind them while they're queuing up at the Virgin Atlantic check-in . . .'

'What did the papers call him?' Richard mused. 'The Croydon . . .'

'Meanwhile, of course, all hell's broken loose back at Lisa's house,' I went on, 'because everyone assumes the worst. The worst being that Roy's come back and kidnapped Kiddie. The babysitter's freaking out, Lisa's freaking out, the police get called. Lisa comes clean about the assault in the light of this apparent kidnapping, right, so the police, they *move*. Whole fucking country's suddenly involved, helicopters flying around looking for Roy and Kid, news bulletins, the works.'

'The Croydon Castaway!' Richard said triumphantly, like he'd just scored a really tricky crossword clue.

Ted looked dumbstruck. 'Don't tell me Kiddie ended up in America?' he said.

'Nah,' I said, shaking my head. 'That would be a bit too good to be true, wouldn't it? He probably *could* have done, if he'd kept his mouth shut and just stuck with his adopted family. But no, Kiddie goes and ruins it by trying to ask the nice lady at the check-in if she knows how to get to the Dagobah System from Washington DC. Then the shit hits the fan. The family Kiddie's been stalking suddenly realize they've acquired a fourth child in their travelling party and they disown him on the spot. Poor Kiddie's whisked away by security while they scour the airport trying to find his parents. His plans all ruined.' I took a deep breath.

'Then what?' Ted went, blinking at me like a dozy dog. I bet you've sobered up now, son, ain't you, I was thinking.

'We-ell,' I said, casually, 'Kiddie, bless him, plays dumb. He's set his little heart on going to the Dagobah System, or at least to America, to find Yoda. So he won't talk. Won't answer any of their questions, won't even tell them his name, just sits there and spouts out Yoda talk.'

'Yoda talk?' Richard said.

'Ted knows,' I said briefly. 'Yoda talk. Everything backwards, in this croaky voice. You can imagine the airport security don't have a fucking clue what to do with him. I mean, this is a six-year-old kid, remember, in a state of delayed shock, talking complete gibberish. No parents turn up to claim him, so they get in the police. Eventually, the clever old Filth put their heads together and realize Kiddie fits the description of the missing boy from Croydon, and bingo.'

'Bingo,' Ted repeated softly.

'The one good thing that came out of it was that Kiddie got to ride in a helicopter back to Croydon. He's never forgotten it. It's the nearest thing to a spaceship he's ever been in,' I said, smiling suddenly at the memory.

'What's Kiddie's real name?' Richard said, unexpectedly. 'I've been trying to recall.'

'Marcus,' I said after a few seconds had gone by. I was strangely reluctant to tell him. 'Marcus Hamilton. AKA the Croydon Castaway. How the fuck d'you remember all that, anyway?'

'Oh, I remember all sorts of things,' he said modestly.

'*Marcus?*' Ted said in an amazed voice.

'What about it?'

'I dunno. It's just weird, Kiddie having a real name . . .'

'Yeah, well, Kiddie suits him better than Marcus. Maybe he'll grow into it one day.'

'He doesn't *look* like a Marcus,' Ted said.

'Well he don't look like Yoda, either, but that ain't ever stopped him from trying to act like him, has it?'

Richard laughed. 'Like you said, there's something extraordinarily logical about the behaviour of children who've developed their fantasy worlds to such a highly evolved degree,' he said sagely. I shot him a look. He lifted his glass to his mouth and took a sip of his drink. 'I mean to the point when everyday life interferes with their own created reality,' he went on. 'Kiddie probably has a very clear idea of what he's doing and why, if he's run away for the same kind of reason.'

'What, you mean all this has got something to do with *Star Wars* too?' Ted asked.

I didn't say anything for a minute, surprised at Richard's insight. Ted was right, the guy was obviously no doughnut. 'You might be on to something, you know,' I said. 'Kiddie sort of manages to fit everything around *Star Wars* in one way or another. In fact, it turned out that the main reason Kid wouldn't talk to the security person who was put in charge of him at Gatwick was because he thought the guy looked like

11

'*Tar*kin, that *baddie*, the one . . .' the child paused here for breath, 'who makes 'em lock up the prin*cess*, they going to *kill* her but Luke comes to *res*cue her and at first she thinks he's a *storm*trooper 'cause they didn't know they were brothers and *sis*ters then.' He seemed to think about this for a minute. 'Not till the end of the last one, they don't,' he added, and nodded as if to indicate that this cleared matters up once and for all.

He was sitting next to me at the table clutching the glass of orange juice I'd given him. 'Thirsty, I am,' he'd said in a peculiar voice, when we'd walked into the kitchen, and then requested lemonade. He looked so disappointed when I told him I didn't have any that I found myself apologizing helplessly, hoping he wouldn't start crying again. But he hadn't, he'd just accepted the juice, opened his mouth and started skittering on in this funny storytelling way.

'The last what?' I asked, looking down at his cropped head. He angled his face upwards and slid his eyes across my face. 'The last *one*,' he said with finality. '*The Return of the Jedi*'s the last one, that's where they find out.'

'Oh, the *Star Wars* films,' I said inspirationally, and smiled to show I understood his reference, relieved to have finally made some kind of connection with his train of thought. Not that I really had the first clue about *Star Wars*. The boy, however, was looking at me as if I might be slightly retarded.

'Do you like *Star Wars*, then?' I asked, in an attempt to keep the communication going. But his bemused expression merely seemed to deepen into one of amazement.

For a moment he didn't speak, apparently battling with the question. Then, 'Which one do *you* like best?' he said, regarding me intently.

'Which *Star Wars* film?'

He nodded.

'Oh,' I said, not wanting to admit I'd never seen any of them, 'I'm not sure. What about you?'

'The second one's the best.'

'Right.'

The phone started to ring then, making us both jump slightly. I knew exactly who it was. After I'd got him settled at the table with his drink, I'd called Estelle, impulsively, but just as quickly changed my mind, and put the phone down before she'd answered. There was no separating this little kitchen drama from my own. I knew that if Estelle came bowling round to take charge of Kiddie for me, I'd probably start wailing again as soon as I saw her face. And I wasn't up to an emotional confession right now. Richard, me, babies. No, no, no.

As I let it ring on questioningly, the boy looked between me and the phone, at first with eagerness, then with increasing disappointment.

'The phone's ringin',' he said pointedly, wagging his head.

I nodded.

'Aren't you going to answer?'

I shrugged, smiling, but this obviously wasn't good enough for him, because he stood up and blithely reached out a hand towards the phone.

'Hey,' I said, startled. I managed to reach past him and grab the receiver just before he got there. 'Hello,' I said into the phone, breathlessly, shooting him a pleading look. His brown eyes were round and innocent, his mouth partly open as he watched me.

'Guess what?' Estelle's voice trilled in my ear. 'I'm eating the most fantastic prawns!'

I cleared my throat. 'Really?'

'There's a new Thai place that's opened up just down the road – I ordered a take-away for lunch. Aren't I frivolous?'

It was an effort to laugh.

'You just called me, darling, didn't you? I checked the number. But you got cut off or something.'

'Actually I dialled you by mistake.'

'Oh,' she said. There was a pause filled with a faint, plump swallowing, then she said, 'Have you got a cold? You sound all stuffy.'

'I think I've got one coming.'

'Well go to bed, darling, and catch it before it catches you.'

'Yeah, I will.'

'Everything else OK, sweetheart? Aren't you working today?'

The kid, obviously an impatient third-party phone listener, chose this moment to demand loudly, 'Who is it?'

Caught, I shook my head at him again, as Estelle retaliated, inevitably, 'Who was that? It sounded like a child.'

'It was,' I said, still looking entreatingly at him. 'Listen, I've got to go, some of the kids from downstairs came up to borrow something. I'll give you a call soon, OK?'

'But, darling, are you sure you –'

'I'm fine, Mum,' I said, my voice rising uncontrollably like a wave that broke on the last word. 'Bye.' And I put the phone down, defeated by my own useless transparency. I waited for a minute, half-expecting her to call back, but she didn't. So I sat back down at the table next to him.

We were so close that I could actually feel the heat coming off his body. I studied him covertly while I tried to think of the best way to frame all the questions I needed to ask him, but after a few moments I became aware that I had stopped searching for words, and was staring at him greedily, literally drinking in all his details. I didn't think I'd ever been so physically close to a little boy before. The longer I looked at him, the more fascinating his own childishness seemed, a mixture of natural self-possession and frailty.

The child himself didn't seem to see me, taking small sips from his glass, kicking one foot against the chair leg. His face had recovered from his initial crying fit much faster than mine had. His nostrils were delicately crusted powdery white and I could still see the tear-marks on his face, silvery trails which wound down to his mouth, but his skin was incredible, pale brown and flawless. Suddenly I wanted to stroke his cheek with my hand, feel the perfect, sculptured quality of his features – the short nose and plum mouth – and touch the thick eyelashes that curled up comically.

I raised a hand to my own swollen eyes, my skin like sore tissue paper stretched tightly across my cheekbones. The kid's legs had stilled. He wasn't looking at me, but there was a feeling of waiting about him.

'Tell me your name again?' I said.

'Kiddie,' he said, eyes fixed on some unreachable distance. His voice had an endearing throatiness underpinning the London accent.

'Kiddie? I thought you said you were called Luke. That's an interesting name. Is it a nickname?'

'It's *my* name,' he said with touching dignity.

I smiled at this. 'My name's Sara, did I tell you that already?' I asked.

He nodded, then in a faraway voice he asked me if I loved him, and without pausing for breath he told me that it was alright, he understood, and that when he came back he wouldn't stand in my way . . .

Richard, I thought for one dazed heartbeat – he's talking about Richard.

'But Han didn't know they was brothers and sisters then,' he finished up. The moment of madness passed. I looked at him, nonplussed. He was still moving his lips. It was starting to dawn on me that he might be a little bit . . . backward. I still didn't understand his garbled account of how he'd arrived outside my front door, but then again, *everything* felt slightly unreal right now. The unnatural darkness of the stormy afternoon sky, the secretive quietness of my flat, as if it had been shocked into stillness by our unexpected entry, the unfamiliar physicality of this small brown boy sitting in my kitchen – everything had a strange, slowed-down quality to it. It was like falling asleep in a chair, the feeling of that split second when everything slides away into unconsciousness, before your body jerks you awake again.

As if on cue, Kiddie lifted the glass to his mouth with both hands and took a loud, sucking sip of juice, swallowed and exhaled a panting breath, tongue protruding. His breath had a grassy, innocent smell that suddenly jolted me to my senses again.

'So then, Kiddie,' I began, 'how are we going to find your family? Does anybody know you're here in Queen's Park?'

'My family lives in Croydon.' He looked up at me noncommittally for a second and then down at his juice.

'*Croydon?* But you said you came here from Paddington. From the hotel?'

'Uh.'

'Well, who was with you at the hotel?'

'Lovell and Ted.'

'Are they your family?'

'Lovell's my Uncle Lovell.'

'Right, your uncle, you told me. The man in the bar.'

'I had lemonade.'

'Yeah, your uncle bought me a drink.' It was like remembering a dream from long ago – the hotel, the bar, knocking back that gin, Jesus. And the quirky face watching me at the bar. Brown skin, like Kiddie's, brown eyes full of warm curiosity. For a second I drifted off again, tracing my steps back from the bar up to Richard's room and the shocked look on his face as I'd turned my back on him, shaking with righteous anger . . .

'OK,' I said, summoning myself. 'So you came straight here from the hotel?'

'On the bus,' he said, with a touch of pride. 'The whole way. While you was cryin'.'

I gave a surprised laugh. 'How do you know I was crying?'

'I saw you.'

'Oh. Well, anyway . . .'

'Why?'

'What?'

'Why was you cryin'?'

'It's a long story,' I said. His eyes, fixed on mine, were an astonishingly clear amber.

'I like stories,' he said, tilting his head and giving me such an innocently inviting look that without warning my own eyes brimmed with tears of absurd gratitude.

'Oh, it was nothing important,' I said, smiling at him, even though my words sounded choked and ridiculous. 'I was just feeling a bit sad.'

Kiddie seemed to think about this for a minute. 'I was sad too,' he said matter-of-factly.

'Were you? Is that why you ran away from your uncle?' I asked, wondering if I'd finally be able to coax some sense out of him. With a sudden guilty stab of shock, it hit me that there might well be a really awful situation underlying Kiddie's inexplicable presence in my flat. How many little kids followed strangers halfway across West London to their front doors? What if he was in serious trouble? Child abuse, mental instability, drug-lord uncles masquerading as harmless wideboys . . . A series of ridiculously dramatic scenarios flashed through my mind.

Meanwhile, Kiddie was whispering again.

'What's that?' I said.

'I was sad 'cause you were in trouble. I'm your last hope, see,' he answered, looking up at me.

'I don't understand, Kiddie,' I said anxiously. 'Are *you* in trouble? It's OK, you can tell me if you are.'

The child grinned at me unexpectedly, showing a row of little square teeth as white and neat as a picket fence.

'It's from *Star Wars*, silly,' he said in a delighted voice, kicking his heels against the chair.

I sighed, relieved. 'How come everything seems to be about *Star Wars*?'

Kiddie, still looking pleased, wagged his head silently, his whole upper body rocking, then swivelled his eyes ahead of him and went back to kicking naggingly against the wood of the chair.

'OK, look,' I said. 'We've got to get in touch with your uncle and tell him you're here, so the best thing is if I call the police and . . .'

'No!' he shrilled instantly, squirming away from me.

'What?' I said, startled. 'What's wrong?'

'You don't call the police,' he said in a panicked voice, his eyes shining with sudden tears.

'But we need them to help us find your parents. Your uncle. They're very good at doing things like that.'

'I don't like . . .'

'You don't like the police? But we have to let them know that you're at my house, Kiddie. Your uncle's probably spoken to them by now anyway, and they'll already have begun looking for . . .'

'I don't *like* the police,' he said in a heartbroken voice, 'an' all their funny hats.'

I couldn't help laughing. 'Come on,' I said, reaching over and putting my arm around him. 'Don't be silly.'

'*No,*' he said, pulling away from me. 'You don't laugh.'

'I'm not laughing,' I said, smiling at him. But it was too late – as I watched, his mouth folded itself into a soundless crease of anguish, and his entire face slowly contorted, pulled by invisible threads into a rictus of sorrow.

'Oh, don't cry, love,' I said, stricken. 'I wasn't laughing at you. Please?'

In response, he let out his first wail, a broken stab of sound that was swallowed up by a long, gathered breath. Watching him prepare noiselessly for the next outburst, I felt my own lips start to tremble uselessly. His grief seemed so pure, so noble, compared to mine, that I almost welcomed it on top of all the stale layers of pain that covered me like damp newspaper. I pressed my fingers to my eyes and tried to stem the flow but it was no good. We sat there, knees touching, and wept.

'Lo-vell,' he said wetly after a few seconds, mid-sob, looking up at me with slitted, teary eyes. 'Lovell, I want.'

I nodded, speechless, and let my own tears wash out, listening with distant amazement to our absurd duet as we sat there sniffing and gulping together, emitting our own incoherent sounds of misery. I had one hand on Kiddie's shoulder, and feeling his small body shaking beneath my fingers made me ache with pity, expanding my own hurt to its very fullest. I was thinking, this is what it must be like to have a child, to be a mother and be part of your children's helplessness, to submit to the fact of their inevitable pain. I thought of Estelle holding the phone and listening to me cry, as she'd done so many times before, and of that strange distance I sometimes felt emanating from within her tenderness. It suddenly seemed as if I understood the key to a great mystery – that love is at its most fleeting when it brings pure happiness, because it's always underscored by the knowledge that you can't prevent pain from happening to somebody you love. That loving other people really guarantees nothing as much as it does your own pain. And I thought to myself, *maybe I should have this baby, because despite all this, it will be the only person who ever truly loves me, the only person who I can truly love back.*

'Why you cryin' again?' Kiddie suddenly said in a voice still clotted with tears. I looked down at him, wiping my stinging nose with my hand.

'Oh, nothing,' I croaked, feeling like a fool and trying to smile. 'Seeing you cry just made me feel a bit upset.'

'Why?'

'I don't know. Haven't you ever felt upset when you see someone crying?'

I felt him grow very still, and glanced at his sober, tear-stained face. He looked at me for a second, and said querulously, 'Turn that frown upside down.'

'What?'

'That's what Lovell always says.'

'Oh.' I got up and crossed to the sink for paper towels, blotting my own face quickly with my back to Kiddie. 'Here,' I said, approaching the table and extending a clean tissue. He tilted his face up expectantly, and I realized he was waiting for me to wipe him down. Gently, I dabbed around his eyes and nose, which were screwed up with comic stoicism. While I was doing it, he opened one eye and regarded me through it, and I felt another pang of tenderness right in my belly. Pregnancy does that to you, I thought automatically, it makes you mawkish and tearful . . . The word 'pregnancy' doubled back and re-entered my consciousness, spreading across my chest like a splash of hot fat. Taking a deep breath I took a step back and looked at Kiddie to survey my handiwork.

'Better?' I said.

'I need to go toilet,' he answered, squinting at me.

'Alright,' I said, relieved to be able to answer such a simple demand. 'I'll show you where the bathroom is. And then,' I said warily, crumpling the tissue in my hand, 'we *have* to make some phone calls. We'll call the hotel first, and see if Lovell's still there. If not, I'm going to call the police, OK?'

Kiddie seemed to consider this for a second. 'I think he's at the hotel, waiting for Ted,' he said huskily. 'It's for a magazine.'

'What is?'

'The rat attack.'

'I don't understand you.'

'We was there this morning, seein' the rat attack, then we went to that hotel place. Lovell and me was waiting for Ted,' he said.

'OK,' I said, confused. 'Well, let's hope he hasn't left yet.'

He nodded and stood up in a businesslike fashion.

'Come on then,' I said, pushing back my chair. He followed me through the kitchen and along the hallway. Justine's bedroom door was tightly closed and I turned and put my finger to my lips as we approached it.

'My flatmate's asleep,' I whispered. 'She's a doctor. She works all night and sleeps in the daytime.' Kiddie looked interested, but kept quiet. There was a palpable stillness emanating from behind Justine's door, the kind of blanketed silence which folds itself around someone's sleep. I could navigate these silences expertly, having learned at my cost that waking Jus up after a nightshift was more trouble than it was worth.

Kiddie was obviously an experienced creeper too. When I glanced back he was intently executing an exaggerated tiptoe in slow motion past the doorway. When we reached the end of the hallway I stopped and pointed up the short flight of stairs towards the bathroom.

'The toilet's up there,' I said in a low voice. Kiddie, his lips folded together as if he was bursting with secrets, gave me a questioning look. I smiled and nodded encouragingly, wondering if he wanted me to take him in. When did little boys learn to go to the toilet themselves? I realized I had no idea how old Kiddie was. Six, seven? It was hard to tell.

'OK?' I asked.

In response, he opened his mouth a fraction and exhaled a sentence, in which no actual words were discernible.

'What?' I whispered back.

'Ssssherpshhersspresser,' he breathed meaningfully.

I bent down and put my head to his. 'Say it again, I can't hear.'

'I'm very good at being quiet,' he said into my ear in a tiny voice.

'I can see that,' I said, straightening. 'Thanks, Kiddie.'

'Yur wulcome,' he said, American-style, without missing a beat.

I let him pass and he started up the stairs in jump-stop fashion, placing one foot and then the other on each step. It was slow progress and I sat down on the bottom step to wait for him, leaning against the wall and listening to the erratic tap of rain on the skylight above my head. Wearily, I looked up at the dark-grey square of swirling cloud. As he rounded the top bannister I heard Kiddie whispering to himself, the creak of the bathroom door being pushed open. I closed my eyes and gave a gargantuan yawn. As I came up for air there was a moment's silence, then a great tidal heaving of water being displaced, accompanied by an inarticulate squawk of surprise which seemed to echo briefly before evaporating into further silence. For an instant I stayed frozen on the stair, then I scrambled to my feet and ran up to the top landing, heart hammering.

'Kiddie?' I called out as I neared the top. There was no reply. I pushed open the door and walked into an oasis of warm, perfumed air. Justine was sitting in the bath clutching a flannel to her chest and wearing an expression of sleepy bewilderment. The floor was covered with water, and Kiddie was standing there, staring at his feet as he shifted from one to the other.

'Hello,' Justine said with perfect composure. 'Delighted you could all drop by.'

'Sorry Jus, I thought you were in bed. This is, er . . .'

'He scared the bloody life out of me, I was just about dropping off in the tub.'

'I need to go toilet,' Kiddie said, politely, but with a note of urgency.

'I *thought* I heard voices downstairs, but I couldn't tell. I'm so tired I'm almost hallucinating.'

'Yeah, there's a bit of, er . . . a bit of a situation going on. Nothing to worry about, though. Just go back to bed.'

'I need to go *toilet*.'

'What situation?' Justine said, looking at me more closely. 'Are you OK? Have you been crying?'

I nodded and glanced furtively at Kiddie, whose rhythmic sidestep in front of the toilet was becoming faster. 'I think we better let him do his thing, if that's alright,' I said, and handed Justine a towel. His bladder forgotten, Kiddie's face momentarily displayed a touching conflict between casual disinterest and rivet-eyed fascination, as she stood up and wrapped the towel around herself, tucking the top into her cleavage. She stepped out of the bath regally, one set of painted toes after the other, and stood on the mat. Steam rose from her shoulders and wisped upwards into her dark red hair, which was piled up and beaded with a misty halo of water droplets. She looked like a damp Valkyrian queen.

'I'm Justine,' she said to Kiddie, looking down on him from her impressive height. 'Most of my friends call me Jus. Who are you?'

Kiddie, stilled by the vision, was apparently speechless.

'This is Kiddie,' I said, leaning against the door in helpless submission. 'He's visiting for the afternoon.'

'Oh,' Justine said. 'Well, nice to meet you, Kiddie. We'll leave you in peace.'

'Right,' I said to him, as if nothing out of the ordinary had happened. 'I'll be in the kitchen when you've finished.' Kiddie flicked me a glance but said nothing, still transfixed by Justine, who sealed things by giving him a huge wink as we left the bathroom. I caught a last glimpse of his face before I closed the door, flushed rosy-beige with pleasure, or possibly fear.

'No doubt you'll be the subject of his first wet dream,' I whispered to her freckled back as we descended the stairs.

'I wouldn't mind,' she said. 'He's adorable. Can we keep him?' I followed her into her room, the curtains still drawn, and sat down on the rumpled bed while she switched the bedside lamp on and slid under the covers, still wearing her towel. Plumping up the pillows, she leaned back and gave a sigh of contentment.

'Go on then,' she said, yawning. 'Tell all.'

For a moment I wavered there in the warmth and the darkness, us squashed on the bed like two schoolgirls exchanging dorm secrets. Part of me longed to share the drama, to fast-forward towards the sympathy I knew I'd get if I told her about the revelations of this morning, but I wasn't ready yet. I wasn't convinced I deserved it, not with Kiddie's own crisis at hand and the impending rescue mission still to come. And up till now it had been hard to share Richard with Justine. The two of us spent so little time together under the same roof that when our paths did cross, conversation was usually limited to domestic discussions about the flat and brief, soap-operatic updates on each other's general goings on. She knew the essentials: he was an old friend of my parents, was middle-aged, married, clandestine, and very good in bed. There was no easy bridge that would take me from a shopping list of basic elements to the complications of my own feelings at this exact moment.

'Come on, spill the beans.' She eyed me searchingly over her quilt. 'What's upset you so much, for starters? Let me guess, Kiddie's your long-lost adopted son returned to claim you?'

I blinked with shock, then tried and failed to remember what I'd done with the pregnancy kit this morning. If I'd thrown it in the bathroom bin, Justine might well have seen it. Although I couldn't believe she'd be teasing me if she had. I stole a look at her, but her face showed only a tired curiosity.

'It's nothing that exciting,' I said, fixing my eyes on the coverlet bunched up beneath me. 'I wasn't feeling very well this morning so I didn't go to work . . . then I got caught up with Kiddie.'

'Does he belong to a friend of yours?'

'Not exactly, no.'

'Where'd he come from, then?'

'Well, I was in Paddington, and I got the bus home, and Kiddie saw me and thought I was someone he knew, a friend of his uncle's, I think. He followed me back here, anyway, and we met outside the door . . .'

'I don't get it,' Justine said. 'Why the hell would he want to follow you home without saying anything?'

'I'm not sure yet,' I said lamely. 'I haven't really been able to get much sense out of him. All he wants to do is talk about *Star Wars*.'

'Sounds very strange,' she said, yawning hugely again and sinking down further into her pillows. 'Where does he live?'

'Croydon, I think.'

'Croydon?'

'Well, apparently his uncle's still in Paddington at this hotel, so I'm going to ring them now and see if I can find him. If he's not there I'll call the police.'

'What, you mean you haven't spoken to *anyone* yet?' Justine said, opening her eyes. 'What've you been doing with him all this time?' From outside, I could hear Kiddie's erratic progress down the stairs.

'Well, it's not that simple,' I said, standing up and moving to the door. 'He burst into tears the first time I mentioned the police. I didn't want to upset him any more than he was already.'

'It's his parents who are going to be upset – they're probably frantic, he could have been gone for hours. Go and make the call, for God's sake. And you can send him in here while you do it, I'll entertain him.'

'Are you sure? He's very sweet, but he's quite hard work. There's something a little bit off-balance about him, I think.'

'I'll give you my diagnosis,' she said, eyes closed again, and waved me off imperiously.

I sighed and closed the door behind me. Kiddie was standing at the bottom of the stairs looking lost, and my heart squeezed at the sight of him.

'Better now?' I said, smiling.

He nodded. 'Where's Just?'

'She's in bed. Do you want to go in and say hello?'

Kiddie looked troubled. 'Is she cross?' he asked in a low voice. ''Cos I saw her with nothin' on?'

'No, of course not,' I said. 'Why don't you go and talk to her while I try and get hold of your uncle, OK?'

''Kay,' he said in a happier voice.

I turned and knocked on Justine's door. 'Jus, you've got a visitor,' I called. There was no response, so I opened the door and peered around it. She was fast asleep, her wet hair spread out on the pillow.

I sat a disappointed Kiddie down in front of the living-room TV and told him I was going to use the phone. Once the box was switched on, he seemed content enough watching one of the interchangeable Australian soaps, although he was wielding the remote control in a practised way when I left the room. In the kitchen I picked up the phone and dialled the Lansdowne. I knew the number off by heart, which was thudding sickeningly at the thought of simply connecting to a building that Richard might still be in. All the time I was speaking to the receptionist and waiting for the manager to come on line, and then explaining myself over a chorus of relieved exclamations from a Mr Something-Something, it was Richard's face I had in my head, Richard's voice in my ears, Richard jerking through my consciousness like a row of target ducks at a fairground shooting range – an endless clamouring for attention. Even after I'd submitted all my details, and the manager had told me that yes, Kiddie's uncle was still in the hotel lobby, and asked me to hold while he went to tell him the good news, I was imagining Richard upstairs in his hotel room, doing . . . what? Packing his overnight bag, writing me a letter, pacing around in a silent fury?

'Is he alright?' The voice was hurried, almost rough, and shook me awake.

'Hello? Is that . . . ?'

'Is he alright?'

'He's fine,' I said guiltily. 'I'm sorry it took so . . .'

'What happened?'

'Oh, well I still haven't really managed to, er . . .' I tailed off, conscious that I didn't have a decent explanation myself. 'I mean, I know what happened, but I don't know *why* exactly.'

'Again please, in the Queen's English this time, darlin'.'

I let out a nervous laugh. 'Well, Kiddie followed me home from the hotel you were in. *We* were in. The Lansdowne.'

'Why though? Did he say why?'

'Not really. I didn't even see him there, to be honest. I saw you though,' I said, thinking I'd better admit it sooner rather than later. I was still mildly embarrassed that he'd seen me in the depths of my post-Richard trauma. Or maybe it was more the fact that I'd taken his drink and run.

'Me? Where?'

'In the bar. Actually, you bought me a drink,' I said, as casually as I could.

There was a pause at the other end of the line, which ended in a quiet splutter. Then, 'No shit! Was that you? Fuck! 'Scuse my language,' he added mock-primly. 'I did buy you a drink an' all, didn't I? I remember you very well.'

I laughed again, despite myself.

'How mad is that, man? Well, where is he, anyway? Can you put him on the line? Just so I can check he's still alive.'

'Of course,' I said. 'I'll speak to you again after you've had a word, OK?'

'You bet!' he said buoyantly. 'Listen, it's Lovell, by the way. Sorry, no manners.'

'I know. Kiddie told me.'

'What, that I had no manners?'

'Um . . .'

'Only jokin' darlin'. Did he miss me?'

'Yeah,' I said. 'I think he did.'

'That's what they all say. Come on then, where's my little goblin?'

'Hold on, then, while I go and get him.' I put the phone down and walked back down the hall with a strange mixture of relief and excitement. But when I got to the living room there was no sign of Kiddie. For a single panic-studded moment, I froze on my toes, then I realized that I could hear voices in Justine's room across the hall. As I pushed open her bedroom door I heard her say, 'That's not very fair,' and Kiddie's corresponding cackle of laughter. The curtains were still drawn, and he was sitting cross-legged on the end of the bed facing Jus, who was propped up against her pillows, arms folded. They were both grinning.

'OK, then, if Lovell's like ham,' Justine said, glancing up at me and back to Kiddie, 'what about this friend of his, Teddy-boy?'

'Why's Lovell like ham?' I asked, nonplussed.

'Han,' Kiddie said reproachfully, acknowledging my presence.

'That's Han Solo, dear,' Justine said in a stage whisper. They both chortled companionably.

'Oh, OK. Well, guess what, Kiddie?' I said, eager to tell him the news. 'Han Solo's on the phone right now waiting to speak to you.'

Justine clapped her hands and gave a little cheer for Kiddie's benefit. 'Sara's found Han!'

I smiled down at Kiddie, who looked astonished. 'He can take it in here,' Jus said, picking up the phone on her bedside table and holding out the receiver to Kiddie, who accepted it hesitantly.

'Come on,' I said in an encouraging voice. 'Don't you want to talk to him?'

Kiddie, saucer-eyed, put the phone to his ear and said, 'Hello?' Then his face burst crocus-like into a smile of pure joy and he began to rock excitedly on the bed. ''Lo,' he said, looking right at me. 'Yeah . . . Fine.' His face brightened and darkened as if by shadows cast by scudding clouds. 'No I ain't . . . I'm OK . . . yeah, she's nice.'

Justine shot me an amused look. 'Well done, princess.'

'That's what Kiddie called me,' I said, remembering. I sat down on the floor beside the bed.

'It seems that he thinks you're a dead ringer for Princess Leia. From *Star Wars*, that is,' she said, and added quietly, 'He lives in a world of his own, this one.'

'What d'you mean?' I asked, listening to Kiddie, who was still absorbed in his phone call. I heard him say, 'I was on the *upstairs* part of the bus.'

'As far as I can tell, that's the sole reason he followed you home.'

'What, because he thought I was that actress, or something?'

'I suppose so. Maybe there's more to it than meets the eye. You do look a bit like her, actually,' she added, squinting at me.

'Do I?'

'Mmm. She was quite sexy, that princess.'

'Well, thanks very much.'

'Consider yourself lucky, anyhow,' Justine said wryly. 'He thinks I'm like Chewbacca. Despite the fact that he's seen my tits.'

Kiddie gave a final 'Uh' into the phone, and then extended the receiver to me. 'Lovell wants to talk to you,' he said. I knelt forwards and took the phone from him. He sat back on his heels with a look of deep satisfaction, wriggling deliciously on top of the bed as Justine began to poke at him from under the covers with her feet.

'Hello again,' I said into the phone.

'Hello, madam.' The voice at the end of the line was noticeably lighter than before, and I had another sudden clear image of Lovell, the wide angles of his face with its constantly suppressed grin, the bottle-blond fuzz of hair. 'Well, you seem to be keeping him happy, anyway. He had me in a right old panic, the police are about to turn up and accuse me of being an unfit parent.'

You and me both, I thought. I said, 'Are you going to come and pick him up?'

'Yeah, you gave your address to whatsisname already, right? Where do you live exactly?'

'Queen's Park.'

'Oh yeah? Up by the Paradise, are you?'

'Near there.'

'Nice bar, the Paradise.' His voice seemed studiously innocent. 'Go there much?'

'Er, sometimes,' I said. 'How are you getting here, do you need directions?'

'I got a lift. I'll find it, don't worry. I know Queen's Park pretty well. I'm a bit of a fan of the Paradise myself.'

'OK then,' I said, thinking irrelevantly, is this the climax to all the drama? A chat about the local?

'Look forward to seeing you again,' Lovell said chivalrously. 'Listen, Sara?'

'Yes?'

'Thanks for looking after Kid. I know he's in safe hands.'

'It's fine.'

'Cheers, then.' He hung up and I put the phone down, smiling. I sat back down on the floor and hugged my knees to my chest, giving another enormous yawn.

'Alright, princess?' Jus asked from the bed, muffled by pillows.

'She ain't the princess any more,' Kiddie said. He was watching me unblinkingly, like a small brown owl.

'No? Why not?' I asked.

He kept on looking at me, rocking slightly on his knees. 'Princess Leia never cries,' he said clearly. 'Not even when they blowed up her planet. You cry all the time.'

'Well, not *all* the time,' I said.

Justine rolled over on to her side, her face glowing in the pool of lamplight. 'Leia was a tough lady,' she said to Kiddie, opening one eye and winking at me. 'But then so's Sara. Even though right now she looks like a bit of an

12

emotional retch. emotional retches are girls who cry so hard that they throw up, i think. they probably cry all the time, not just when they fall over and hurt themselves or have a bad dream. once i heard my auntie lynn sayin to lovell that my mum was an emotional retch after she visited her in hospital. after that i was afraid to see my mum because i thought she might smell all pukey, but in the end i wasnt allowed to see her anyway because her mouth was all busted up. she had stitches in it like sewin, and they said it would upset me.

grownups think everythin upsets you, even when it dont. after i ran away to the airport they said i done it because i was upset about my mum bein in the hospital. they said i talked about star wars all the time cause i was upset about things-at-home, but it aint that, its because i just really *like* it. they always want to know *why*, whenever you get upset. why you cryin, whats the reason, why you so sad? they get all annoyed if you cant explain, but when i asked sara why she was cryin, she said, because i was just feelin a bit sad, which is a stupid answer. it aint fair, really. dont think she was tellin the truth but you cant say that to a grownup or they get even more annoyed.

saras lyin on the sofa pretendin to watch telly while im waitin for lovell to come and pick me up, but really shes just starin at the ceiling and bitin her fingers. after a while she puts her hand in her bag on the floor and takes out a tissue to blow her nose, so i reckon shes probably cryin again. theres nothin good on tv and she doesnt have any videos or games so im pretendin to watch telly, too. i wanted to play with just until lovell came, but just said she needed her beauty sleep or she was really gonna start lookin like chewbacca. so i had to leave her room and come in here.

when i said that just was like chewbacca, it dont mean she *really* looks like chewie, just because shes got red hair and shes all tall. but when other people *do* look a lot like princesses or jedi masters, if you try and explain it, grownups think they got to tell you about the difference between real and pretend in case you forgot. thats when they say things like, its only a film, dont take it so serious. but it aint very helpful, because i *know* its a film. its just that i *want* people to be princesses and jedi masters because they re a lot better than normal people.

it dont matter as much now anyway, cause lovells comin in a bit and lovell knows. i stop pretendin to watch telly and get up and stand by the window to see if hes here yet.

you ok KIDDIE? sara says from the couch with her eyes closed.

yeah.

he ll be here soon.

yeah.

its going to be funny seeing him again.

why?

well, it seems like so much has happened since i met him in the bar.

i had lemonade.

i didnt see you there though, you were hiding.

i wasnt hidin. i saw you.

did you?

you looked different.

how?

cause you wasnt cryin then.

sara touches her face and says, i must look like a right old mess.

yeah. because you been cryin a lot.

then she gets off the sofa and says, im going to go and use the bathroom for a minute, will you be alright here?

yeah.

ok. let me know if lovell arrives. sara goes out of the room and i hear her walkin up the stairs all slow like a granny.

i look into the street. outside its rainin and theres big puddles in the road which would be good for jumpin in if i had boots. cars keep turnin into the street and i get all excited each time in case its lovell, but none of the cars are the right car. lovell bought his car off my mums friend denise, and its a big blue bmw with a red yellow green sticker in the front window. lovell always says the sticker has got to go, and when i asked why, he said because it means people will think hes from jamaica and he aint, hes from chelsea.

i wait for ages and ages but i still cant see lovells car, and then a cartoon comes on telly so i watch that, and when its finished i stand up again by the window. outside the house i can see a brown car slowin down, and even though it aint lovells car, i can see lovells face peerin out the back window, and i shout out, they re here, and i wave but he doesnt see me.

i run out of the room, and shout upstairs to sara, theyre here, again. after a minute she opens the bathroom door and calls down, ok im coming, try not to wake justine up. then i go back into the front room and look out the window again, and watch lovells yellow head duckin out the car door, and i run back out and along the landin past justs room and past the kitchen and then down the stairs i go thud thud thud and i open the door at the bottom of the stairs that creaks, and i jump into the hallway and skid towards the front door and i can see lovell walkin up the path towards the door, even though hes all blurry through the glass.

saras comin down the stairs behind me. i turn around and she looks different because her face aint red any more and her hair aint stickin up and her lips are all shiny an nice and she smells like perfume.

then lovells ringin the doorbell which i can hear somewhere high up in saras house, and then hes knockin on the glass, rap rap, and it sounds all loud because me and sara are so quiet, waitin in the hallway.

arent you going to let him in, sara goes? its really raining out there.

i open the door. lovell rushes inside and says YOW, and grabs me and makes a funny noise like a cross between laughin and yawnin but my heads all pressed into his jacket and i cant see or hear that much, i can only smell his wet leather coat and feel his sweatshirt stickin in my mouth. after a bit of squeezin he pushes me away and holds me by the shoulders, and says, hello trouble, and he starts grinnin and i grin too and then my eyes get all hot so i press my head against lovells tummy and shut my eyes tight and the cryin slips out by accident.

lovell just keeps squeezin tight, and above my head i hear him say, we must stop meetin like this.

sara laughs. im sara, she goes.

lovell goes, i hadnt forgotten. then he shuffles me forwards still holdin me to his chest with my eyes hidden in his sweatshirt till my back bumps into part of sara, and i hear a kissin noise and lovell says, we re almost family now, arent we?

sara coughs and says, i suppose we are, and you can tell that shes smilin when she says it.

i owe you one, lovell goes, for services rendered.

dont be silly, sara says. then she goes, is he ok?

lovell gives me a shake and says, you ll be fine wont you KID? then i hear the front door swingin open and i lift my face off of lovell and see ted step into the hallway too. he shuts the door behind him and looks at me and smiles and says, KIDDIE! as if hes all excited to see me. he reaches one hand out towards my head and then stops and puts his hand back in his pocket.

hes just parking the car, he goes to lovell.

so, this is our guardian angel from the hotel, lovell says to ted, rubbin my head with both hands.

ted says, hi.

sara says, hi.

then ted steps forwards and shakes hands with sara and lovells still grinnin and rubbin my head and sayin, ted, sara, sara, ted, we all meet at last, and then everyone stands there for a bit lookin at each other and smilin a lot, except me, because i only just finished cryin.

sara says, well at least this time i can offer *you* a drink.

i could murder a cuppa, lovell goes, what dyou say, KIDDIE?

sara says, KIDDIE, you know the way dont you?

i feel all proud, and i say, follow me please.

everyone laughs a bit and i go through the doorway first and up the stairs, and lovell and sara and ted follow me up to the top and into the kitchen.

ted and lovell sit down at the kitchen table and i stand between lovells knees and he puts his hands on my shoulders.

sara goes to fill up the kettle.

so this is where you been hidin out, lovell goes, lookin round. you got good taste, KIDDIE, i ll give you that.

sara says, everyone want tea?

please, lovell says, strokin the curtains on the window next to him, which are all shiny with lots of tiny bits of mirrors in them.

i like these, he goes.

sara goes, i had those made in india, actually, out of my favourite sari. i went to goa for christmas.

then ted says, AH! and points at me, knockin over a glass thats on the table and spillin some juice.

shit, sorry about that, he goes.

sari about that, lovell goes.

um, ted says, wipin the juice away with his sleeve, talking of christmas, you ve reminded me that i ve got this great star wars joke i ve been meaning to tell KIDDIE.

what you on about teddy? lovell goes.

its a good one, ted goes, do you want to hear it?

lovell says, go on then, winkin at me.

ok, ted says, luke skywalker and darth vader are on the deathstar having a battle with their light sabres, right, when all of a sudden vader says, luuuke, luuuke . . .

lovell starts laughin.

ted goes a bit red but he keeps on in a moany deep voice – luuuke, vader says, i know what you ve got for christmas. so luke puts down his light sabre and says, what do you mean, vader?

and vader says (deep moany voice), the force is strong within you luke. i know what you ve got for christmas. so luke says again, vader, how can this be, how do you know what i ve got for christmas?

right then the doorbell rings again.

someones here, i go.

lovell says to ted, thats your man, and says to sara, its the guy who drove us here.

sara says, does he want to come in?

i suppose so, lovell says. go and open the door ted, and then you can give us all the punchline.

ted looks a bit annoyed, but he says, ok, and goes out the kitchen and down the stairs.

theres a bit of a pause and sara smiles at me and lovell, and then lovell says, this is a really nice place. isnt it KIDDIE?

yeah.

yeah, i love this flat, sara goes, its very peaceful.

i hear the door slam downstairs and footsteps comin up the staircase, and then the kettle clicks off and sara bends down and starts takin cups out of the cupboard. i hold on to lovells knees and look at ted, whos comin into the kitchen with a big tall man behind him.

alright? lovell goes to the tall man. thats our gentleman showfer, he says to me, squeezin me with his knees.

hello, the big tall man says, lookin straight at me, you must be the croydon castaway. he winks at lovell and smiles and says to me, my name . . . and then he glances round and sees sara standin in the corner by the sink with a carton of milk in her hand, starin at him hard. he stops smilin and his scary spider eyebrows go into a frown.

. . . is richard, the man says in a puzzled voice, still lookin at sara.

sara moves her lips a bit but no sound comes out except a chokin noise.

ted says in a rush, anyway, KIDDIE, so luke goes to vader, how on earth do you know what i ve got for christmas? and vader says, because, my son, i can feel your presence.

for a second its all quiet, and then lovell laughs and says, not bad, man, whatcha think KIDDIE? and i say, not bad, man, even though i dont get it, and ted looks all pleased and the big tall man looks all confused, and then i hear the sound of sniffin and its comin from sara and i look at her and shes cryin *again* and still starin at the tall man, and she says all shaky, is this some kind of sick joke?

i thought it was quite funny, says just.

everyone looks round at the voice who said it, and there she is, standin in the doorway wearin a long white dressing-gown.

im justine, she says to the whole kitchen. do you have to be a star wars nut, or can anyone join this party?

part three

13

If you could be anyone you wanted in the whole world, who would it be?

This is the question that came to me as I was standing in Sara's living room looking at her CD collection. Behind the spatter of rain on the windows and the murmuring of Kiddie, who'd been sitting in the far corner of the room talking to himself since Justine had dragged Lovell away for a private chat, I could hear the sound of distant sobbing drifting up the hall from the kitchen. My eyes skated across the racks of album titles, acknowledging the cheerful familiarity of some, noting the unknown, a few challenging me to take them out for closer inspection. But I didn't, I just stood there looking at the rows of famous names, and listening absently to the human background noises, which were gently washing over me with waves of nostalgia. It seemed to have an echo of some scene from deep in my childhood – the tap of rain, the woman crying in a close yet unreachable place, the questioning chirrups from the kid, cross-legged on the carpet. And underneath it all, the plaintive sound of silence that is waiting to be filled with music.

Rooms give off a residue of the music that's been played in them. Especially during that mid-afternoon wasteland when the surrounding quiet takes on a dead quality. I'm an expert on the varying acoustics of time – depending on what part of the day it is, the same piece of music can sound quite different. Mid-afternoon, for example, was often when I ended up listening to records that I wanted to absorb fully, without distraction; it made for better articles and reviews. But it was also a time when I was inclined to pull out some old favourite album I hadn't played for ages, just to hear it really cleanly again. And right now, in the midst of all this singing quiet, my eyes had arrested on a CD copy of *Imagine* and I was suddenly hearing the song 'Oh Yoko!' so clearly in my head that I ached to take out the disc and put it in the stereo and let the tinkling riffs of piano and guitar and those yearning vocals fill up the room. Maybe because it somehow felt like a perfect accompaniment to the hidden scenarios that were taking place down the hall.

These were all something to do with Justine, I'd decided. Everything had been relatively normal in the kitchen up until her entrance. One minute everyone was laughing happily at my joke, the next, this voluptuous girl with her mane of twisted red hair was standing in the kitchen doorway, robed in white, and delivering her scene-stealing line. After she'd spoken, there was a stunned silence, then Kiddie wriggled out from between Lovell's knees and trotted across the kitchen to stand in front of her, as if trying to protect her from some kind of madness that was about to ensue.

If he was, his timing was perfect. While Justine stooped and dropped a kiss on the top of Kiddie's head, causing him to flinch with delight, Sara put down the milk carton she was holding and gave a heartfelt sob, as if she could hardly bear to be parted from it. It was so incongruous that I felt a wild urge to giggle rising in my chest. Her eyes streaming, she made a series of blind groping movements towards Richard, and with theatrical uniformity, everyone in the room turned their heads towards him. He seemed to waver for a second or two, then took a step towards her, stopped, and said to the kitchen at large with a simple, yet commanding authority, 'Could you give us a minute alone, please?'

Sara tottered forwards and collapsed against his chest like a dying balloon. His arms went up around her and in the gaping silence that followed, I noticed Justine's face glaring at Lovell and me. She jerked her head towards the door twice in quick succession, and in turn, I nudged Lovell, who was eyeballing Sara and Richard with a kind of appalled fascination. He turned a pair of startled brown eyes on me, then we both stood and pushed our chairs back.

The scraping of wood on the floor sounded unbearably loud. As we crossed the kitchen I stole a last look at the couple embracing next to the fridge. Sara was almost completely hidden behind Richard's towering frame, except for two small hands with silver-tipped nails clutched around his neck. Stepping as quietly as I could across the cork floor, I followed the strange procession out of the kitchen and up the long hallway, while the sound of Sara's crying and Richard's contrapuntal soothing noises receded into the background.

In the front room, no one said anything for a few seconds. We stood in an awkward circle, avoiding each other's eyes. Then Justine sat down on the sofa, tucking her knees up under her, while Kiddie plopped on to the carpet at her feet.

'Well, guys,' she said, 'who'd like to tell me what the hell's been going on?'

I looked to Lovell for help, but he was deep in thought.

'Er,' I began, 'we just came to pick Kiddie up . . .'

'I mean, sorry for barging in on your little reunion and everything,' Justine went on, ignoring me, 'but I thought it was supposed to be a happy occasion. Except Sara didn't seem to be crying for joy.'

'No, right.' I cleared my throat.

'What's she so upset about?' She folded her arms.

'I've got no idea,' I said truthfully. 'We only just got here ourselves.'

Justine, wide-eyed, turned to Lovell. 'Can you shed any light?' She paused. 'I take it you're Uncle Han Solo, by the way.'

'You what?' he said, looking up, then his face softened. 'Ah, I see you been talking to Kiddie. Flattery will get you everywhere, Kid,' he said, throwing him a wink. Kiddie ducked his head, blinking with pleasure.

Justine glanced at me. 'And you're Teddy-boy, otherwise known as C3PO.'

'I'm a robot?' I said, eyeing Kiddie. Lovell let out a splutter.

'Apparently so,' she said. 'So who's the other guy – the man with the ears?'

'He's a friend of ours,' I said.

'He's someone we just met,' Lovell said at the same time.

'Is it Richard?' She was studying her nails, put one in her mouth, and removed it again without looking at either of us.

'Do you know him too?' I asked, surprised.

'Not personally. But that doesn't answer my question.'

'What question?'

'Well, what the hell's he doing here with you?'

In answer, Lovell barked out a laugh, sat down in an armchair against the opposite wall and crossed his legs. I followed his lead and took a seat on the huge sofa, a good two feet away from Justine. I wished like hell we'd at least managed to get the tea made before we'd all had to troop out of the kitchen. There was a foul taste in my mouth, and I felt bleary and disorientated, if a little less shit-faced than before. I let my head fall back on to the cushions, stifling a yawn.

'What's so funny?' Justine said to Lovell.

'Nothing. Ask Ted, he's Richard's friend. Right Ted?'

'Come on,' I said, tiredly. 'He just drove us here, that's all.' I didn't quite see why Justine was interrogating us. Or why Lovell was in such a weird mood all of a sudden. 'Does Sara know him, then?' I asked.

She snorted. 'Sara might be sensitive, but she doesn't usually go around hysterically hurling herself at men she's never met. Not even after hearing a joke as bad as yours.'

'I thought you said it was quite funny.'

Justine gave me a withering look. Lovell, though, stopped frowning for a minute and flashed me a grin. 'You know how to pick your moments, anyway, Teddy-boy.'

'You know how to pick your nose, anyway, Teddy-boy,' Kiddie said, rapid-fire, and waited for a reaction from Lovell before allowing himself to dissolve. I looked down at him – he was rocking slightly in his cross-legged position and his usually blank expression had been replaced by one of cartoon hilarity. It struck me that he was having a whale of a time now he'd been rescued, he probably hadn't had this much attention for years. Then again, he was the Croydon Castaway, he was an old hand at all this stuff. His name should really be updated now, I thought to myself indulgently, my mind drifting. The Queen's Park Ranger? The Kensal Rise Kid?

'Oh well,' Justine was sighing, 'I can see I'm not going to get any sense out of any of you.'

'Listen,' Lovell cut in, 'if Sara's got a problem with old Dickie Boy in there, it ain't got nothing to do with us. Firstly, it's none of our business. And second of all, she was absolutely fine ten minutes ago when she let us in.'

'No she wasn't.'

'Oh yeah? How d'you know?'

'Because I live here, remember?' Justine said. 'And this has been going on all afternoon.' She paused.

'Go on,' Lovell said grudgingly. I watched them, puzzled by the stand-off that seemed to be unfolding before my eyes.

'Well,' Justine began, 'I came home from my hospital shift to a normal, empty house. Then I got ambushed in the bath by a little runaway . . .' Here she stroked Kiddie's skull, and he twisted his eyes up in his head at her touch. 'And *then* I discovered that sometime during the morning, my flatmate had apparently had a nervous breakdown – causes unspecified.'

Lovell was concentrating hard on the arm of his chair.

'I tried to find out what had got her so upset,' she went on, 'but she just told me some mad story about being followed home by an under-age stalker. And the next thing I know, she's crying her eyes out in the kitchen with three strange men standing around watching.'

'And you're asking *me* for answers?' Lovell asked.

'Absolutely.'

He tipped his head back against the wall and studied the ceiling. 'Well, all I can tell you is, that wasn't the first time I've seen her cry today.'

'Oh?'

'Yeah. The first time I laid eyes on her, at the hotel, she didn't exactly look like she was having a ball.' Lovell sounded as if he didn't give a toss either way, but I knew his line. He'd turned on the charm the minute we walked in the door, and Sara had showed every sign of being suckered in, like most girls were. Even Justine, in the throes of her Big Nurse routine, seemed to be hinting with each glance at Lovell that she had suspenders on under her uniform. I sighed to myself, disadvantaged as usual by his mere presence.

'And what was she doing at this hotel, exactly?' Justine asked, raising her eyebrows.

'Search me . . . We hardly spoke to each other. We had a drink, then she hopped it.'

'Lemonade, lemonade,' Kiddie interjected.

Justine reached down and rubbed his head again. 'Was Richard there too?'

'Yeah, I was interviewing him,' I said. 'For *Fisch*. I'm a journalist.' I glanced sideways to catch her reaction, but she didn't look very impressed.

'What the hell's Fish?'

'It's a magazine.' OK, so she wasn't the type who read the underground arts press.

'Strictly top-shelf material,' Lovell added in an absent-minded voice. I followed his gaze to the top of Justine's dressing-gown, which had slipped down to reveal a few inches of cleavage.

Justine, who didn't seem to have noticed the view she was affording us, gave me the full benefit of her blue stare. I opened my mouth, but she spoke for me.

'Which hotel was it, by the way?'

'The Lansdowne,' I said, careful not to let my eyes wander from her face. 'Do you know it?'

'No. Should I?'

'Er, no.'

'Well, what goes on at the Lansdowne?'

'Dunno,' I said, shrugging. 'Nothing too exciting.'

'What do you mean, exciting?'

'It ain't exactly a five-star gaff, or anything, is what he means,' Lovell said impatiently.

'Well, that's why I'm asking,' Justine shot back. 'I thought most Paddington hotels were full of prostitutes and . . .'

There was a loaded pause.

'No, no, no,' I jumped in, shaking my head. 'It's not that kind of place.' My eyes met Lovell's, and his widened for a moment, then his face split into another grin.

'What?' I said, embarrassed, but he just shook his head in an infuriating way. Justine, watching us, raised her hands in supplication, but said nothing either. She shifted her position on the sofa and once again the silky gown slid off her skin, offering a glimpse of creamy thigh.

My head was beginning to throb again. In between what looked to me like Justine's deliberate attempt to seduce one or more of us, and the implication of Sara as some wretched fallen woman, my sense of reality had become completely skewed. And where the fuck did this leave Richard? I was trying to square my image of him in the hotel room, animated behind the curtain of cigar and whisky fumes, with the harrowed face I'd seen in Justine's kitchen. More and more my hour with him at the Lansdowne seemed like a hungover dream from long ago.

'Listen, there are things I'd like to ask Sara, an' all, you know,' Lovell was saying to Justine. 'She ain't the only one who's had a bad day.' Glancing at Kiddie, he lowered his voice. 'I haven't even got to the bottom of Kiddie's disappearing act yet. Sara didn't get round to explaining exactly how he ended up in your gaff.'

'Oh? Well, I can tell you that,' Justine said.

The under-age stalker immediately got up and skittered away across the carpet, stationing himself at the window. '*Look*, it's stopped rainin',' he said with great interest. 'Lovell . . . ?'

The diversion worked. 'Alright, Kid,' he answered, and shook his head at Justine. But she wasn't to be deterred.

'Hey, Kiddie,' she said, 'how about staying here for a second with, er . . .' She looked at me helplessly.

'Ted,' I said with resignation.

'With Ted, while I show Lovell something next door?'

Lovell threw me a lightning look of mock horror.

'What you gonna show Lovell?' Kiddie asked in an aggrieved voice.

'Just my room.' Justine stood up and tightened the belt of her dressing-gown.

'Why?'

'Because,' she said, 'it's important evidence in the story.' Kiddie looked confused, but impressed. 'It'll only take a minute, anyway. Come on Han Solo,' she said, and Lovell rose obediently, his lips suddenly smooth with suppressed glee. As he followed her out of the door he turned and winked at Kiddie and me.

'If I ain't back in half an hour, call a doctor,' he whispered, and vanished.

That had been five minutes ago. It was in the midst of the silence following their departure that it occurred to me that a lot of music had been listened to in this room. There was a serious musical ghost hanging around, and you don't usually get that in girls' rooms. I mean, I'd seen all the CDs when I'd first walked in, but girls are always doing something when they're listening to music; I've never met one yet who was happy just sitting still for a reasonable period of time and *digesting* a record, without having to talk or knit or water the plants.

The room we were in was fairly ordinary, although comfortable – pale-yellow walls, the oversized blue sofa with silk cushions scattered around, bookshelves and a long low table with lots of candlesticks and incense holders and the sort of ethnic crap that girls collect obsessively. Then in the corner, next to the decent sound-system, the stacks of music. No vinyl, of course, but a good few hundred CDs.

I got up and wandered over to have a closer look. Kiddie gave up his position at the window and returned to the corner by the sofa, murmuring to himself. In the background, very faintly, came the odd crescendo of Sara's muffled weeping. I wondered whether she and Richard would be able to hear the music if I played something in here, as a sort of sympathetic gesture. I started scanning the shelves for inspiration, drawn irresistibly towards the silent hum of the boxed-in albums.

There was an eclectic mixture on those shelves, but after a few minutes of scrutiny, I knew I was right about the musical ghost. For a start, there was a fair amount of classical, which can generate a particularly heavy atmosphere if played loudly enough. But it was a pretty solid display altogether, more than a few years' worth of accumulated phases and explorations and discoveries. The lack of vinyl was frustrating, actually, because it was almost impossible to sequence the actual musical development of the listener from a CD collection alone. LP sleeves acted like carbon-dating; they not only indicated the age and disposition of their owner as well as wrinkles or idiom might, they also allowed you to trace the links between each musical milestone and work out the underlying *structure* in their acquisition.

I had a go at hashing together some sort of chronology from the CDs, anyway, starting from childhood with all the Beatles albums lined up in a solid block. From there you found the seventies American staples so beloved of studious, teenage middle-class girls – Crosby, Stills & Nash and *Tapestry* and Joni Mitchell and Steely Dan. This was followed up with a safe assortment of soul (Aretha, Marvin, James Brown box set), punk (PiL and the Clash, mainly, but enough of the albums to make the sneers felt) and hip-hop (only compilations, but decent ones), all of which represented the rebellious, physical awakening. Pleased with my interpretation, I kept looking for clues. It took a while, because the CDs weren't alphabetized, unforgivably, but I managed to find the subsequent rediscovery of the intellect (with a slightly feminist slant), as seen in the smattering of highbrow jazz, Patti Smith and Laura Nyro, and even to isolate a possible latent Gothic period denoted by the proliferation of eighties and early nineties Cs (Cocteau Twins, Nick Cave, Curve, the Cure). Also visible was the cultish devotion to one singer-songwriter whose career was long enough to encompass all these changes in the listener and more – in this particular case, Dylan. I had to say, I was impressed.

There was plenty of the predictable twenty-something easy-listening in there too, of course – the down-tempo dance acts and one-hit British indie albums with art-school titles, but I came upon enough curious musical sandwiches to make me wonder exactly who all the CDs belonged to. Loudon Wainwright III between the Stooges and the collected works of Love? Terry Callier and the Five Stairsteps alongside John Cale's *Vintage Violence*? Surely it wasn't Justine? I imagined her engaged in some late-night seduction with a visitor, poised on the same sofa, candles flickering, curtains drawn. But she wouldn't be sharing a bottle of wine with him and listening to Callier crooning 'What Colour Is Love?' More like doing a striptease to a Janet Jackson record, dance steps optional.

Somehow, I had to admit I wouldn't quite have credited the range of music to Sara either. Funny, because she was obviously bright, and nice, and had taste . . . it's just that she didn't seem that . . . musicky. It was sort of tantalizing. You couldn't help but be interested in someone with a collection like this. Unless, of course, she had a boyfriend who worked at a record company with a decent back catalogue.

Kiddie's voice piped up. 'What we doing now?'

'I dunno, Kiddie.'

'Where's Sara?'

'She's in the kitchen?'

'Why?'

'She's talking to her friend.'

'The gentleman chauffeur?'

'Yeah.'

'The gentleman chauffeur's her friend?'

'It looks like it.'

'What they talking about?'

'I don't know.' I went back to my scanning.

After a few minutes of quiet, I turned around to check he hadn't fallen down a crack in the abundant sofa and suffocated himself, but he was merely leaning against it with his back to me, fiddling with something in his lap. Meanwhile, I took out the Lennon album and looked at the cover.

If I could be anyone I wanted in the whole world, would John be a contender for the job? Very possibly. Except, of course, he got shot. But then he also got the chance to become canonized. It went without saying that you would want to be a musician over anything else. When I was at secondary school the popular question for one whole fifth-form term, among certain friends, was whether it would be cooler to name your dog Hendrix or Zappa, given the choice you obviously didn't have, as your parents had exercised the usual suburban lack of imagination years before. This simple question subsequently developed into a passion for debating the relative attractions of various musical geniuses that lasted right through sixth form and into university. I even tried playing it with Lovell once, but he didn't get it. 'Why would I wanna be anyone else?' he'd said, before launching into an anecdote about the legendary size of Jimi Hendrix's dick.

Lennon had always had a lot going for him as a candidate in my personal short-list, despite all the pain – the fucked-up childhood, the failed marriage, the documented struggles with all the usual demons of fame and rock 'n' roll excess. But then great music *was* pain, as much as it was a celebration of life. And imagine creating a piece of music like 'Oh Yoko!' I mean, this is a man who made a work of art out of telling the world he called out his wife's name in the middle of a shave. Jesus, when about the most romantic thing you could do for a girl these days was give her a line of coke, forget the bunch of flowers.

That was the power of music, though, the illusion it created in you that the big, grey, amorphous clouds of real life – of fear and unknowing and disappointment and longing – actually counted for something. And although you were probably as incapable as the next person of expressing your own feelings in a way that came even slightly close to the purity of a great piece of music, listening to it let you believe that there was some kind of nobility in the most ordinary of lives, including yours.

I thought of Richard's misjudged comments about the lack of freedom songs in this age of insignificance, and then something else he'd said to me up in the hotel room came floating back. *The point of living is to flourish.* I remembered thinking it a strange phrase to use at the time, a weak sentiment floundering about among all the big philosophical terms he was throwing around.

But now it seemed to capture something important. If I substituted 'music' for 'philosophy' in his argument . . . I struggled to complete the train of thought . . . then music allowed you to flourish despite your own insignificance. Was this complete bullshit? Or was it, as Richard had said, remarkably simple? I caught another echo of his words. *I can be both insignificant in the greater scheme of things and valuable in my own tiny corner of the world* . . .

Because even Lennon was just a guy, after all, right? It can't have been bed-ins and transcendental love and works of genius all the time. Even if he was the creator of immortal music, John was still a normal man who undoubtedly suffered bad hangovers and the occasional row with his wife about whose turn it was to do the washing up. Just like Richard, in fact, with all his weighty words, his warnings and his theories and his eloquent projections, now reduced to a grumbling voice in a kitchen full of tears. We might all be doomed to failure, but men were always going to make women cry, and women were always going to want to be comforted, and most importantly, there would always be music to make people feel better about things. Maybe this was the only answer to any of the big questions, the only safe resolution. The questions may have been ever harder to articulate, the fears that hovered in the space for their answers ever more shadowy, but music still plugged holes, mended rifts, bonded people together – it was the generational glue, just as it had been in Richard's day.

That was something he would probably never understand, I thought, even if I could have put it into words. It would be a bit like trying to explain to your mum exactly what you found pleasurable in listening to *White Light/White Heat* at high volume. Right now, though, it was somehow enough for me to know that I might have infinite problems but I also had an infinite world of aural painkillers to help me deal with the pain. I found myself thinking that it all seemed somehow tragic, and yet deeply reassuring.

'Can I put a CD on?' I said slowly, without turning round. There was a second of silence in which I remembered Lovell and

Justine were in her bedroom behind a closed door, then Kiddie's throaty voice.

'Have they got any Stevie Wanderer?'

'What are you smirking at?' Lovell asked as he sauntered into the room alone, wearing an expression of extreme satisfaction.

'I could ask you the same question,' I said, slotting the Lennon CD back into its place on the shelf. He sat down in his favoured armchair and allowed the grin full range of his features.

'Where's Justine?' I asked, back on the sofa.

'Upstairs, having a shower. It got a bit hot and sticky next door.'

'Yeah, yeah,' I said, not entirely sure he was bluffing.

Lovell ran a finger under the collar of his sweatshirt and shivered. 'What a woman!' he said, closing his eyes and leaning back in the chair. 'And I thought red-heads were supposed to be shy . . .'

'Come on,' I said. From upstairs there was the sound of a toilet flushing, and I had a startling, fleshy vision of Justine – de-robed, fair-skinned, and advancing with slow determination.

He opened his eyes and winked at me. 'Had you there for a minute though, didn't I, son!'

The vision faded. 'You wish,' I said.

Lovell exhaled a delighted laugh. 'Don't worry, mate, she's yours for the taking. You'll be eaten alive, though.'

'Cheers,' I said dryly.

'Not that you couldn't do with a bite,' he added, and turned his attention to Kiddie, who had crawled into the space between the wall and the end of the sofa and was kneeling there, facing out. Only his head was visible, which he wagged at us in a conversational way.

'And as for you, my young Jedi . . .' Lovell said.

Kiddie gave him an untroubled look. 'What?'

'You've made my day, that's what, Kid,' he said. 'Once again, you've made my day.'

'Wednesday?' Kiddie asked earnestly.

We both laughed. 'Yeah, that's right,' Lovell said. 'I won't forget this Wednesday for a long time.'

'Why?' said Kiddie.

'Why d'you think?'

He considered the question. 'Because I got in trouble?'

'Not with me, darlin'. You were on a mission.' He shot me a look. 'Looks like Richard was right about Kid having a logical explanation for going off skywalking again.'

Kiddie's head dropped down and out of sight.

'What is it, then?' I said. Lovell, however, just winked. He apparently had the jitters, as if Justine had just slipped him a line of something pharmaceutical in her room.

'What d'you think of all this, Ted, eh?' Lovell said. 'It's fucking mad, innit?'

'Sara and Richard, you mean?'

'I mean, Jesus, man. How more convoluted can things get? What about you and Justine? That would tie things up nicely.'

'Yeah, right,' I said, blushing as Justine swished through the doorway, still in her dressing-gown, and resumed her seat on the sofa. I caught Lovell's almost imperceptible wink.

'How you feeling?' he said to Justine, as soon as she sat down. Kiddie appeared again from behind the back of the sofa, and reverently touched a finger to Justine's toes, which she wiggled in recognition.

'I'm fine. Why?'

'You look knackered, darlin',' Lovell said innocently. Unable to help myself, I emitted a nervous sniff of laughter.

'What?' Justine turned to me. I shook my head, not daring to speak.

'Justine's been up all night, you know, poor girl,' Lovell said.

'Oh, yeah, you're a nurse, right?' I said, trying to restore my standing.

'A doctor, actually,' she said, eyeing me with disdain.

'Er, right. Sorry.'

'Hey, Kiddie,' Justine said, ignoring my apology. We all watched as Kiddie, holding a lipstick like a crayon, began to draw a picture on her naked foot. 'Where did you get that?'

'Down the sofa,' he said, intent on his artwork.

'Well, glad we cleared things up, anyway,' Lovell said to Justine. 'Let us know when you want to go back to bed.'

Justine raised her eyebrows.

'To catch up on your beauty sleep, that is,' he added, and they exchanged a brief smile, which seemed like the first friendly look that had passed between them. 'What d'you think, Ted?' he went on. 'Should we take Kiddie home and leave the girls in peace?'

It occurred to me that I hadn't considered we might be putting Justine out, or Sara for that matter, by hanging around their flat with the rescued runaway any longer than we had to. But I didn't want to go, not yet. This sofa was far too comfortable, for a start. My bones had turned to sponge.

'But . . .' I started.

'But what?' Lovell said.

'What about Richard?'

'What about him?'

'Well, are we going to take him with us?'

'He's the man with the van, Ted. If he's gonna be tied up here for a while,' and he looked sideways at Justine, 'then we'll just call a cab. Which reminds me.' He took out his mobile and switched it on again. I almost felt disappointed – it was like a sign that the crisis was officially over and things were running as normal.

'OK, then,' I said, as he listened to his messages, a frown on his face. 'We'll get a cab. Camden's not that far from here, anyway.'

At this he looked up from his phone. 'Oh no you don't, mate. I got to go back to Paddington, and you're coming with me. My car's still clamped, remember? Bang goes your commission from *Fisch*, son.'

'But I've got to go home and write my piece,' I said, imagining hours spent sitting damply in Lovell's motor and waiting for the clamp-busters.

'No fucking chance, Teddy. Not until I'm sorted. The trip to Paddington was for your benefit, remember? It ain't my fault the whole thing turned into a Carry On film.'

'Look, there's no rush,' Justine directed this comment at

Lovell. 'I'm not going to be able to sleep now anyway. Not after all the excitement.'

I glanced at him, expecting to receive a visual nudge, what with Justine lying there flashing her legs and practically inviting him to spend the night, but his playful mood seemed to have evaporated. I myself had no desire to go out into the rain and then back to Paddington, or even to the gloom of my flat . . . the flat, Christ, with its embalmed rodent still centre-stage. I closed my eyes at the memory shock, and as I did, a series of random freeze-frames of the day's events clicked through my mind – Kiddie and Lovell laughing hysterically at nothing in my kitchen, the congealed eggs on my plate in the Parkway Diner, Richard holding court in the hotel room, waving a miniature whisky bottle around for emphasis, the sight of Kiddie's face in Sara's hallway, expectant with fear and joy. It all sped past in an almost comic montage, and I felt a strange rush of pleasure that I'd ended up here, in this living room, with this odd collection of people and CDs.

All in all, the day hadn't turned out so badly, considering how it had started. I'd done some work, I'd got unexpectedly drunk, and I was in a warm flat with half-naked girls flitting around. Plus there was the bonus of finding Kiddie again, of course. Not to mention all the weird goings on with Richard and Sara. Daniel would probably be thrilled when I told him how they'd ended up falling into each other's arms in the kitchen.

It suddenly struck me that if I was clever, I might even be able to use the whole chain of events to structure the piece I was going to write – a kind of literal guide through *The Losers' Manual* . . . I supposed I'd have to ask Richard if he minded, that is if I got to see him again before we had to leave. I hoped I did. As well as everything else, I was dying to know what was going on down the hall.

And then there were footsteps in the hallway.

Sara came into the living room first. I don't know how I was expecting her to look, but it gave me a real jolt to see her puffy eyes, and red, swollen cheeks. I tried not to stare, but it was difficult. When Richard entered the room behind her, my eyes automatically went to his face in the sheer relief of having someone else to look at. He gave me a guarded smile as he walked in, taking a place next to Sara at the end of the coffee table, in front of the semi-circle created by the rest of us. Apart from the state of her face, they looked like a couple about to give speeches at a wedding – a little nervous at the formality but doing their best to seem as if they were enjoying the experience.

'Hi,' Sara said in a bright but tremulous voice.

'Hi,' we all chorused back.

She smiled and swallowed. 'Um, I'm sorry about before . . .' she began, looking at the carpet. There was an accommodating silence, then she looked around and said, 'Oh. Where's Kiddie gone?'

Kiddie, who'd hidden himself behind the sofa, popped up again, bright-eyed.

'Boo,' he said, as an afterthought.

'Feeling better?' Lovell said to Sara, and I could tell he was having a hard time taking in her altered appearance. 'Ready for another gin?'

She let out a watery laugh. 'I don't know about that,' she said. 'That's probably what set me off in the first place.'

Everyone tittered politely. Kiddie's shrill cackle came fractionally too late on the crest of the adult laugh and rang on into the silence that followed it.

Sara waited until he'd stopped and said, like the perfect hostess, 'So, does anyone still want that cup of tea?'

'I'll do it,' Justine said. 'Why don't you sit down?'

'No, no, I'm fine. Lovell, tea?'

'Yeah, lovely,' he said, glancing at Richard. I realized I was waiting for Richard to speak, to guide us towards some kind of appropriate response to the fact of them standing there together before us. But he showed no signs of needing to explain anything, which made a significant change.

'Tea?' Sara said to me.

'Er, thanks.'

'I'll give you a hand, then,' Justine said, and Sara nodded vaguely.

'What would you like, Kiddie?' she said, and smiled, 'Don't tell me . . . *apart* from lemonade. We've got some juice, anyway. Want some more of that?'

'OK.' He emerged from his crawl space behind the sofa, dragging a black shoulder bag behind him, and took up his position next to Justine, emptying its contents on the floor.

Sara's smile became slightly fixed. 'That's my bag,' she said. I followed her gaze. She was staring at the little pile of things that Kiddie had placed between Justine's lipsticked feet like some sort of religious offering. Noticing the attention focused on his toys, Kiddie bent his head, and picked something from the top of the pile.

'What's *that*?' he asked with great interest, holding up a toothbrush-sized piece of white plastic that looked like part of a kitchen appliance, and waving it under Justine's nose.

Mechanically, everyone looked at it, then at Sara, as she emitted a strangled noise.

'Oh, love,' Justine said softly from the sofa after a couple of seconds had struggled by.

Sara, stock-still, seemed mute.

'Oh, Christ,' Richard sighed, and raised his eyes to the ceiling as if expecting a Messianic vision.

Sara's pink eyes had the hunted look of a helpless rabbit, darting wildly around the room but refusing to rest on any one person.

'What is it?' Kiddie demanded.

'It's a . . . thermometer,' Justine said, her brisk self again. 'You can measure temperatures with it.'

Kiddie was studying the plastic thing with an intent face. 'And you put them in your mouth and suck them when you got a cold,' he said, and raised the object to his lips.

'No!'

'Don't!'

The girls' blended exclamations seemed to shock the room into a still deeper silence. Then Justine reached down and plucked the thermometer from Kiddie's hands, dropping it back into the bag. He blinked with surprise.

'It's best not to touch things that have been in other people's mouths,' she said, and flicked her eyes up to Sara, who was still frozen to the spot. Richard, his hands behind his back, switched his gaze from ceiling to floor and rocked slightly on his toes like a schoolteacher embarrassed by a stupid answer. I glanced over at Lovell, wondering why they were making such a fuss over a thermometer, but Lovell himself had the most peculiar expression on his face, as if someone had just told him

14

he was gonna be a father. Richard. The old fucking goat. I
stared at him as he stood there in the middle of the room, my
gob wide open, then my eyes flicked over to Sara for a split
second. I couldn't see her face, and I was glad I couldn't, but I
could see his clear as day. And Richard, the sower of seed, the
impregnator, the spawn-monger, Richard just looked so fucking
unmoved by the whole thing, so mildly inconvenienced –
standing there with this expression of polite annoyance on his
face, as if he'd just had his cab hopped on the street by another
punter – that I thought to myself, you don't deserve it, mate. The
girl, the baby, none of it.

As far as bombshells went, it was a good one. I did a quick
recce of the room to see who else had put two and two together,
and everyone in it seemed totally paralysed, except Kiddie, bless
him, who was still blithely smearing lipstick over Justine's feet,
while the rest of us stood or sat around in dead silence,
completely unaware he'd put his size one foot in it. I'm no
stranger to drama, myself, I been caught up in plenty of personal
soap operas that were a lot worse than this, believe me. But as I
sat there letting it sink in, all these mad things started rushing
past me in an endless stream of obviousness. Things I should
have noticed before. Things that made me realize the whole day
so far was actually something completely different to what I
thought it'd been. It was like finding a pair of x-ray specs and
putting them on and discovering a parallel universe operating

right in front of your eyes. And that made me feel like a right mug.

There's nothing like a bit of a shock for jolting your brain, because mine, which was generally all up for bunking off school early, was suddenly catching up on its homework. First off, as soon as I managed to get a good look at Sara, I suddenly saw that Kiddie was dead on – she really *was* a bit of a ringer for Princess Leia, or the actress who played her, whatsername. I couldn't believe I'd missed it now, though of course Kid was going to zone in on the fact before anyone else. The big brown eyes and the dark hair and the rounded cheeks, right down to her stupid white outfit – it was Her Worship, all right. I couldn't help but take my hat off to Kid for putting it all together.

It also didn't help matters that somehow all the bawling had made her look incredibly sexy. The outline of her mouth was all red and blurred as if she'd just been snogged within an inch of her life, and she looked sort of half-drugged, with her swollen eyelids and flushed face. Clocking all this, I felt like an even bigger fool, remembering how nice and easy it had been flirting with her earlier on. Thinking I'd been doing great, when all along she'd been tangled up with Richard, of all fucking people, Mr Helpful with his shitty old Ford full of old *Guardian*s and Sainsbury's carrier bags. And now she was up the stick as well. Jesus.

So much for my great instincts about women. I mean, you didn't have to be a genius to suss that something was going on between the two of them, just as soon as Dickie Boy had sauntered into the kitchen during our little afternoon tea-party, and she'd become stuck to him like a wet tissue. But I kept thinking back to the hotel, to Sara necking her drink in front of me with swimmy eyes, while Richard had been holed up with Ted in his room. The fact is, all of us were sort of already connected at that point by our own agendas, including Kid. We just didn't know it yet. None of us had the faintest that we were gonna end up in a room together sorting through each other's dirty laundry. In Queen's Park, for fuck's sake.

I couldn't help feeling a bit cheated, too, as if all along

someone had been trying to distract me from seeing the bigger picture. Of course, now I could see the bigger picture, well, I wasn't sure if I even *wanted* to see it, because it overshadowed everything – even the sheer relief of finding Kiddie again, the euphoria of dodging catastrophe. When Justine had got me next door and spelled out exactly what Kid had been up to, stalking the princess, I'd felt almost high with pride that he'd pulled it off in such style. I'd have been quite happy to leave the story there and call it a day, maybe with Sara's phone number in my pocket. Only now there was a whole new fucking sequel to deal with.

All of this flashed through my head in a couple of seconds, and as I was taking it in I was thinking, whatever happens next, it can't get any weirder than this.

I was wrong, of course.

The *very* next thing that happened was that Sara legged it. As she crossed the room, head down, Richard's arms jerked, and for a second it looked as if he was gonna go after her, but he didn't. In the vacuum that followed the slam of the door, Kiddie said, 'Where she going?'

Right on cue, my mobile started ringing from inside my jacket pocket. Everyone looked around for the source of the noise. My phone doesn't have a normal ring, see, my mate Stewart had programmed it to play the theme from *Star Wars* instead. What else? Didn't sound quite the same, of course, but you got the idea, and it made Kid giddy with joy every time someone gave me a bell. I took it out and looked to see if there was a caller ID.

'Shit,' I said, and stood up. Lisa's name was flashing on the phone like a warning signal. I'd been anticipating this moment – she'd already left two messages moaning at me for not calling her, but I really wasn't that crazy about having to fill her in on Kiddie's second Great Escape right here and now, not in the middle of all the drama. My sister was a prize panicker. I didn't feel up to more female hysterics, even from the outer reaches of Croydon.

'Have a seat, mate,' I said, gesturing to Richard and backing towards the door, the phone still beeping manically. 'Kid, back in a minute,' I added. His face twitched uncertainly, and I gave him a wink.

Above him, Justine rustled on her throne. 'Well,' she said to the room, when my hand was on the doorknob, 'does anyone have anything else they'd like to share with us before we pack up for the day?'

'Ted used to be a woman,' I nearly said over my shoulder as I went through the door, not wanting to waste such a great offer, but I thought better of it. Pushing the door shut behind me, I flipped open the mouthpiece and put the phone to my ear.

'Alright, Lisa?' I said.

'You took your time.' I heard her exhale smoke. I could just picture her sitting in her front room, fag in hand, cup of tea on the table. Enjoying the peace and quiet without Kid, but not quite knowing what to do with it either.

'Yeah, well. You got me now, haven't you?'

'Your phone's been switched off for ages. You screening your calls or something? Girl trouble, is it?'

I laughed. 'Nah, not quite.'

'Everything alright?'

'Fine, yeah.'

'Kiddie?'

'Kiddie's great.'

'So what you been doing all day?'

'Uh, just visiting a few friends, bombing around town.'

'Where are you now?'

'West.'

'I hope you're not round that mate of yours, Wally, or whatever his name is. Kiddie got nightmares about him last time you took him there – he told me he had dreadlocks and a snake.'

I laughed. 'Yeah, Wally's got a python.'

'Oh, lovely.'

'S'alright, he keeps it in a box.'

'Well, as long as you haven't been getting stoned in front of him again.'

'Fuck's sake, Lisa,' I said, remembering I actually had a one-skin in my trouser pocket and thinking I could really put it to use right now.

She sighed. 'Stick Kiddie on then, will you?'

'Hold on.' I covered the mouthpiece with my hand. This was my big chance to own up honourably to this afternoon's little escapade. If I didn't, and bottled it, Kid was bound to say something to Lisa on the phone, and the cat would come yowling out the bag. Maybe I should just make an excuse and tell her that Kiddie was in the garden, playing. Or on the toilet, straining over one of his famous two-hour floaters. On the other hand, how much worse was it gonna be when she found out, as she was bound to, that I hadn't told her about it all at the first opportunity? A lot, potentially. When Lisa got pissed off with me for being slack with Kiddie in some way or other, she punished me by doing the worst thing she could. She stopped sending him over.

'Listen, I'll get him, alright?' I said into the phone. 'And then I'll speak to you again after. There's some stuff I got to tell you.'

'What stuff?' Immediate suspicion.

'Hold on to your garter, just let me get Kid first,' I said, and went back into the living room, banging straight into Kiddie, who was lurking behind the door trying to look as if he hadn't been earwigging. Ted, who was now kneeling in front of the stereo, studying a CD booklet with his typical trainspotter's scowl of concentration, looked up warily.

'Only me,' I said, gazing down at Kiddie, who gave me a shifty smile and started bouncing from the knees, like he always did when he'd been caught out. I held the door open with one hand and the phone aloft in the other, waving it at him.

'Guess who wants to speak to you?' I went on, taking a step back into the doorway. Kid made a grab for the phone, and I held it up further out of his reach, grinning. Then, suddenly, he froze. I'd heard it too – the sound of a doorbell ringing down below in the bottom hallway. He fixed his eyes on mine and I saw him weighing up his choices. If there was anything he loved more than yakking on the phone, it was answering the door.

Before I'd had time to speak again, there was a rush of air as Kid jumped through the doorway and shot off down the landing.

'Get it I will,' he said as he went.

Fair enough. You can't ignore a doorbell, it could be the Fire Brigade. Or a strip-o-gram. Or the drug-delivery man.

'Did you hear that?' I said to Justine, poking my head back into the room of doom. 'Someone's at the door.'

'God, what now?' she said, standing up, while Lisa's voice started buzzing out of the phone like a trapped fly. 'Lovell? *Lovell?*'

'Hang on, he's just run downstairs,' I said to Lisa. 'I'll get him to phone you back in a minute, OK?' I rolled my eyes at Ted and he smiled vaguely, going back to his booklet. Yeah, mate, everything's fine, I was thinking. You just go on memorizing more obscure facts about dead rock stars in the hope that it gets you laid one day.

'Run downstairs where?' Lisa was saying.

'Don't worry about it,' I said into the phone, back in the hall and watching Kiddie swing round the bannister at the top of the staircase and start thumping down to the ground floor. 'Call you straight back.'

'Wait a minute, Lovell . . .'

'Gotta go, Sis,' I said, and hung up, as Justine brushed past me, dressing-gown flapping, and swooped away in hot pursuit of Kiddie like the angel of death. I followed her to the top of the stairs and waited there as she ran down and disappeared through the door at the bottom, out into the front porch. There was the clucking sound of women greeting each other, overlaid with Kiddie's voice, and I wondered who he'd managed to freak out now. I didn't have long to wait – a few seconds later, Kid, looking well chuffed with himself, emerged through the flat door and started up the staircase, followed by Justine, who looked a bit grim, and a middle-aged woman with auburn hair and matching lipstick who was clutching a Burberry umbrella. I backed up towards the kitchen as they arrived on the landing one by one, receiving a grin from Kiddie, a glare from Justine and an interested once-over from the mystery lady.

'Hello,' she said, a little breathlessly, and flashed me a smile. 'Who are you?'

'I'm Lovell,' I said, and flashed her one back. 'I'm the new butler.'

Kiddie let out a gurgle of laughter. 'And Kiddie here's the new cook,' I added, which made him stop laughing. He put on a wounded face.

'I ain't the cook, I'm . . . the gardener. No, I'm the chimney sweeper,' he announced. Satisfied, he looked up at the red-haired woman for approval.

'Well, what lucky girls to have you both waiting on them,' she answered sportingly, and stretched out a hand to me. 'I'm Estelle.'

'She's the mother,' Kiddie said, as we shook, and the woman gave an ironic, tinkly laugh.

'Justine *said* so,' he added defensively, glancing at me.

'And she was absolutely right,' Estelle said to him, nodding and unbuttoning her raincoat.

'Yeah,' Kid went on, placated, 'she's the mother, and Just's the . . .'

'I'm the doctor, remember,' Justine finished for him, as I looked Estelle over. Of course – Justine's old lady. As red-haired, bright-eyed, and by the looks of it, bushy-tailed as her daughter. I glanced at Jus and noticed that she had the red imprint of Estelle's lips on her cheek. Paired with her white dressing-gown and her sudden air of awkwardness, she looked like a little girl who'd just gatecrashed her parents' cocktail party. I had to admit it gave me a kick to see the abrupt transformation.

'So,' Justine said to her mum, in a voice that was bright with fake lemon-freshness, 'How are you?'

'Oh, I'm wonderful,' Estelle said, and looked critically at Justine. 'You look rather tired, though, darling. Working far too hard as usual, I suppose?'

She nodded and I smiled at Estelle, thinking, half an hour ago I was holed up in your daughter's bedroom and being lectured on child psychology while she practically flashed her Alans at me. No wonder she's tired. It must be a full-time job being that much of a woman.

'And where's Sara?' Estelle went on, smoothing down the front of her blouse. I couldn't help noticing that she had a nice figure. Bit more Richard's scene than mine now, but she must have been something when she was young.

'Sara's the princess,' Kiddie said, inevitably. 'And she's been . . .'

'Uh, Kiddie,' Justine interrupted, 'why don't you and Lovell go and wait in the living room while I make some coffee.' His face fell. 'Sara's having a nap, actually,' she said to her mum, and batted me a warning glance. 'I'll go and wake her up in a bit.'

'OK, lovely.' Estelle adjusted her hair. 'Poor darling,' she added, 'she told me she was feeling rotten.'

'Oh, really?' Justine said. There was a pause, and I felt their female radar tuning in and out, looking for a common frequency. Jus turned to me. 'Go and see if the others are alright in there, OK?' she commanded, nodding towards the living room.

'*I* want some coffee,' Kiddie piped up.

'Coffee isn't good for chimney sweepers, you know,' Estelle said, smiling at him, and adding, 'Which others?' as she followed the direction of Justine's eyes. 'I'm not interrupting anything exciting, am I?'

'No, no,' Justine said, and began shepherding her mum towards the kitchen. 'It's just a couple of friends. I'll tell you about it in a minute . . .'

I gave Estelle a little wave as they went through the kitchen door. 'See you later,' I said, and winked, which seemed to delight her.

'Do you want coffee too, Lovell?' she began, but Justine answered for me by stepping in front of her and pulling the door shut. I only wished I could be there to hear her come up with a decent explanation for what we were all doing in her flat. That would be worth any amount of dirty looks.

'What they doing?' Kid said plaintively, straining at the end of my arm towards the kitchen.

'Come on,' I said. 'We've got to call your mum back.' I steered him towards the living room, but before we'd even reached the door, my phone started ringing again.

'Lisa?' I said into the mouthpiece, making an ominous face for Kiddie's benefit. 'Yeah . . . OK, OK, just hold on.' I cut her off in mid-squawk and handed the phone to Kid, wondering if I should brief him not to say anything incriminating. Bound to backfire, though. 'I need to talk to her afterwards,' I told him. 'Don't be too long, eh?'

He nodded, and gave his first shy ''Lo?' into the phone.

I left him outside the door. Inside the living room, Ted and Richard were sitting opposite each other, deep in conversation.

'Yes, yes, I see that,' Richard was saying impatiently. 'But you can't tell me that music's a coherent philosophy in itself, can you?' There was obviously nothing like a bit of pontification to get your pecker back up.

'Sorry to interrupt the seminar,' I said, straight-faced.

'Hello there,' he said calmly, as if I was a student come knocking on his office door to ask him for an extension on an essay, just like Ted told me he'd always done at college.

'Everyone alright?' I asked.

Ted gave me a weak grin. 'We're just trying to do a bit of catching up from before.'

'Cool,' I said, sitting down on the arm of the chair furthest from them. 'Well, don't let me stop you.'

Ted flicked his eyes back to Richard, who'd hardly taken a breath. 'I mean,' he went on, 'essentially I'm saying that it's a connection to the world of *ideas* that's missing from our everyday experience – ideas that predate your own private reality. And music doesn't function, generally speaking, within the realm of ideas. Do you see what I mean?'

Jesus, I thought. Kiddie got lost for this?

Ted opened his mouth, but stopped as the door swung open again and Kid himself sidled into view.

'Mummy wants a word,' he said to me, glum-faced, and handed over the phone. He wouldn't meet my eyes, and I guessed that Lisa must have rumbled some of what'd happened today during their conversation, in which case Kid knew I was in for it.

'OK, wait in here with Ted,' I said, and exited once more before he had a chance to argue. Wanting a bit of privacy for the leathering that was about to come, I went halfway up the stairs to the top floor and sat down before I put the phone to my ear.

'Lise?'

'What's been going on, Lovell?' she said, straight off.

'Nothing. Well, we had a little problem before, but it's all under control.'

'What kind of little problem? Kiddie said he got lost on a bus . . . what the hell's he talking about?'

'Let me ask you something,' I said patiently. 'Does Kid sound OK to you?'

'He sounds confused. What happened to him?'

'Well, alright, he ran off for a bit, but we found him again, so it's all cool.'

'*Ran off for a bit where?*'

'Lisa, d'you really think I wouldn't have called you if something bad had happened?'

'What *did* happen?'

'OK, look . . .'

'I might have known,' she went on, her voice rising. I moved the phone away from my ear an inch. 'He always gets these ideas in his head whenever it's you that's supposed to be looking after him.'

'Jesus,' I said, wounded. 'I'm trying to tell you, he got a bit lost, but it wasn't for long. He's alright, Lise, he's totally fine. Will you please stop fucking worrying?'

'Don't start bloody cursing at me! I'm his mother, for fuck's sake!'

I took a deep breath. 'Just calm down a bit, Sis . . .'

'I still want to know what happened to him.'

'It's complicated . . .'

'I don't care, Lovell. Tell me!'

'OK,' I said, dropping my voice, and hoping she'd follow suit. 'Just listen to me, right?'

It worked. 'Alright,' she said in an almost normal tone. I heard her light a cigarette and suck on it hard.

'Good,' I said. Then I gave her the plot. It took me five minutes to get it all straight, and it sounded pretty ridiculous, even as I was telling it, but she didn't make a squeak while I was talking, just inhaled and exhaled her Silk Cut. I knew what she was thinking. Just like before, she didn't believe that Kiddie could possibly have come up with such a mad scheme on his own – her Kid wasn't brave enough, or daring enough, or clever enough. But there are things you can't see in your own kid. It wasn't about being brave or daring or clever. It was about being in your own head so much that you could be deaf, dumb and blind to the real world. Thing is, no one knew enough about the inside of Kiddie's head to know if he was a freak or a genius.

At the end of my speech, there was a silence, then she said in a heavy voice, 'Just bring him home, Lovell, OK?'

'Lisa . . .' But she'd hung up. Lisa never hung up on people.

I sat slumped on the stairs for a while, feeling a bit shit. More specifically, equal parts of guilt and frustration, mixed in with the overwhelming need to take a piss. I heaved myself upright and walked up to the top floor, which was little more than a small landing with two doors – the bathroom on the right, the one beside it closed, a blank face. I knew Sara must be behind it, and I stood there for a moment, gazing at it. There's always something a bit exciting about a closed door, specially when you know there's a girl on the other side. It reminded me of being a kid and standing outside Lisa's bedroom, listening to her getting dolled up on Saturday nights with the muffled stereo playing in the background. Eventually, if I stood there long enough, she'd always sniff me out. Depending on her mood and whether she had any of her friends in there with her, she'd either let me in so I could watch the preparations, or tell me to fuck off. It was a gamble, but once you were in, it was paradise.

I listened a second longer for sounds of life from inside Sara's room, but there was nothing. Only rain on the roof, and the men's voices from the room below. Anyway, my bladder was threatening to give out. Even though the bathroom door was slightly ajar, I knocked on it anyway before entering, thinking about the time a few weeks back when I'd been at a girl's house late one night, and after she'd disappeared to change into something more comfortable (so I'd thought), I'd walked into the bathroom for a slash, only to surprise her squatting in the bath in the hunter position, giving herself a rinse-out. She was more shocked than I was, but it's the kind of impression that's going to eclipse any one-night stand . . .

I unzipped, grinning at the memory, and stood there in front of the toilet, but it wouldn't come straight away. Waiting for inspiration, I looked down at my knob and found myself wondering, not for the first time, if I had a kid myself somewhere in the world without knowing it. There'd certainly been a few near misses over the years. Plenty of kids got born without asking for the privilege, unplanned and unallowed. Just like me. Kiddie too, for that matter.

I let out a groan as my bladder began to empty, then stifled it in case Sara could hear me next door. It was funny thinking of her now with this extra baggage in her stomach. When did a baby become a person? When Lisa was pregnant with Kiddie, even when she was huge, I still couldn't really think of the bulge as a potential kid. Once he was out, of course, it was different. His character was stamped on him from day one, and whenever I thought about the pregnancy I had a picture of Kiddie all squashed up inside Lisa talking to himself.

I finished off, flushed the bog. Rinsing my hands, I thought about Kid, cooped up again downstairs and being ignored, no doubt, while Richard let the bullshit flow. The guy may have been clever, but no one who took himself that seriously could expect anyone else to. I couldn't figure out what the fuck Sara saw in him, specially after how he'd acted around her this afternoon, like she was a threat to his professorial image, or something. Like when you were a kid and you bumped into one of your school teachers down the shopping centre with his wife and kids on a Saturday afternoon, and he'd pretend not to notice you because he knew damn well that the shock of seeing him acting like a normal human being might stop you being scared of him. Which meant that back at school he'd lose his power over you.

As I stepped through the bathroom door, deep in thought, Sara's own door flew open, and there she stood, the princess with the bun in the royal oven. It was all I could do not to stare at her belly.

'Hi,' I said, trying not to look surprised.

'I thought it was you in there,' she said. She looked alright, considering.

'Sorry to disappoint you.'

'I didn't say I was.'

I grinned at this. 'You OK?'

'I'm fine.'

'Good.'

There was a bit of a pause, then she said, 'Were you just having a row with someone? On the phone?'

'Yeah, I was talking to Kiddie's mum.'

'I couldn't help hearing a bit of it.'

'I'm in the dog-house, anyway.'

She laughed, moving away from the doorway and into her room. I followed her, not sure if I was invited or not, but she didn't protest, even when the door swung shut behind me.

'Wow, nice up here,' I said, looking around me. It was a big, airy attic room with skylights, grey with drowned afternoon light against the white slope of the ceiling. It smelled nice, too. On the floor by the desk there was a massive glass bowl full of white flowers, lilies, maybe. Come to think of it, the whole house was full of flowers, vases in all the rooms. There was the bed and a clothes rail, and in the far corner, next to the French windows, lots of blank canvases stacked against the wall. Or maybe they had pictures on their other sides.

'Are you an artist?'

'Sort of.' She sat down on her bed. 'So, what happened? Did his mum get upset?'

'Yeah.'

'But none of it was your fault, was it?'

'Nah, but it don't make any difference to Lisa. She's very protective about Kiddie, you know? She overreacts.'

'Well, all mothers would get like that if their kids ran away.'

'Yeah, only this ain't the first time he's escaped. I was babysitting him that time, and all.'

'Why d'you think he does it?'

'I dunno, really. I mean, he's had a bit of a rough time and all that, specially with his dad, but lots of kids have it tough, and they don't go skipping off trying to rescue princesses.' She smiled at this, as I'd hoped she would. She had a lovely smile.

'Well,' she said, 'Kiddie's definitely a bit . . . unusual.'

'You're not wrong. I reckon it runs in my family. God only knows what my own kids'd be like . . .' I stopped mid-sentence. Sara didn't seem to join the dots though and I gave her a bit of a grin, thinking I'd swerved it, but then she sighed and said, 'It's alright, Lovell.'

'What?'

'Everyone knows, don't they?'

'What, about you and . . . ?'

'The baby. Not hard to guess, really, was it?'

I went and sat down on the bed, not too close. 'Sorry,' I said. 'Don't blame Kid, eh? He didn't mean any harm, you know.'

'Poor Kiddie,' she said, and gave me the ghost of a smile. Then she added, 'What's going on downstairs, anyway – are they all fussing around?'

Hardly, I thought, not wanting to tell her that Richard and Ted were practising for a slot on Radio 2, Justine and her mum were having a coffee morning, and left to his own devices, Kid was probably rummaging through someone's knicker drawer by now.

'I wouldn't worry about them,' I said. 'We'll be out of your hair soon, anyway – I should take Kid home to his mum, before she sends the Old Bill after me.'

She nodded, but said nothing. We sat there in silence for a bit longer, but it was a comfortable kind of silence. I love talking to girls in their bedrooms. Sit a girl down on her bed and ask her questions, and if you're lucky she might just open up like a flower. I didn't quite know where to begin with this one, though – I felt like I'd already had an unfair head-start. After a while I got up and walked over to the glass doors and stood looking out. There was a sodden rooftop garden, and beyond it an aerial city of satellite dishes and sagging eaves and swirling white cloud. It

205

was wicked, actually, it felt miles from the street. She must get woken up by birds singing in the morning, unlike my dawn chorus of wankers honking the horns of their BMWs on the Kings Road. You could cultivate a great crop of weed up there, too.

At which point, I thought of the spliff in my trouser pocket again. I walked back over to the bed and sat back down, wondering if she'd go for it or not. I didn't want her thinking my timing was off or nothing, but the opportunity seemed too fucking perfect to waste.

'Tell you what I fancy right now, Sara?'

'What?'

'A smoke.'

'Yeah?' She looked puzzled.

'Yeah. It's about that time of day.'

'Oh . . . you mean pot?'

I laughed. There's a certain type of girl who still calls grass 'pot', usually the kind who hasn't got stoned since university. The kind of girl Ted usually goes for.

'Yeah, pot.' I raised my eyes to gauge her reaction.

'Well, go ahead if you want to,' she said. 'I probably shouldn't, though.'

'Yeah,' I said instantly, 'course,' then tried to cover myself, like the moron I was, by adding idiotically, 'My sister smoked weed when she was pregnant with Kiddie.'

There was a pause. Then she said, 'Maybe that accounts for his vivid imagination.'

We both giggled a bit. I felt like a dickhead, but some of the tension had gone, anyhow. She shifted her position on the bed so we were sitting side by side, knees almost touching, like kids on a school bench.

'You know what?' I said, forgetting the joint idea. 'I never really said thanks for taking care of him today.'

'What, Kiddie? Don't be silly.'

'I owe you one, that's all I'm saying.'

'Well, don't worry about it. He's a sweetie.'

'I know, but having him follow you around probably wasn't

exactly what you needed, was it? I mean, you've got enough on your plate, right now, what with all this . . . you know.'

Men are pathetic cunts, sometimes. I couldn't even bring myself to say the word 'baby'. Sometimes, when Kiddie was ill or upset about something, he'd do anything to avoid saying what it was out loud, for fear of jinxing himself. He still referred to the scene of his first getaway as ''Atwick Airpoo'. Now I knew how he felt.

Sara shook her head, unfazed. 'It's funny,' she said, 'but when you spend time around a kid, you always start thinking what it would be like if you had one of your own. I wouldn't mind having one like Kiddie.'

'You'd change your mind after a couple of days, trust me,' I said. Thinking about people having babies always led *me* back towards the shagging part, and as far as Sara was concerned, that was something I didn't want to dwell on too much. Richard was probably the sort who'd be into dressing up like Batman or tying her to the bedposts.

That was the problem, see – I already knew far too much about this girl. I still couldn't quite get my head round the fact that this bird in her princess disguise had started off as a nice-looking girl in a bar, only to reappear throughout the day transformed into the patron saint of lost children, Dickie Boy's secret shag, the heir to the galactic throne, and finally, a mother-to-be. And after all of it, I still couldn't decide what I really thought about her – if I was setting myself the ultimate challenge by trying to score with someone's pregnant girlfriend, whether I was just letting Kiddie's fantasy rub off on me, or even if I had some sort of mad sympathy crush on her, considering what she was going through right now.

'I take it you haven't got any kids, then?' she asked, breaking the silence.

'Not that I know of. Kiddie's the closest thing.'

'Do you want to, though?'

'Yeah, eventually. No rush.'

'That's what I always thought.'

'Yeah, well. You've still got loads of time, whatever happens,' I said, a bit awkwardly.

'You never know, though, do you?' Sara said. 'I mean, if you'll get a second chance to do things properly.' She shot me a look. 'D'you know what I mean?'

Jesus, I was thinking, talk about setting me up in a moral dilemma. Part of me wanted to shake her and tell her to kick Richard out the door on his corduroy arse, the other part of me knew I should keep my trap firmly shut if I didn't want to make even more of a total wanker of myself.

'Well,' I began, 'even if this is your only chance, it ain't worth taking it if you're not happy about it from the beginning.' Not bad, I thought.

Sara didn't seem to be overwhelmed by my diplomacy. 'It's not always that simple, though. Knowing if you're happy or not.'

I thought about Lisa and Kiddie, then, and how hard Lisa had it. I'd never really stopped to really ask myself if she was happy or not, despite everything – I mean, whether she was happy having Kid and just making the most of it. Maybe Ted was right, and I'd always had it too easy to really understand.

'Doesn't help you though, does it?' I said.

She shook her head and gave me a rueful smile. I felt really sorry for her, then – it all suddenly hit home somehow in a really tangible way, much more than it had in amongst all the tears and drama.

'I never wanted to do it on my own, you see,' she said. 'Have kids, I mean.'

'How d'you know you'll have to?'

'Well, Richard and I aren't exactly a functional couple,' she said. 'I only get to see him once a week.'

'Oh, right. That's a shame,' I said lamely.

She gave a little choke of laughter, or maybe it was tears. 'You can say that again.'

'That's a shame.'

There was a pause, then a weak giggle. 'Don't try and make me laugh.'

'I'm just doing what you ask me,' I said.

She wiped her nose on her sleeve unselfconsciously. 'God,' she went on, 'today's been the strangest day of my whole life.'

'You and me both, darlin'. Not to mention Kiddie.'

Our eyes met for a minute, then she dropped her head. In the longish pause that followed, I glanced around the room and my eyes alighted on her white rubber shoes, sitting side by side near the door. Ridiculous fucking Minnie Mouse shoes. I nearly laughed out loud at the sight of them, they just looked so clumsy and forlorn, waiting to be stepped into. But something shifted inside me, and I stopped myself, because they were Sara's shoes and I didn't want to offend them. That was the point at which I realized things were getting way out of control. *Sara, I'm in love with your shoes*, I imagined myself saying, and found myself grinning like a cat.

'Come here, princess,' I said. It was now or never. I reached across and put my arms around her upper body. She looked surprised, but sort of allowed herself to be drawn towards me. Her own arms stayed at her sides, the hands folded in her lap. Slowly, I felt her relax. My mouth was in her hair, which smelled damp and perfumed. I could feel her shoulders digging in my chest. There was that same clean scent again, giving me a memory-flash of gin and wet eyes . . .

'Lovell,' she said, in a muffled voice.

'Yes, darlin'?'

'Um, it's a bit uncomfortable . . .' She straightened up, disengaging herself, but her left hand strayed over and rested on my knee for a second. She didn't look at me. I patted her back once, and we sat there for a bit longer, sort of slumped against each other. It was nice like that, peaceful, listening to each other's breathing. My brain started wandering, trying to imagine what the others were all doing downstairs. It felt like we were in another galaxy up here. A galaxy far, far away . . .

'Shit,' I said suddenly, breaking the spell, 'I better check on Kiddie.' I patted her again and stood up. 'D'you need anything from downstairs?'

'No, I'm fine.' She looked slightly dazed.

'Shall I see you in a bit, then?'

She nodded and we exchanged wary grins. I crossed the room, went out on to the landing and started down the staircase, feeling a bit stirred not shaken, but I didn't have a rat's chance to think about any of it too much, because there was Justine at the bottom of the stairs, hovering outside the living-room door. Automatically I found myself debating the best explanation for what I'd been doing in Sara's room, but there was no need, because as soon as she saw me, she narrowed her eyes and hissed at me, 'He's out!'

'Eh?' I said, jumping down the last two steps. 'Kiddie? Where the fuck's he gone now?'

'Ssshhh. Not Kiddie, Richard,' she whispered, rolling her eyes. 'He's gone into the kitchen. I was hoping you'd keep him in the front room so I could try and get either him or Estelle out of here before they collided.'

'Why?' I whispered back, clueless.

Justine glanced around conspiratorially, and opened her bedroom door, beckoning me inside. I followed, wondering if she'd gone completely off her maracas or whether she was just about to have a second crack at me, and gave her a sort of knowing look, but she was having none of it. 'I thought you were the clever one,' she said, once the door was safely shut.

'I am.'

'Well then, you might have figured out that Sara didn't exactly plan on having Richard and her mum pay her a visit on the same day, right?'

'Hang on,' I said, 'Estelle's *Sara*'s old lady?'

'Who the hell did you think she was?'

'I thought she belonged to you, sweetheart,' I said, unable to help my grin of disbelief. 'You know, the red hair and all that.'

'Well, she doesn't belong to me. And thanks to you, her and Richard are now swapping stories at the kitchen table.'

'Wait a minute,' I said, a bit nettled. 'It ain't my fault her mum turned up. How the fuck was I supposed to know? Anyway, it's not the end of the world, is it? He don't have to tell Estelle he just banged up her daughter.'

'Listen to me,' Justine said, staccato, 'Estelle is *not* supposed to know about Sara and Richard . . .'

'OK, OK.'

210

'No, it's not OK,' she said, sitting down on her bed. This time I really could see her knickers, although I didn't have the heart to tell her. 'That's what I'm trying to explain. Richard's an old friend of Sara's parents,' she went on. 'That's how Sara met him, through her mum and dad.' She looked at me almost imploringly. 'Now do you get it?'

'Oh, *man*,' I said, leaning against the door. 'It gets more and more twisted by the moment.'

'You should have seen their faces when they saw each other, Lovell.'

'What did Richard say, for fuck's sake?' I asked, trying to picture it.

'Not much.'

'That makes a change.'

'He didn't really get a chance. Estelle freaked out when she saw him. He just stood there looking shellshocked, while she jumped on him and started shrieking about how long it had been since they'd last seen each other and what the hell was he doing there. I had to answer for him, practically.'

'So what happened? What did you say?'

'Well, I'd already told Estelle the real story about how you and Kiddie and Ted ended up here – so I tacked Richard on the end.'

'How d'you mean?'

'I told her that Richard was a friend of yours, before he had a chance to say anything. Pretended I didn't know he and Sara had ever met.'

'Nice one.'

'Well, what was I supposed to tell her? That he'd actually come round to see her pregnant daughter, instead?' She clocked my expression and gave her head a little shake. 'God,' she said, 'this is a total mess.'

'You're not wrong.'

'What's Sara doing up there, anyway? Is she still crying?'

'Nah, she's fine. We were just having a little chat.'

It was Justine's turn to dish a knowing look, but I didn't rise to the occasion.

'How come Richard ended up in the kitchen, anyway? He was

getting all deep with Ted last time I saw them,' I said, wondering exactly how I was supposed to have kept him in the living room all this time, as Justine had intended. Held him down by force? I had a sudden picture of me and Dickie squaring up to each other while Ted and Kiddie looked on. It was par for the course, really – after all we'd been through today – tears, booze, pregnancies, kidnappings – the only thing we needed to finish everything off was a really good punch-up.

'He went to get his cigars,' Justine said. There was a moment's stifled silence, and then, for no real reason, we both spat out a laugh.

'Sshhhh,' she said, covering her mouth. 'Oh Christ, what the hell am I going to tell Sara?'

'Do you want me to?'

'Why? You're being very responsible all of a sudden.' She raised her eyebrows.

'No skin off my nose,' I said, shrugging.

'Well, mine neither. I've dug myself in deep enough already.'

'So what you gonna do?'

'Get it over with. You can wait in the front room,' she said dismissively.

'Cheers.' Justine didn't even seem to hear me. 'I better see if Kid's alright, anyway,' I added.

'Yeah,' she said in an absent-minded voice, as I stood up and made my exit. Women are fucking geniuses at creating entire matinées out of the smallest bit of emotional upset and then just when they got you interested, they tell you you're not invited to the show. I went into the hall and put my head round the living-room door, but there was only Ted sitting there on his Jack, listening to a CD and singing tunelessly to himself. He stopped when he saw me.

'Where's Kiddie?' I asked.

He shrugged. 'I thought he was with you.'

'Oh shit,' I said, and withdrew my head, leaving him to his music. Justine was already heading up the stairs to Sara's room, and I followed her, having a pretty good idea where Kiddie was hiding out.

'What are you doing?' Justine whispered, annoyed, as I met her on the landing. I nodded towards Sara's door and we both stood there, listening to the muffled sound of Kiddie's monotone, interspersed with the odd comment from Sara. Justine sighed and shrugged. 'That means my job's already probably done.'

She knocked once on the door, and pushed it open. I half expected to see Sara prone on the bed in hysterics, but her and Kid were both just sitting there side by side. Kiddie gave me a sideways grin when he saw me.

'Alright, Skywalker?'

He nodded, kicking his heels.

'Hello again,' Sara said. 'Look who I found. Or who found me. What's going on downstairs?' she added, directing the comment at Justine. 'Kiddie's convinced he's just met my mum.' She smiled round at us, including me in the joke.

'I *did*,' Kid said, glancing at me for confirmation.

'Well,' Justine began smoothly, in a voice I reckoned she'd practised on patients who were about to be told they were getting an enema, 'the thing is, he did, actually. They're both here.'

'Who?' Sara said, with delayed confusion.

'Richard and your mum. I'm sorry, love. They're having coffee in

15

the kitchen? In *my* kitchen, for Christ's sake? The idea of it seemed so ridiculous, I think I actually laughed when Justine said the words, chortling at the image of my mother and Richard freeze-framed in shock across the kitchen table while the rest of us camped out upstairs like naughty children hiding from the grown-ups. But when I looked at their three faces, innocent and anxious and intrigued, the quick spray of panic that hit me dried as instantly as it had come, leaving behind only a faintly stinging residue on my skin. And I was suddenly, blindly furious.

Somehow I found myself on my feet, only dimly aware of the three of them now, because inside my own head I was saying very clearly and loudly to myself, THAT. IS. ENOUGH. The anger seemed to inflate me; I floated across the room towards the door without any thought in my head other than that I wasn't afraid any more, I didn't give a fuck what anybody thought any more, I just wanted the carousel to stop turning and the tinny music to stop blaring and the crowd to stop oohing and aahing and gaping at me while they waited to see how I was going to react to the next disaster.

'Are you OK?' I heard Justine say, from a great distance. She embarked on a complicated explanation of how she'd covered for me when Estelle and Richard had surprised each other, but I wasn't really listening, intent on my trajectory. Through the door, out on to the landing, then on into the bathroom where it was quiet. My reflection in the mirror over the sink stared back at me through malevolently swollen eyes. I looked shipwrecked: squinting, slack-jawed, my hair sticking straight up in some places and cat-flattened to my skull in others, and two raw red patches high on each cheekbone. I almost felt a perverse sort of pride, imagining what Estelle would think when she saw me.

I left the bathroom and padded down the stairs in my bare feet. There was music coming from behind the living-room door, which was closed. Someone was playing 'Alone Again Or'. Listening to Arthur Lee singing that he could be in love with almost everyone, I allowed myself a grim smile, heroine-like, before the denouement, her big scene. Silently I waited for him to complete the verse, not missing the irony. He wasn't the only one who was going to be alone again tonight. Then I walked on down the hallway, past Justine's bedroom, past the bannister, where I could see Estelle's coat and umbrella hanging, and then on to the final stretch towards the kitchen door.

Voices from inside, low and casual. Her fluty laugh. My fingers were on the handle, exerting pressure, then the door was open and I was on the threshold, looking in at the two faces, which were both regarding me through a haze of smoke.

There was the tiniest pause. Then Estelle said, 'Hello, darling,' serene-voiced. Her face betrayed nothing. 'How are you feeling?'

It was supposed to be my moment of power. Standing there framed by the doorway, arms folded, I thought about consolidating it with a choice response. *Pregnant, thanks, Mum.* As the words flashed through my head, so did an instant vision of Estelle's answering expression, full of the shock I'd previously longed for. But that wasn't what I wanted any more. Just seeing them sitting side by side amid the friendly clutter of coffee cups and ashtrays, twin plumes from cigar and cigarette forming a single canopy of smoke above their heads, was enough to throw sand over the fortifying anger that had brought me to the kitchen door. I could almost inhale their familiarity along with the tobacco fumes.

Estelle didn't seem put out by my silence. 'Can you *believe* this one?' she said, gesturing at Richard, who smiled benignly from his seat. 'Strolling in here with his cigar, cool as a cucumber. He didn't even have the nerve to look surprised to see me. For a moment I felt like I'd lost about thirty years and we were back in Leeds,' she added, and laughed girlishly.

I closed the kitchen door behind me and leaned against it, suddenly weak. The two of them had been friends when they were both younger than me, when Richard and Ben were students in their final year, and my mum had used to drive up from London in her Morgan convertible to visit them in their Chapel Town digs, bringing food and brandy and her own bed linen, as she refused to sleep on Ben's tattered sheets. They had a dog in Leeds, a stray they'd adopted called . . . Lenin, that's right, who I'd loved without ever knowing for the fact that it had apparently lived on leftover fish and chips. Ben had a beard then. Estelle wore dresses she made herself – there was one particular one, silk, with stripes in shades of blue; it was Ben's favourite, and she made a cushion out of it for him when the dress finally fell apart.

It was a wave of secondhand memories that I'd inherited from my parents and Richard both, a recounting of that most tantalizing part of the family mythology – Before Me. Only now, breaking coldly over me, they were an unassailable reminder, too, that everyone knew Richard better than I did. Everyone had a greater claim to him than me, even my own mother, whose hands were laid flat on the tabletop. My hands, only older, and ornamented with the diamond ring she'd been wearing on her right middle finger as long as I could remember, the single ruby band next to it.

'Do you want a cup of tea?' Estelle said brightly.

'Yes please,' I said, deflated further by the inevitable question. My voice came out as a half-croak, and I was suddenly bitingly aware of my scarecrow-like appearance. She stood up, collecting dirty cups. 'Richard and I were just working out that we haven't seen each other for over three years, you know,' she said, laying a hand on my shoulder briefly as she passed me, a gentle pressure preceding her perfumed wake. 'Not since Claudia's gallery opening. Did you come to that, darling, or were you still up in Glasgow then?'

I managed a nod. Richard glanced at me and said, 'Your mother's just trying to make me feel guilty for being so bad at keeping in touch.' I observed the humour in his eyes, the lines surrounding them, the unruly brows and springing hair with a kind of distant interest, as if recognizing his face from old family photographs, slightly blurred and naked with youth. Looking at him, I was suddenly reminded of Ben again. It was just the way he spoke about Estelle sometimes – that dry 'your mother', both intimate and ironic, the arm's length it signified from those familiar, bejewelled hands. I wondered if he was doing it for my benefit, or for Estelle's.

I was half-glaring at him by then, but he carried on, unperturbed. 'Anyway, it's far more exciting to meet up by accident than at some deadly cheese and wine party, don't you think?' He picked up his cigar and put it between his lips with unhurried pleasure. 'We'll be dining out on this story for weeks.'

My mum tittered in her corner.

I cleared my throat. 'It must have been quite a shock,' I heard myself saying, surprised at how ordinary I sounded.

'It certainly was,' Estelle remarked, with her hands in the sink. 'Although I'm sure there's no such thing as coincidence. You just run into people again when it's the right time.' She twisted round to smile at Richard.

'You were always inclined to the romantic view, Stelly,' he said, and she rolled her eyes in fond exasperation.

Stelly? I moved away from the door and sat down at the end of the table, equidistant from the two of them. Neither seemed to carry the slightest hint of acknowledgement that I was implicated in Richard's presence here in my house; we were a bizarre triangle of familiarity who in our various combinations both were and weren't supposed to know each other very well.

Estelle, though, was saying archly, 'Oh, I'm far too old to be romantic,' and pushing back her hair with a forearm which ended in a lurid yellow rubber glove. In a moment of surreal understanding, as if all those tutorials she'd given me about how to handle the opposite sex had finally paid off, I realized she was flirting with him. A hiccup of incredulous laughter nudged into

217

my throat, but as I looked at Richard, smiling back and inhaling a measured mouthful of smoke, it stifled and died. Everything that had ever passed between us seemed to have been cancelled out, just by seeing him sit there while my mother did the washing up.

The kitchen lapsed into silence for a moment, filled with steam from the kettle and fresh waves of cigar smoke. I stared at the ashtray, at Estelle's abandoned cigarette with its lipsticked tip and snaking ash, and experienced one of those juvenile impulses you get in quiet public places to scream at the top of your voice. I was saved by my mother's act of placing a cup of tea in front of me. As my nose filled with the scent of Earl Grey, I was suddenly ravenous, remembering with a separate kind of impotent wrath that I'd barely eaten anything at all today, as though I'd been intentionally starved. There was nothing in me, I thought, a little hysterically, except a baby and a shot of gin. Maybe a sip of orange juice, too, that I'd shared with Kiddie . . .

'Hungry, I am,' I announced.

Richard, blowing smoke, coughed. Our eyes bumped together and then away again, but not before I'd managed to shoot him twin jets of ire across the table.

'Why don't you come home with me then, darling, if you're feeling better?' Estelle said, busy putting the milk away. 'I've invited Julia over tonight for supper, you can eat with us.' She glanced at her watch. 'In fact I must dash soon, I've got a lot of garlic to peel.'

'Julia?' Richard interrupted in a ruminative voice.

'Did you ever meet her?' she asked, and answered for him, 'Yes, of course you did, at my wedding! She came wearing the most enormous hat, like a cartwheel. Do you remember?'

'I never seem to remember much about weddings,' he said, 'other than the quality of the champagne the morning after.'

'I suppose that includes your own?' she said, and winked one blue eye at me theatrically.

It was a classic Estelle wink – wry yet artless, the practised work of a motherly impresario attempting to cheer up her ailing child. Suddenly I knew absolutely that she had no idea about the sordid details of me and Richard, whatever she'd made of my tear-battered face, and I was so instantly, surprisingly relieved that I felt a rush of generous love for her. Hot on its heels came a fresh surge of rage at Richard – *for always getting away with everything*. So when Estelle said in her most impetuous, redheaded manner, 'Richard, you must come for supper too, of course. It'll be a hoot – Julia will be thrilled to see you after all these years,' I caught his eye, and my mouth smiled but my brain said, *Oh no you fucking don't*.

'Well,' he said carefully, 'it sounds wonderful, but I'm not sure if I really . . .'

'Oh, come on,' Estelle said. 'You're not getting away from me that easily. A couple of hours, then we'll let you disappear again. Ben would never forgive me if he found out I'd missed an opportunity to feed you one more time.'

I took a moment to thank the gods that Ben was away on a business trip, otherwise she would probably have tried to insist on a full family reunion. 'Why don't you get going then, if you're running late,' I suggested. 'Richard can drive me over a bit later. When Lovell and the others have gone.' I studiously avoided looking at him as I said it, and received instead a darting, tender glance from Estelle at the mention of Lovell's name. I almost laughed again as I caught the implication, it was such a perfect convolution, although I wished Lovell a silent apology, because I wasn't going to correct Estelle's assumption that he was the bad boy just yet. Not that I thought he'd take too much offence at the mistake.

'Perfect,' she said, as if a champagne cork had just been popped. 'What do you say, Richard?'

'I've never forgotten your culinary mercy missions, you know,' Richard answered, smiling. He added for my benefit, 'If it wasn't for Stelly, Ben and I would've probably starved to death in Leeds.'

I didn't even flinch at this, just smiled determinedly into the centre of the room. Estelle said in a pleased voice, 'I'll take that as a yes, then. Well, let me just go and say goodbye to that sweet little boy before I go off and rattle my pots and pans.' With that she marched across the kitchen and towards the door, tossing a 'Back in a bit' over her shoulder like a scarf.

I could hardly wait for the door to close behind her. When it was done, however, Richard merely tapped his cigar into the ashtray, leant back in his chair and said, 'Nice to see your mother again.'

I gaped at him.

'Oh, come on, Sara,' he said. 'What did you expect me to do, shin down the drainpipe when she walked in? It was just as much of a surprise for me. Anyway, I've known Estelle for ever. Longer even than you have,' he added, raising his eyebrows bemusedly.

'Yes, you made that clear enough,' I said in a deadly voice.

'Look, I can see it's a bit awkward for you, us all being thrown together like this, but really, it's the least of our worries. And even if she found out what those particular worries were,' he added, 'she's hardly some kind of Victorian matriarch, is she? You've been looking at me as if you're expecting a public flogging.'

'That's not the fucking point,' I burst out in a spitting whisper. 'How would you feel if your mum turned up at the end of a day like I've had and started trying to turn it into a dinner party?'

'I can't answer that.'

'Well, what a luxury for you.' My voice was slowly rising. 'Are you *laughing*?

'Calm down,' he said, smiling at me. 'I can't talk to you like this.'

'Don't tell me to calm down, you pompous . . . old . . . Oh *Christ*.' I clenched my fists under the table, feeling a sort of strange, howling delight at finally letting it all out. Richard looked startled, but didn't interrupt. 'What the hell is there to talk about, anyway?' I went on furiously. 'You made your feelings about everything absolutely clear when you kicked me out of your hotel room this afternoon. So now you've had your little catch-up with my mum you can fuck off back to the countryside and your poor ignorant wife and pretend it all never happened.'

'Jesus,' he said, almost admiringly.

'I'm glad to know that you'll be dining out on the story for a few weeks, though. At least you won't go hungry. Whereas I'm . . . fucking . . . *starving*,' I ended, both triumphant and stunned at my own conclusion.

Richard stifled an indeterminate splutter. 'Look,' he said in a reasonable voice, 'quite aside from your appetite for drama, don't forget there *is* a very competitive story circulating around your flat. We've already explained to your mother that it was pure coincidence I turned up here today with Lovell and Ted; you know perfectly well I had no idea it was *you* that Kiddie had followed home.'

Unable to argue this point, I picked up my cup and took a rapid gulp of tea, burning my tongue. 'Shit,' I said, in pain and irritation, then, 'Have you got any idea what it was like to walk in here and see the two of you chain-smoking together over your coffee without a care in the world? When I'm having to hide out in my own house from a bunch of strangers who all want to know why I'm feeling so sorry for myself. Poor little princess! Poor little cry-baby!'

He was regarding me with an odd expression on his face. 'Don't look at me like that,' I snapped self-consciously. 'If you've got anything else to say, then spit it out.'

'There are plenty of things that still need to be said . . .' he began, but got no further. Estelle chose that moment to bustle back through the door, brandishing her umbrella. For a wild moment I thought she'd been listening outside the room and was about to brain Richard with it, but she merely beamed at the two of us, stiff in our chairs, and said, 'Right, I've said my farewells, so I'd better get going. Are you sure you don't want to come with me now, before it gets dark? You could follow us in your car, Richard.'

'Not yet,' I said. 'I can't just leave Jus here with the others. She hasn't been to sleep yet and she was on call last night.'

'Poor thing,' she said, adjusting the cuffs of her raincoat. 'Well, pack her off to bed then.' As she raised her head, she added slyly, 'She's not the only one who needs it, either, by the looks of things. That fair boy's practically asleep in her lap.'

'Too much whisky,' Richard said in an amused voice. 'I'm afraid I'm probably to blame for that.'

I gripped my cup silently. Earlier on, when everyone had left us alone and we'd been standing in the kitchen, I'd smelled it on his breath, too. Squashed red-faced against his chest, I'd inhaled the tang of it and wondered if he'd been drowning his sorrows back at the hotel after I'd walked out. As a solitary, perhaps slightly tragic figure, though, not part of some boozy little scout club with Ted. In fact, I'd caught a hint of the same smell around Lovell as well, now I thought about it . . .

I was still chewing over the implications of male conspiracy when Estelle said, 'Well, I'll expect you both in a little while, then. Drinks in an hour? You might want to pick up some wine, too, if you have time.'

'White or red?' Richard said smoothly.

'Surprise me,' she answered. 'You seem to be awfully good at that.' She hummed with laughter, twiddling her fingers at me. 'Bye, darling. Don't get wet, it's still pouring outside.'

'I won't,' I said, willing her to hurry up and leave again so we could continue.

With a final wave, she turned and disappeared, leaving behind a diminishing but jaunty trail of trilled farewells as she moved through the hallway and started down the stairs. I waited in prickly silence until I'd heard the final, distant blam of the front door before I spoke, and suddenly I'd fast-forwarded from where the two of us had left off, from schoolgirl to nagging wife. 'Having a bit of a piss-up with the boys, were you?'

'Eh?' he said. 'Oh, well. We had a couple today, yes.' He glanced round at me, and taking in my expression, added with a faint grin, 'It's amazing how much you remind me of your mother, sometimes. She used to give me that exact same look of disapproval, too.'

'Why?' I retorted. 'Did you manage to knock her up as well?'

There was a stifled pause, and then he let out a roar of laughter. I blushed to the roots of my hair, and then forced my face back into a scowl. It didn't really want to stay there, though, so I hid my mouth behind my teacup while Richard's laughter reduced itself to a series of slow grunts and a prolonged hacking cough.

'No,' he said eventually. 'Nothing like that. She thought I was a bad influence on your father, though, when we were at college. Ben and I used to hide from her when we'd been out boozing all night. He wouldn't answer the door, couldn't cope with the hangover *and* Estelle.'

'Well, at least you don't seem to have that problem,' I said tartly.

'Oh, I was always better than Ben at drinking,' he said, a trace of humour still on his face, 'and deflecting your mother when she was on the warpath.' Slowly, his eyebrows came together. 'Nothing much changes, you know. When I first met your parents, we were all just beginning, just starting out. I was completely in the dark about the real world – about myself, about women, just about anything. I had some big ideas and not much else.' He picked up his empty cup and gazed into it. 'Seeing Estelle again today, I remember how we were, years ago, and I wonder what's really changed.' The cup went down, accompanied by a dry laugh. 'Sod all, that's what. *I'm* still the same, anyway. Bigger ideas, perhaps slightly better worked out. And yet still no real answers. Still in the dark.'

I stared at him. 'Am I supposed to feel sorry for you?'

'God, no. Save your sympathy for someone more deserving.'

'Like myself, you mean?'

He was quiet for a moment, then said, 'I'm not an entirely heartless old bastard, Sara, but I can't alter the facts of what's happened simply by being penitent. I mean, my taking the blame for it all might make you feel better temporarily, but it's still not going to change anything, is it?'

'But *I'm* the one it's happening to,' I snapped. 'And so far, everyone in this entire house has been more help to me today than you have. Kiddie included.'

He sighed. 'I've no doubt that Kiddie's probably better equipped than I am to supply you with some solid answers, if that's what you're looking for.'

223

'There you go,' I said. 'Lovely. Pass on the responsibility to a lost seven-year-old boy.'

'Getting lost occasionally is a small price to pay for being able to determine your own truth so single-mindedly, don't you think?' Richard said thoughtfully.

I let out a slow moan. 'What?'

'Well, Kiddie's so ruthless about preserving this fantasy world of his – he'll go to such extraordinary lengths to protect it. Of course, eventually he'll grow up and it'll crumble naturally, but in the meantime, I can't help but envy him his freedom, existentially speaking . . .'

'For Christ's sake!' I exploded. '*Will you just drop the fucking philosophy for once in your life?*'

There was an eyebrow-filled silence. 'I'm just trying to establish some sort of context for what I want to tell you,' he said, surprised.

'*Tell* me? Tell me what? What is there possibly left you can tell me that would shatter any of my remaining illusions, Richard?' I was actually beginning to enjoy myself. 'Kiddie isn't the only one today whose fantasy . . . crumbled, did you say? I mean, it's one thing to find out that the person you thought was a beautiful princess is merely a . . . a part-time fucking florist who's so over-emotional she bursts into tears when she sees a thermometer.' At this he gave me a slightly bewildered look. 'Well, anyway, imagine what it's like for the *princess* to have the same revelation,' I went on, undefeated. 'Don't try and lecture me about defending the truth, or whatever the hell it was. You wouldn't know what the truth was if it smacked you round the face with its handbag.'

He didn't respond for a minute, staring upwards, and then he said in an unexpectedly gentle voice, 'Believe it or not, I *am* a great defender of the truth.'

'Yeah, right,' was my sophisticated parry.

'But to defend your *own* truth sometimes means you have to make choices, Sara. And those choices are sometimes necessarily at odds with what other people expect or want or come to believe they need from you.' The eyes came down from the ceiling and rounded on me. 'Kiddie's lucky – people still tolerate his right to defend the truth he's chosen, because he's a child. If he was my age, he'd probably be institutionalized for it.'

I threw him a warning look. 'But this isn't about Kiddie, Richard. It's about me. And you.'

'Kiddie's an example. I'm using him metaphorically.'

'I don't have time for fucking metaphors!' My entire body felt as though it was wired with strings, singing with tension.

There was another pause, and Richard's shoulders sagged a little. 'Oh, Christ, I'm no good at this,' he said ruefully. 'I'm not trying to be deliberately obtuse. But you don't have all the facts, Sara.'

'I think I know all I need to know.'

'But you *don't* know everything, Sara. How could you? That's precisely the point.'

'What *point*?'

He gave a great sigh, then. 'Well, do you know anything about Huntington's career, for example?'

'No,' I said irritably. 'Who the hell's Huntington?'

'It's not a who, it's a what. A disease.' He spelled it out. '"Chorea"'. A bit more than just any old disease, really. My mother died of it. It was the great tragedy of my childhood – well, I was a teenager, really.'

'So?' I said, thinking, *if he's angling for pity, he's not going to get it.*

'So, when my mother had been diagnosed, they told me that the same thing might happen to me, too, one day. Or it might not. I was a child at the time, but I understood those were the best odds they could give me.' He flashed me a smile. 'I suppose it's no surprise that I was drawn to philosophy when I grew up, really – a discipline based on elegant conjecture.' The smile slipped away as he took in my shrug of impatience. 'Anyway, Huntington's is a bit of a lottery, unfortunately . . . if it's in the family genes.' He shot me a look.

'I don't get it,' I said shortly.

'If one of your parents is carrying the Huntington's gene, there's a 50 per cent chance you'll carry it too. And if you are,

225

you become affected.' He was studying his packet of cigars. 'There's a test that tells you if you're positive.'

'Oh?' I said, somewhat thrown, but determined not to soften. 'And have you had it?'

'I couldn't, when I was younger,' he said, extracting a cigar from the box and holding it between his fingers. 'Testing for Huntington's used to be quite complicated, certainly in my mother's day; you had to get lots of blood samples from different family members. I'm an only child though. My mother was too. All the relatives were on my dad's side, strong as bloody horses, of course, most of them. It wasn't until a few years ago that they developed the individual test, when I was coming up to fifty.'

I was beginning to get impatient again. 'Yes?' I said. 'So? What was the result?'

'Hold on a minute,' he went on carefully. 'Believe it or not, there are plenty of people who decide never to have the test, even though they know they might be carrying the gene.'

'Why?'

'Well, can you imagine the psychological pressure of living with the knowledge that you're a physical time-bomb waiting to explode? For some people that would simply negate any quality of life they might have.'

'Wait a second, Richard,' I interrupted. 'What exactly is it you're telling me? You might get this . . . thing when you're old? Perhaps? But you still don't know?' I looked at him, genuinely puzzled, and to my surprise he let out a snort of laughter. 'What?'

'Just the flat note of disappointment in your voice, that's what. I admit that 50 per cent odds don't make much of a premise for drama, do they? OK, let me be more specific, so you know what we're dealing with here.' He sat up straighter in his chair. 'First of all, it's usually middle age when Huntington's hits. About my age, although my mother was quite a bit younger.' He tapped the cigar against his fingers. 'Secondly, it's incurable. Sometimes it's fast and sometimes it's slow, but the symptoms are the same. To begin with, you lose your sense of physical and mental judgement. Then you develop these strange muscular spasms – that's the chorea part. Epilepsy too, sometimes. Basically, you start to lose the ability to control your body. And then your mind. Then you die,' he added impassively.

I said nothing for a minute, shocked into silence by the absolute neutrality of his tone as much as by the words themselves. 'Is that all?' I managed to get out.

He gave me a sad smile. 'Thirdly, it's extremely distressing to watch. My mother was a little woman, and by the end she looked like something not quite human, like a goblin, all wizened. Hunched over in her wheelchair, shaking, hands like claws.'

Caught up as I was in the sudden horror of it all, I was still distracted by the movement of the door, which seemed to have pushed itself open a crack. Richard didn't notice though, he just kept on talking.

'She lost her power of speech quite early on, so we never knew the extent of her senility, although they told us it was probably advanced. Luckily she died fairly quickly, as cases go.' The cigar was being rolled back and forth, back and forth between his fingers. 'That's all you can hope for, really.'

My eyes were still fixed on the door, which seemed to be floating fractionally on its hinges. I realized he was waiting for me to speak.

'Oh. Well, I'm sorry,' I said, dragging my eyes away unwillingly, and my voice sounded dry. I was torn between genuine sympathy and a nagging feeling that it was all just a bit too . . . *convenient*, the fact that he'd managed to pull a bigger tale of woe out of nowhere.

'Well, don't be. Like I said before, save your grief, at least until I can give you my personal guarantee that it's going to happen to me.'

'So you *don't* know, then?'

'Like I said, it's only been a few years since this new test was developed, and the knowledge there for the taking, so to speak.'

There was another waiting silence while I struggled to come up with the right response, then he added, 'The problem with knowledge, of course, is that it's indelible. Everything physical life isn't, in fact.' A tight smile appeared briefly. 'I mean, I suppose I've come to terms with my situation intellectually, but then I've never had a problem getting to grips with abstractions, you should know that.'

There was no avoiding his eyes, then. They held me fast, darkly, their expression unreadable. 'I don't want it, you see,' he said.

My heart jumped at the words I'd been anticipating hearing all afternoon. 'The baby?' I said flatly.

He gave a laughing sigh. 'Not the baby. The test, love. I don't want to have the test.'

I was flooded with relief and irritation. 'Oh God, the test, the test. Look, I took a fucking test too this morning, Richard, remember? But I don't have any choice whether or not I want to deal with it, do I?'

'But this is different, Sara. I've spent the whole of my adult life trying to prepare for the possibility of ending up a Huntington's casualty. Just try and imagine what it's like for a minute, will you?' he said, and suddenly his voice had a grating note I'd never heard before. 'Every headache, every twitch, ever fucking hangover, for God's sake . . . constantly watching for signs that it's going to happen. It's enough to drive you insane, long before your brain properly turns into jelly.'

'Don't start shouting at me,' I said crossly. 'You told me you're just as likely *not* to have it. Make your mind up, for fuck's sake.'

'Christ on a bike!' Richard said, looking amazed. 'Aren't you listening to anything I'm saying?' He stopped, seeming to check himself. 'Look, I'm doing my best to explain that having this . . . this *test* is one leap of faith that I'm just not prepared to take. Do you understand? It's the biggest question there's ever been for me, overriding all others. And it's the only one with a ready-made answer that I just do not want to know.' His eyes probed mine.

'But,' I said, and my head was trying to search out the apex of all this information, all the words – only a crucial part of my brain seemed to have slowed right down. 'That's ridiculous. I mean, what about your family? What about your wife? What about *me*?'

He sighed again. 'Sara, you're not getting it. All this is precisely why I don't have any family.'

I looked at him, frowning. The softness of his voice made me suddenly afraid. 'Both times I've been married,' he said, 'we decided jointly not to have kids right at the beginning, because of the possibility of Huntington's. Taking the test was never an issue, then, because I couldn't have it. Of course, both times we ended up regretting not having children, too – it's certainly what broke up my first marriage, and made my second . . . difficult, to say the least. But it's too late for us anyway, of course, Claudia's past the age. Except now . . .' Our eyes locked again. 'Except now there's you and this baby. And for the life of me, love, I don't know whether to be delighted or terrified about it.'

Everything shifted focus in that split second. There it was, finally, achingly clear and cold in my mind, and I didn't understand why it had taken me so long to see it.

'The baby,' I said, for the second time in as many minutes. Only this time there was no question in the words, they were just a flat sound that was absorbed into the frozen wastes of my own thoughts. Everything was still and quiet around me, but my head had started numbly singing with figures as I sat there staring at Richard and trying to calculate the odds of the baby's eventual survival, trying to work out what 50 per cent of 50 per cent amounted to, pushing the concepts of probability and confirmation and likelihood away in disbelief and then feeling them flood back again. It was impossible to think clearly, like shovelling snow in a blizzard – as soon as I created an opening, it was covered instantly with the obliterating white of shock and anger and icy dread. The percentages and numbers just kept whirling inside my head, decreasing in size again and again until they were reduced to nothing . . .

'I'm sorry,' Richard said simply, breaking the silence.

My eyes unglued themselves from his face. And out of the nothingness I saw it properly for the first time. The baby. Half mine, half Richard's, and now, it seemed, already potentially half dead. But above all, suddenly human, if only a tiny shrimp, floating inside me. It had passed into the realm of existence, of substance, pushed there by the threat of this far-off death, and it struck me as obscenely pompous to be conceiving of the shrimp's significance only in so far as whether I wanted it or not. It was alive, regardless of my opinion, its primitive heartbeat pulsing away, insistently demanding protection as long as it chose to beat its steady tattoo: I am . . . I am . . . I am . . .

The scattered sound of rain tapping its own rhythm on the windows brought me back to myself, and with it, the searing pain of thawing frostbite, of numbed senses coming back to life.

'Why didn't you tell me before?' I said across the table. My voice was unsteady.

His was quiet. 'Because it's nothing that should ever have affected you.'

'Because it's nothing that should ever have affected me,' I repeated stupidly. 'But it *has* affected me.'

'I'm well aware of that,' he said wearily, and all the practised composure was gone. His face was grey in the fading light, its lines deeply drawn, the eyes shadowed with tiredness.

'All those clever justifications, then,' I went on almost mechanically, 'for burying your head in the sand, for not wanting to know the truth about yourself. They're no good, now, are they?'

'There's nothing clever about them, Sara. They're a fact of life for me. An unfortunate necessity. They make life bearable, and I can't make any apologies for that.'

'But it's not just your life we're talking about any more.' Saying it, I felt it even keener than before, stabbing in my chest. 'It's not just up to you to decide what's necessary, either. It's up to . . .' I was brought up short by the dreadful irony of that unspoken 'us' – the two of us finally, legitimately united as I'd always wanted.

There was a moment's silence. 'I understand all that, of course,' he said, without looking at me. 'But doesn't everything rather depend on what you decide to do about the baby?'

I shook my head, dazed by the question.

'Come on, Sara, at least talk to me about this.'

'There's no decision.' How could I explain it to him – the baby had become real, it had fully entered my consciousness, my conscience – swimming down through every level of awareness. It couldn't be unwished or unimagined. *Nothing has any real value until you realize you might lose it*. The words echoed back from somewhere. Who had said them to me? I closed my eyes for a moment as the memory returned: Richard on the hotel bed that first time, his hand holding mine.

'For crying out loud, will you stop being so triumphant about it all for a minute?' he snapped then, and my eyes flew open. He took a deep breath. 'Look, I know this is a great shock, it's a lot to take in at once, but –'

'Oh, it's too late to start rationalizing everything now,' I interrupted, in a louder voice. 'If you want to be rational, you should have told me about it at the beginning, then we wouldn't be having this conversation, would we? In fact you shouldn't have come anywhere near me.'

Richard grimaced. 'I can see there's no getting you over my appalling refusal to brand myself the very first time we met. What would you have me do? Wear a badge? Huntington's Chorea Club?' I noticed with a small shock that his mouth was folding in on itself ominously. 'Make sure I warn everybody I meet that they shouldn't come too close, just in case they end up getting infected with my bad . . . fucking . . . genes?' He choked over the last word, and lowered his head, but I saw the muscles of his face struggling to control themselves. On the table, one hand clenched itself around the unlit cigar, the knuckles pale and taut. The other hand was pressed palm down, and as I looked wordlessly at the blunt nails, the spray of black hair on each finger, an unexpected memory floated into my head. A time five or six years ago, when my father took me to Paris to see the Matisse exhibition I'd nagged him about for weeks. On our last night we stayed at the already overflowing house of Ben's friend Dominique, and ended up having to share a double bed. It was an awkward family intimacy – Ben wasn't like Estelle, who had always walked around the house half-dressed and luxuriated in her own voluptuousness – I was hardly used to seeing him without his glasses, let alone in his Y-fronts. When the lights were out we lay chastely and with a certain rigidity in our pyjamas, side by side on the mattress. But halfway through my wakeful night, peopled with Ben's quiet grumbling snores, he turned in his sleep, and one soft, naked foot crept across the bed and curled against mine. For an instant I froze, my heartbeat bubbling in my chest, then he turned again, and the foot was gone. The next morning, looking at the thinning crown of his head as I sat down late for breakfast, I'd felt an odd pang of tenderness as I remembered it – his vulnerable foot – almost like a separate being, a lonely creature looking for warmth in the night.

Richard's sense of his own physicality had always been at the core of my attraction to him, it seemed like such a strong component of his character, compared to someone like gentle, ineffectual Ben, who tended to turn the dimmer of his presence down when he wasn't needed. Only now, staring at his hands, it was as if I was gazing down at Ben's balding head again and seeing my father's own physical frailty for the first time, recognizing that our roles as child and parent had begun their slow and inevitable reversal. I tried to imagine Richard's vigorous body silenced by illness, summoning all the anger and fear and resentment I was holding inside my chest, but I couldn't. Instead my brain said distinctly, as if it was presenting a gift, *I don't love you.*

The words trembled on my tongue as I lifted my head to meet his eyes again, only to dissolve in the quick surge of relief that spread through me, chased by a wave of pity so strong that everything else was washed away for a second or two by that blur of emotion – pity for him, for me and the shrimp, too. It seemed like the saddest thing I'd ever felt, an acceptance of every possible grief that might come, and yet there was a strange kind of excitement in there too. I was thinking, this is the beginning of that defining experience you've always been waiting for, this thing you expected to be able to somehow plan and execute like a still-life, to hold up and admire as an expression of your own will, to show that you'd made your mark. And now it's finally happening, the first thing to go is the illusion that you created the circumstances of your existence through judgement and skill. Good or bad, they're as random as a gene pool, whirling with infinite variations of life.

Richard raised the unlit cigar to his mouth. I watched as he struck a match and held it up, the quick flare illuminating his face during a rapid succession of small puffs. Then the first long draw, his head tilting back as he shook out the match and dropped it in the ashtray. A holding silence followed by an exhalation, ceilingward, his eyes closed.

'I suppose Estelle knows, too?' I said, wreathed in sweet smoke.

'About the Huntington's? Oh yes. She and Ben have always known.'

My mind became tangled with a strange assortment of people's faces as they heard me announcing I was going to have Richard's child, damaged goods as it might be. Both my parents, the wife with invented features, the barman at the Lansdowne, Chloe and Justine – all silently mouthing phrases about me: *devastated . . . poor darling . . . bastard . . . emotional wretch . . .* Lovell's face appeared in the fray for an instant, and winked at me, banishing the rest of them. Suddenly I wished I was upstairs again, sitting next to him on my bed, so I could tell him about all the things that had become clear in the last hour or so. He'd hardly believe I'd learned so much, I thought.

'This is it, then,' I said across the table. The words had an echo of previous endings from my history, which had been full of drama and recrimination and bitterness, but this time I felt nothing, or rather a fullness and an emptiness both, which were some way off connecting with my live senses. The silence, the tea-cups, the ghost of dead cigar smoke were all still present, only everything was different, too, the sky outside now darkening imperceptibly against the wet trees.

Richard said tiredly, 'This is what?'

I looked at him, trying experimentally to summon back some of the old feelings, but they'd packed their bags and left. 'This is where we say goodbye,' I said. 'And you leave. Right?'

He returned my look with the faintest suggestion of the old quizzical humour. 'I'm not quite as bad as all that, you know,' he answered. 'I didn't bring all this up so I could ride off into the sunset with a satisfied conscience and never have to think about you again.'

'What *do* you think about me, Richard?' I said. It was odd how easy it was to ask, now that I didn't care so much.

He paused, then said unexpectedly, 'I only wish you could see yourself through my eyes, sometimes. You're so bloody young, you don't realize . . .'

'Not any more,' I said painfully.

'Oh yes, love. Why do you think I was so drawn to you in the first place?'

I let out a sigh. 'I don't know. Because I had tits?'

He didn't even smile. 'Probably more because you reminded me of myself, somehow. You still don't know what it is you want, but you want it badly enough to look in all the wrong places.'

'Yourself being one of them.' He cut his eyes away from me, and I found myself feeling unwillingly sorry for him again. I was aware of the space between us, cool air where there might have been a reaching out, a need and its answering gesture. Instead my hands had found their way to my stomach and were curved around it, feeling the slow rise and fall of breath. I wondered what conversations I might have with my unborn baby when it eventually grew up, describing how I became involved with its father, and why it didn't work out. But it was impossible to imagine. How could you ever make another person understand the impetus behind their own beginnings, the jumble of urges and hopes and crossed purposes that caused it to exist? I thought of Kiddie, of all his confusion and delight in being a child, and how much more valuable that seemed than any philosophical rationalizations of life or death.

The rap at the door was so sharp that I jolted in my chair. Before I could answer, the door swung open and in walked Lovell.

'Easy,' he said into the silence. 'Everyone alright?'

I looked at him, at the door, astonished by the space, which had been empty and was now suddenly filled with him.

'Blimey, it's dark in here,' he said, peering across the room. 'Fancy some illumination?'

Richard laughed quietly. 'I think we've had about all we can take for one day.'

'Eh?'

234

'Next to the fridge,' I said. He flicked the switch, and I blinked in the instant brightness, feeling exposed.

'Sorry for barging in and that, but I think we're going to split soon.' His eyes swung between the two of us, his pale head shining silver under one of the spotlights above the sink. 'I wasn't sure if you was gonna surface again.'

I found myself saying, 'It's OK. Richard's about to get going too.'

'Back to the old whisky den, are you?' Lovell said to Richard casually, who was looking at me with surprise.

'Actually, he's going to have dinner at my mum's,' I said. 'You better get a move on or you'll be late, Richard.'

He seemed to think about this for a second, and then bent his head in acknowledgement. 'Alright then. Are you coming with me, Sara?'

The silver head and the grey head were both inclined towards me, waiting.

'No,' I said. 'Not tonight.'

Richard nodded, expressionless, then gave me one of his sideways smiles, which pierced me for a second. 'We'll do it another time.'

'Just tell her I'm not feeling up to it,' I said. 'No need to go into too much detail.'

He gave me a swift, shrewd glance. 'Of course.' He picked his cigar box off the table, sliding it into his jacket pocket, and I noticed Lovell looking at us both curiously.

'Right then,' Richard said abruptly, and stood up. 'I'd better go and pay my last respects to the Croydon Castaway. Is he still awake?'

Lovell laughed. 'Oh yeah. Kiddie'll probably outlast us all. He wouldn't have missed a single minute of today.'

'Oh, me neither,' said Richard, as he passed me on his way out of the room. 'There's certainly been something for everyone, hasn't there?'

The map that I drew for Richard to direct him to Estelle's was a work of art. I'd made its execution last a full five minutes, right up until he came back down the hall from having said goodbye to Ted and Kiddie and Justine. While I sketched roads and roundabouts, Lovell perched on the counter next to me, swinging his legs and keeping up a lighthearted patter. Somehow I was able to listen and laugh in the right places, pushing everything else to one side. I found myself thinking, *everything's so easy with him*, and experienced a momentary urge to blurt out everything that had just happened, as if just the telling might somehow absolve me from the worst of it.

When Richard walked back in, Lovell slid down from his seat, and after I'd handed over the map, the three of us stood in a little hesitant crowd by the door. Richard took my hand and kissed me carefully on the cheek. I flinched at the touch of him, the strange politeness of his lips there – I didn't mean to, but it must have showed, because he let go and took Lovell's hand instead. I watched as they shook, and after all the right words had been said, thankful and congratulatory and perhaps with a touch of cheerful male relief that they weren't obliged to see each other again, Richard turned and walked out into the darkness of the hallway.

'We'll talk soon, then,' he said, his face in shadow, and I merely nodded. I'd never had his home number and he didn't have mine, as far as I knew, but it hardly seemed worth bringing it up now. In any case, my mouth suddenly seemed too tired to form itself into words. We exchanged a final wary smile before he disappeared down the stairs, and then Lovell and I were left standing in the middle of the kitchen, as if caught together once again between the scenes. Only this time, after I'd heard the front door closing, the whole house seemed completely still – as still as it had been when I'd first arrived home with Kiddie. And just being able to stand there in silence with Lovell seemed like a sort of luxury, now it was all over. The quietness felt so thick and pure, like a feather duvet, that I wanted to stand there, wrapped in it, for as long as I could.

'You alright, princess?' he said, after a few seconds had passed.

'I think so,' I said, as if I was pressing down on an abscess to test for pain, and feeling only the disorienting numbness of dulled nerves.

'Good. Kiddie'll be pleased – he was convinced you were in a bit of trouble.'

'What?'

'Poor Kid, he went for a wander round the house, and after a bit he comes rushing back in the front room, pulling on my sleeve and whispering that something bad was going down.'

'Oh?' I said with trepidation. 'What did he say?'

'Well,' he said, deadpan, 'let's see. He said he reckoned that Richard's old lady had been turned into a goblin or something, but not a good one like Yoda. A baddie with great big claws, it was. Either a goblin or a wizard, I think, but definitely a baddie. Scary, huh? He seemed convinced that you were gonna be next. All Richard's fault, I s'pose.' He allowed his face to show off its extrovert grin. 'I thought I'd better check on you, anyway.'

'I'm still in one piece,' I said. 'Just about.'

He leant against the fridge, still grinning, arms folded. 'You hungry, by any chance?'

I was overtaken by a colossal yawn, and put my hands to my face. 'Famished,' I said hollowly, through my cupped fingers.

'I was going to ask you if you fancied a bite to eat somewhere before I take Kiddie home. My treat, of course. But we can do it another time if you're not feeling too hot right now.'

'Oh,' I said. My mind flew to Estelle's kitchen and hovered outside the window – half-drunk glasses of red wine, cigarette smoke, perfume, anecdotes. Her and Julia sitting around the table swapping histories, the empty seats waiting for me and Richard. I suppressed a shiver and was overtaken by a great childlike longing for every kind of comfort: for food and wine and heat and sleep, and perhaps someone to lean against, but it wasn't my mum. I studied Lovell's face, the tiny chocolate-brown freckles that sat across the bridge of his nose. Maybe if I got a pen and joined the dots I'd find the answer, I thought, vaguely, although I wasn't quite sure what the question was. Richard would probably know . . .

'What d'you reckon then?'

237

I came back to my senses. 'OK,' I said automatically. 'Where do you want to go? Are we taking Kiddie with us?'

'Don't worry, I ain't gonna drag you to McDonald's. How about the Paradise, since we're round the corner? They're alright with kids, I reckon.'

'Sounds good,' I said, and put a hand to my face, a little self-conscious suddenly, as I pictured the three of us sitting around a table together. 'Um, should we ask the others if they want to come?'

Lovell already had a hand on the door. 'I got a hunch Justine ain't going nowhere. And if she's not, nor's Ted.' He looked down at the floor for a second, shaking his head, then lifted it again, while the grin took another curtain call.

'Tell you what, though, darlin'. You might need something on your feet. It's wet outside. Why don't you go and pop into your clogs?'

When I entered the front room, fully shod, he was standing in front of the fireplace with a proprietorial air, hands behind his back.

'Here she is,' he said, and I smiled carefully at Ted and Justine, who were sitting side by side on the sofa. Kiddie was back in his usual position at Justine's feet. At the sight of me, his brown eyes grew rounder in his solemn face, but then he dipped his head and went back to fiddling with the buttons on someone's mobile phone, glancing up every few seconds at the Simpsons, who were mutely clowning on the silent TV screen. The music had changed again. Dusty Springfield, crooning 'The Look of Love'.

'Hi,' Justine said, with a tired answering smile that was part question, part welcome. She was still in her silk dressing-gown, languorous on the sofa, and seemed to be playing a part to go with the song.

'I can't believe you're still up,' I said, sitting down next to Ted, who glanced up in a friendly way. I noticed that the carpet by the stereo was littered with CD cases that had been pulled off the shelves. The whole room seemed strange in its very ordinariness, the people sitting around in various relaxed poses. *It's as if none of today ever happened*, I was thinking. *Just another Wednesday evening hanging out with friends. Food at the Paradise, a few drinks, maybe there's a good film on later, no work tomorrow, so I can sleep in . . .*

The undertow of my new knowledge tugged at me briefly, but I announced, 'We're going out for dinner,' as if it was the most normal thing in the world. 'Anyone interested?'

'God, no,' Justine said, yawning. 'I'm about to pass out. You can take my car if you want, though, keys are in the kitchen.'

'Nice one,' Lovell said, looking around at Ted. 'Teddy, get your arse in gear if you want your face feeding.'

'Um, I think I'll just catch a cab straight home from here,' he said airily from the sofa, and then immediately ducked his head as if in apology for his daring. 'You don't mind, do you? I know you've got to sort your car out, but I've got to get started on this piece for Daniel.' He turned to Justine and gave her a crooked grin. 'I may stay a little while longer, though, if that's OK. I've got nothing to go home to except a dead rat.'

She looked puzzled. Lovell was shaking his head with mock despair. 'That's gotta be the worst chat-up line I've heard all year, man.'

Jus, though, merely yawned again and said, 'I might not last too much longer, but be my guest.'

'You be careful he don't keep you up all night,' Lovell said to her, at which Ted actually blushed.

'I can't, anyway. I've got work to do,' he said, and patted his pocket, which bulged.

Lovell caught my eye. 'Transcribing Richard's words of wisdom, are you?'

Ted nodded. 'There's a lot of tape to get through,' he said, and then added with a quick, private grin. 'I dunno how much of it's going to make sense, but it sounded good at the time.'

With an odd sense of dislocation I remembered that while I'd been dripping tears on the bus, watched by Kiddie, Ted must have been talking to Richard in our usual hotel room. I looked at him with distant curiosity, wondering if he knew what I'd just found out.

'Well,' Lovell said, 'I'd make sure you've dried out before you start listening to your tapes. Everyone sounds like a genius to you when you're out of it.'

'Maybe he is,' Ted retorted. 'We'll know soon enough, anyway – his book's coming out in a couple of months, isn't it?'

'What's it about?' I heard myself asking.

He blinked at the question, then looked thoughtful. 'Lepers,' he said in a dreamy voice. 'Lepers, losers, all sorts of mad things.'

'Come again?' Lovell said.

'It's hard to explain, really,' Ted said to me, suddenly serious. 'That's part of the problem, posing the right question in the first place. According to Richard, none of us ask enough of the right questions, philosophical or otherwise, to really . . . *flourish*.'

'Flourish?' Lovell interrupted. 'Are you sure it ain't a book on gardening? Maybe you were drunker than you thought up there.'

Justine snorted at this, but Ted just looked peeved and said, 'Well, you'll just have to wait till I've written it, won't you? You might be quite surprised.'

Lovell was grinning from the fireplace. 'I'll look forward to it. Rather you than me, man, anyway.' He turned to me. 'Ready, Sara? Kiddie? Chop chop, sunshine.'

'Where we going?' Kiddie asked plaintively. 'It's all dark outside.'

'Somewhere nice. You, me and the princess. How 'bout that?'

'What's somewhere nice?'

'It's a surprise. Sara's takin' us on a magical mystery tour of Queen's Park.'

The child's face lit up. 'Is it the fairground?'

'No, darlin'. Not this time.'

Kiddie dawdled across the carpet in a disappointed fashion, still clutching the phone.

'But I want to stay with Just,' he said. 'We can watch telly with the sound up.'

Justine waved a hand from the sofa, eyes half-closed. 'Fine with me,' she said, although I noticed that for an instant, an expression not unlike Kiddie's passed over Ted's face. This wasn't lost on Lovell either, who threw me a wink.

'Well, it's up to you, Kid,' he said, nodding towards the sofa, 'but I think you'll have more of a laugh with us. Come on, I'll let you

16

sit in the front seat. but when we go outside and get in the car, lovell makes me go in the back, instead. he says its because he needs to help sara navigate the ship, but i reckon he just wants to sit next to her himself.

ok, KID? he says as we drive off down the road.

yeah.

dont worry, you ll be glad you changed your mind and came with us.

why, are we goin mcdonalds?

nah, somewhere much better than that. we got a princess at the wheel, remember?

i dont say nothin, but there aint that many places better than mcdonalds. sometimes they even give you presents in there, toys and stuff. lovell says they only do it because they want you to keep goin back when you re grown up, but im gonna go back anyway.

what do they have where we re goin?

uh, how bout some worm pie? lovell says.

yuk.

KIDDIES a bit of a worm pie fan, he tells sara, turnin and winkin at me.

i dont think its on the menu at the paradise, she goes.

whatsa paradise?

lovell says, oh, you must have heard about paradise. its a wicked place, man. up in the sky. full of happy people singin songs and that.

thats heaven, silly.

same thing.

and it aint like that, anyway.

theres no foolin you, is there KID? lovell says. well, we re goin to paradise tonight, anyway. it aint just a stompin ground for angels, its a restaurant as well, see.

so i can have mcdonalds, then.

huh?

you said paradise is the same thing as heaven. well you can have whatever you like in heaven, cant you?

he laughs. nice try, darlin. lets hope you re right about that, anyway – not that i reckon i ll ever be able to test out your theory.

why?

uh, cos you have to be very very good to get into heaven. its a bit like what i told you about the english football team, KID. more women in it though, i hope.

i don't get it, but i laugh anyway with lovell.

sara dont laugh though. lovell looks over at her and says, you re very quiet. feelin alright?

oh, she goes, yeah. its been a long day, thats all.

you re not wrong. which reminds me . . . lovell looks at his watch. im due for another earful any minute now.

what, from your sister?

bingo. he takes out his phone and turns it off. there, he says, as it beeps goodbye, twice in one day, its gotta be a record.

wont she get even more upset if she cant get through to you? sara goes.

nah. it just makes her feel better if she can let off a bit. im a highly responsible childminder really, arent i KIDDIE?

uh? i say, because im busy navigatin. the back of saras seat is the controls with all the buttons and stuff, and when i squeeze my eyes closed a bit, the lights on the side of the street go all blurry, like the stars do when you go into hyperdrive.

its alright, im just singin my own praises, lovell answers, over his shoulder.

sara says in a low voice, does your sister actually know what happened today?

yeah, sort of. as much as any of us do, anyway. i reckon KIDs the only one with the real answers.

ha.

whats so funny?

nothing. you just sounded like richard.

yeah? maybe theres more to him than i thought.

oh, there is, trust me.

lovell goes, he made a bit of a speedy exit today, didnt he?

sara sighs and says, yeah. i wanted him to, though. its alright, really.

what you lookin so worried about, then?

well . . . things are a bit more complicated than i thought, thats all.

yeah, well . . .

ok, they re a *lot* more complicated.

lovell pauses. to do with your mum, right?

my mum? not really, no.

shes cool, your old lady. it cant be that bad.

thats what you think, sara says, stoppin the car at a red light so some people can cross the road.

listen, lovell goes, if your family are cool, you ll do alright. there were so many baddies in my own family its a flippin miracle i turned out as well as i did, let me tell you. aint that right, KID?

yeah, i say, but im not really listenin, im watchin the people start walkin across the street and takin aim so i can zap em.

lovell says, in fact, bein in a familys about the only thing im really good at.

i cant believe that, sara goes.

well, maybe you re right . . . theres a couple of other things i can think of.

she laughs quietly. the people outside are wearin protection and they keep walkin, dodgin the laser fire.

lovell says, you ll be ok, darlin, scouts honour. dont worry so much about everythin. i ll give you a hand, you know?

with what? sara says.

with whatever.

244

the car starts movin again, at lightspeed, an all the baddies get left behind.

after a minute sara mumbles, you just might end up with your hands a bit fuller than you expected.

lovell puts his arm round the back of her seat. dont try and put the frighteners on me, lady, he says. you cant get shot of me that easy.

im not trying to, goes sara.

good. i told you, im the best at all the family stuff. just ask KIDDIE. you ll give me a nice reference, wont you KID?

whats a nice reference? i ask, in case its somethin stupid.

its a vote of confidence.

uh?

its like sayin that, uh, luke skywalkers a good pilot or somethin.

hes the *best* pilot.

yeah, but no one knew that, did they, until his mate gave him a nice reference. told the rebel captain that luke was the best pilot on his planet, right?

yeah. so he could blow up the imperial fleet.

sara goes, what are you two on about?

star wars, lovell says, what else? you should know by now.

not really, she goes, i ve never seen it.

you ve never seen star wars?

just then sara pulls up at the side of the road, and turns the car off.

no, she says, and its all quiet in the car. never.

lovell looks at me over his shoulder with his mouth wide open. jesus, he goes, as she opens the door and starts to get out. hear that, KIDDIE? you ll have to initiate her.

uh?

you can lend her all your videos, at least.

the second ones the best, i say. no one hears me, though, because now lovells gettin out of his door, too, and then they re both standin on the pavement, close together. part of me dont want to have to get out, because its warm in here and im a bit sleepy, and its nice just drivin around at night, never gettin to the

245

place you re supposed to be goin. but then lovell comes over and reaches through the back door and pulls me out into the cold.

lets go, champion, he says, takin hold of my hand. sara comes around and takes hold of the other one, and we start walkin towards the door of the paradise. when we get to the step, they lift me up high either side, and swing me over it, like im flyin through the air. it was me that did it though, really. just usin the force.

Acknowledgements

Special thanks to Geoffrey Ames, Dan Bernstein, Roz Bernstein, Stephen Bracco and Tony Fletcher, writers-in-arms throughout. To Charles Hawkins III, original downtown pop philosopher, for lending me certain ideas from his Dustmite Manifesto. To Gerry and Paul Kennedy for ranting on demand in kitchens across the UK. To Anya Waddington for getting it going, Clare Alexander for steering, and Mary Mount for tying it up.

Love and thanks for you know what: Kat Aguirre, Stephen Bass, Esta Blechman, Max Fish, Alex Gifford, Kate Harrison, Nate Krenkel, Kath McDermott, Jenine McKay, Mike Mooney, Claudia Nicholson, John Toba, Wall of Sound, Chloe Walsh, Tanya Walters, Sioux Z and my family.

refresh yourself at penguin.co.uk

Visit penguin.co.uk for exclusive information and interviews with
bestselling authors, fantastic give-aways and the
inside track on all our books, from the Penguin Classics
to the latest bestsellers.

BE FIRST

first chapters, first editions, first novels

EXCLUSIVES

author chats, video interviews, biographies, special
features

EVERYONE'S A WINNER

give-aways, competitions, quizzes, ecards

READERS GROUPS

exciting features to support existing groups and
create new ones

NEWS

author events, bestsellers, awards, what's new

EBOOKS

books that click – download an ePenguin today

BROWSE AND BUY

thousands of books to investigate – search, try
and buy the perfect gift online – or treat yourself!

ABOUT US

job vacancies, advice for writers and company
history

Get Closer To Penguin ... www.penguin.co.uk